CW01391805

Walking Out of This World

Stephen Ford

LEAF BY LEAF

Published by Leaf by Leaf
an imprint of Cinnamon Press,
Office 49019, PO Box 15113, Birmingham, B2 2NJ
www.cinnamonpress.com

Print Edition ISBN 978-1-78864-989-6

British Library Cataloguing in Publication Data. A CIP record for this book can be obtained from the British Library.

Designed and typeset in Adobe Jenson by Cinnamon Press.
Cover design by Adam Craig © Adam Craig.
Cinnamon Press is represented by Inpress.

About the Author

Stephen Ford is Walks Secretary for the Surrey branch of the Long Distance Walkers Association (LDWA), whose membership relishes longer distance treks at a brisk pace over challenging terrain.

The son of a geologist, he had a varied and nomadic childhood in Africa and the Middle East. From childhood, Stephen has been inspired by wild places, mountains, rivers and forests, places where nature reigns, not people.

Now, inspired to write, Stephen explores these themes: What is nature? Is nature alive? What is life? What distinguishes a human from an animal? Do people have spirits? If people have spirits, then perhaps animals do too? Can spirits exist also in inanimate entities, rivers, trees, mountains, valleys?

Walking Out of This World

Walkers Rendezvous

At precisely 8:30 am on a drizzly Sunday morning in mid-October, Eddie—a purposeful man in his early sixties—manoeuvred his elderly Jaguar off the narrow lane into a muddy rutted car park. Set in the woodland clearing in an unspoiled corner of the Surrey hills, the wheels crunched over crumbling, fungus-encrusted remnants of an old log.

Momentarily, Eddie glimpsed a figure in a brightly glowing outfit lurking in the damp shadows of the surrounding trees. It was as if the light from the figure shone through his eyes into his head, seeking crevices in his mind unlit for years. In his mind's eye was an outline of a familiar young girl. For an instant, he glimpsed her face, not long enough for recognition but sufficient to sense a relationship between them. Once he could swing around to make out the figure in the trees, he could see only the autumnal brown of fallen leaves, and the image of the girl had vanished.

He pulled alongside the one other car, a compact city runabout belonging to Liz, a fellow Far and Fast Walks Society (FFWS) Surrey branch committee member.

Eddie swung his athletic frame out of his mud-spattered limousine, the well-defined features of his long face topped by a full head of shaggy white hair.

Liz, in her mid-fifties, was sturdy rather than elegant.

After brief greetings, Eddie rummaged in his car boot for his requirements as walk leader: his rucksack that included such essential items as a map, compass, rain gear, extra layers of clothing for cold weather, emergency first aid kit, packed lunch, head torch in case they were unable to complete the walk before dark, an electronic navigation aid and route recorder. Finally, he fastened his gaiters over sturdy hiking boots.

'Weather's not going to be good,' observed Liz.

'No, looks like rain.'

'I've mapped the Christmas walk, so you can put it on the programme.'

'Oh good, lunch is booked for 1.30 pm. When do you think we should set off?'

'Let's go for 9. It's about 10 miles, and we've a stop for mulled wine and mince pies.'

Eddie scuffed his feet on yellowish mush shed from the tread of his tyres. Looking up, he again sensed the brightly clad figure among the surrounding undergrowth of holly, brambles and ferns. The light shone through once more into the recesses of his soul. The young girl was there, but now with a second girl, brassier and more overtly sexy. She seduced him while the first girl looked on frowning.

Eddie glanced at Liz and looked back, but the figure in the shrubbery was gone, along with the mental images dragged from his long-lost past.

Two more cars swung in, further squashing the mouldering log, partially obstructing the car park entrance.

Jenny, a bright, attractive divorcee in her forties, bounced out of her modest hatchback waving to Liz.

'Lizzy, that pumpkin and garlic soup recipe was brilliant. I loved it. You're a genius.'

'More where that came from. I'm buried under pumpkins this year.'

'Fantastic, love them. What happened about the roof?'

'I had someone in, but it's still leaking.'

'How awful for you. Couldn't they come back and do it properly?'

'I called, but he fobbed me off. Anyway, I don't trust him now.'

'Shame about that, but I'm sure other folks can fix it.'

'My Trevor would have sorted it.'

'Yes, I know,' Jenny commiserated. 'Must be awful for you without him. How are you bearing up?'

Eddie left the two in conversation, turning his attention to the battered four-by-four off-road vehicle that had pulled in a little distance away.

The occupant was a tall, powerfully built man in his early thirties. He did not catch anybody's eye, focussing on gathering what he needed for the walk. Eddie vaguely recognised the face but couldn't quite place who he was or where they might have met.

'Hello, I'm Eddie.' He put out his hand.

'Tim Drenbold,' said the man, without accepting the handshake.

'Er… I'm thc walk leader for today.'

'Oh, right.'

'Have you been out with us before?'

'No, I usually walk with Thames Valley.'

'Ah, so you must be from over that way.'

'Yes, Slough.'

'So not that far then.'

'No.'

'I think I remember now; you've been on one of our challenge walks?'

'Yes, the Founders Memorial Challenge, last year and the year before.'

'That'll be it, must have seen you then.'

Eddie was relieved to break from the stilted exchange when cars came into the car park, further pulverising the log, reducing much of the attractive yellow glow of the toadstools to a beige pulp.

Eddie could now clearly distinguish the figure of a man in amber-orange clothing standing behind brambles in a cleared area just beyond the car park. Once again, the searchlight shone through into his mind. He was with the second girl between a high fence and racks mounted with bicycles. A third figure emerged, a powerfully built boy in football kit. There was anger and accusations. Eddie felt the impact of the boy's fists pummelling his body and smashing into his face. Then he was on the floor, the boy's heavy boots thudding into his body. Eddie screwed his eyes to see better, but the memories disappeared.

He tried to process the fleeting impressions that had briefly yet vividly intruded, but he had to greet a flurry of new arrivals.

Stan and Mary Potterswell were happily married and longstanding FFWS members. Reg and Ivy Nettleberry were another couple who had met through their hiking activities late in life after losing their original spouses. The two couples were happy chatting, so Eddie turned his attention to the others.

Larry Bettersby arrived in his flashy Porsche, a relentlessly athletic, thrusting individual in his mid-thirties competitively obsessed with setting record times.

Superficially, Karen Doddleston, another arrival, had much in common with Larry. She was obsessively sporty, fast, taut and wiry, sleek in her tight-fitting lycra, always quickly among the leaders in challenge events, a committed vegan, her diet sparing almost to the point of starvation.

Larry and Karen faced each other like boxers in a staged pre-fight weigh-in.

'Hello, Larry and Karen,' said Eddie. 'Glad you could come along.'

'Glad to be here,' acknowledged Larry. 'Sounds like it'll be a good walk.'

'Picnic lunch, I understand,' said Karen.

'Yes, no café or pub, I'm afraid,' said Eddie.

'So, you won't be getting your massive steak today,' remarked Karen, looking in Larry's direction. 'Surprised you're here, in that case.'

'I come for the walking.'

'Not from what I've seen,' Karen retorted. 'Always stuffing your face and guzzling ale whenever I've seen you anywhere.'

Eddie found an excuse to duck from the barbed comments. That log blocking the car park entrance was getting on his nerves. He wandered over to deal with it. The crumbling remnants of crushed rotten wood and slippery mangled yellow toadstools slithered in his hands as he picked it up to toss it to one side. The damp mess landed with a thud onto a heap of wet leaves and moss, releasing a cloud of fungal spores that blended into the miasma of clammy autumnal decay permeating the drizzle-soaked air.

As he wiped his hands on his trousers to remove the clinging wet mush of fungus and moss, Eddie made out the luminously glowing figure emerging from the trees bordering the car park, a man in bright yellow anorak and distinctive amber-orange hiking trousers.

Eddie reflected that he was the most brightly dressed of those present. If they happened to be out after dark and obliged to walk along any road, the man's clothing would qualify as high visibility, which could only be good.

A strong feeling overcame Eddie that there was something more to this man. He was some messenger, but the nature and origins of the message remained a mystery.

He noticed that by a remarkable coincidence, the colours of the man's clothing matched the strange toadstools growing on the rotting log. The man's jacket harmonised with the glowing lemon flecked with white around the toadstool's rim, while the trousers matched where the toadstool darkened at its centre.

The figure almost glowed as he advanced to Eddie. 'I'm here for the FFWS walk.'

'You're in the right place. I'm Eddie. I'm leading the walk today.'

'I'm Miles.'

'Is this your first time out with us?'

'Yes, though I hope there will be others.'

'Well, yes, I hope so too. We're always pleased to welcome new walkers.'

The man had emerged from nowhere rather than driving in, but this did not faze Eddie. He may have arrived earlier, walked around, popped into the woods for a call of nature, parked a little distance away, strolled, or had a lift. Nor was Eddie the least surprised he did not recognise the individual. Many unfamiliar people attended social walks, including new members and members from other FFWS groups such as Thames Valley or Sussex.

Eddie had a nagging feeling Miles was familiar. He

didn't want to ask outright if Miles was a new member, or perhaps not even a member, lest he might make Miles feel unwelcome or cause offence by failing to recognise him.

'Have you come far?'

'I'm over from the other side.'

It was not a detailed reply, so Eddie indicated with his hand in one direction. 'You mean from that way?' Eddie imagined Miles could have meant the other side of the nearby trunk road.

'I'm entirely from the other side.'

Eddie looked quizzical and turned to peer diametrically opposite to where he had first gesticulated. Still, Miles gave no hint as to whether he was looking in the correct direction. Eddie felt that this place Miles referred to was somewhere else entirely, a different place, yet Miles seemed to imply it was nearby.

'Do you know anybody else from the group?' Eddie inquired, gesturing to the others who, in the main, stood chatting—an exception being the taciturn Tim from Thames Valley.

'I am familiar with some of them,' Miles replied cryptically.

'Perhaps I could introduce you to Tim,' said Eddie, hoping the two newcomers might have something in common.

Leaving them together, Eddie rejoined the main throng.

Liz and Jenny paused their animated chatting. 'That gentleman you were just talking to,' enquired Jenny. 'Is he someone we should know?'

'I don't think so. It's Miles. New member, I think, or potential new member.'

'Great, we need new members. Liz and I were just saying we thought we knew him but couldn't quite place him.'

'I had that feeling,' Eddie admitted.

'Funny,' said Liz.

'Must be Alzheimer's,' quipped Eddie.

'Odd thing is,' observed Jenny, 'it wasn't only Miles who seemed familiar, but when I saw him, I recalled other things as if he had reminded me of them.'

'Yes,' said Eddie.

'What sort of things?' asked Liz.

'Things from long ago. I had forgotten until I saw him just now.'

Liz frowned, half opened her mouth, then closed it. 'I've got a few things to share.' She stepped over to her car and emerged with a tray of special homemade plum and gooseberry flapjacks.

Perceiving the large shaggy dogs peering from back windows and the attire of the drivers, it was clear to Eddie a couple of new approaching cars were unlikely to be participants in the FFWS walk. He reflected that dogs were a valuable health aid, encouraging regular exercise and toughening immune systems with the dirt they brought into households.

It was 8:50 am, time for the tedious but necessary administrative task, collecting the names and details of those present as stipulated by the FFWS's insurance company for health and safety. He passed around his clipboard and ballpoint pen.

Eddie hoped this exercise might have yielded information about the mysterious Miles. When the list returned to him, dampened by the light rain, he saw his full name as Miles Miteby, but in the contact location, all he had was The Other Side, and there was neither a membership nor a mobile phone number. Whatever the insurance company might have thought about the lack of detail, Eddie did not feel moved to question the matter.

It was coming up towards 9:00 am, the scheduled start, for which the FFWS was always punctual. Eddie shepherded the group together.

He was about to explain his plans when a large 4x4 all-terrain vehicle pulled into the car park. Eddie checked in case it was another last-minute walker arriving. It wasn't. There were two chunky trail bikes strapped onto the back. Cyclists, concluded Eddie. He hated cyclists on footpaths. They chewed up paths, disturbed the peace and ran people down. He frowned. Shouldn't be allowed.

Eddie returned his attention to his expectant audience. 'The route will be muddy today, in view of the recent weather conditions. There are some hills, but not too bad. About 22 miles to cover, with around 2,900 feet of ascent, that's just under 900 metres for those who prefer metric.'

No doubt someone would verify, using their smartphone app, thought Eddie, looking toward the keen Larry Bettersby.

'No pub or café stop today, but a nice woodland spot is just over the 11-mile mark. Forecast isn't good, so waterproof clothing advised.'

'It might be sunny on the other side,' Miles remarked.

'Shouldn't think so,' said Eddie. 'The forecast is for increasingly heavy rainfall during the day over the whole area.'

The ominous dark grey cloud blanketing the heavens from horizon to horizon supported Eddie's prediction.

With everybody gathered and ready, Eddie set off purposefully onto one of the footpaths leading from the car park into the damp misty gloom of the woods, the others following, including the mysterious Miles, from the Other Side, glowing a bright yellowy amber.

Wet in the Woods

Led confidently by Eddie, the walkers wended with practised confidence through the uneven woodland terrain, stepping over and around tree roots, sliding off stones treacherously greasy with wet mud, snagging feet on brambles, traversing the junctions of branching paths with only densely packed trees, clumps of brambles and a few dips and hollows to serve as navigation landmarks.

Some leaders would have constantly checked their map and taken compass bearings, while others tracked their progress via mobile phone and GPS. Eddie had a feel for where he was within the landscape. Lacking his sense of direction, others were mystified, putting it down to extra-sensory powers. It could have been subtle signs like the shapes formed by tree stumps, a fallen log, a distinctive rock protruding through the path, spiritual guidance, or instinct.

Taking the occasional wrong turn in the woodland maze did not worry Eddie. He would confidently head towards paths that felt likely to rejoin his intended route. In the unlikely event of his losing the plot entirely, they would eventually hit the edge of the woodland from where he could steer around the perimeter, justifiable as an opportunity to enjoy the lovely view over the neighbouring valley.

Through the woods, Eddie was not only preoccupied with navigating the twists and turns but, as a sheepdog, with keeping the group together and accounted for. He could relax and converse with companions when they broke out along a more defined path in open country.

Some walkers are more talkative. Many walked for peace and seclusion. As one misanthrope put it, a man from the north of England who favoured remote and rugged wilderness, preferring animals to people and liking solitude best of all because 'there's no bugger there.' Nevertheless, those who attend a group walk, while not always the most sociable folk, might be assumed to enjoy at least a modicum of social interaction with their companions.

Eddie's life was governed by structure, routine, healthy living and physical fitness, which he applied diligently in his role as the FFWS Surrey branch Walks Secretary. Pedantry had accentuated his naturally meticulous nature demanded in his long career in information technology, a vocation he had been obliged to take early retirement from to care for his now departed wife, Margot, in her final years. He was not naturally chatty but, particularly in his role as a walk leader, considered himself obliged to make an effort.

The two close friends, Liz and Jenny, kept up a more or less continuous chatter, but being so wrapped up with each other, did not facilitate drawing the less connected members into the conversation. Likewise, the two married couples, the Potterswells and Nettleberrys. were self-contained with each other in lively chat.

The mysterious Miles was keeping close behind Eddie, so it was natural for Eddie to engage with him. Besides, Eddie was curious.

Whenever there were newcomers, it was a concern for walk leaders as to whether they would sustain the pace of the group and cover the distance because it was not unusual for those used to more sedate rambles to overestimate their capability, struggling to keep up with the FFWS's relentless tempo. Eddie need not have worried about Miles, who glided with an effortless gait.

Except for his colourful attire, the remarkable thing about Miles was that there was nothing remarkable about him, a blended composite of twenty thousand randomly selected men who morphed into whatever you imagined.

'You're still working, I suppose,' said Eddie to draw him out.

'I'm an Energy Prospector.'

'You mean solar, wind, geo-thermal, that sort of thing?'

'No, another sort of energy.'

'Nuclear?'

'No.'

Perhaps it's some exotic new technology, Eddie imagined, something commercially sensitive he didn't want to discuss.

'Do you have any family?'

'In a manner of speaking.'

'But married, I suppose.'

'No, not married, but I come from a large family over on the Other Side.'

'Do you do any other sports or anything apart from hiking?'

'Not specifically, only what's necessary to fulfil my mission.'

Oo-er, thought Eddie, we'll be getting into religion. Better be careful.

'Your mission. That sounds intriguing.'

'My mission is to restore what has been lost from people's lives.'

Well, it was an explanation of a sort, but it left as many

questions in Eddie's mind as it answered.

'You shouldn't have let Susan slip through your fingers,' said Miles quietly.

Eddie was taken aback. He should have had no idea what Miles was talking about. Yet instantly, he knew what and who he was referring to. It was Susan Sensberry, who had been his first all too brief love of his life as a teenager. In the same instant, he knew who Miles reminded him of. Jez Jackdaw, a schoolmate who, when they were both sixteen years old, urged him to do whatever it took to restore his relationship with Susan, as much wooing and grovelling as it took after he had abandoned her in a vain, ultimately humiliating pursuit of the teenage sex siren, Lucy Lansburg.

In that moment of recognition, Miles became Jez. Yet logic said Miles could not be Jez because he would have been the same age as Eddie, sixty-two, and Miles couldn't be as old as that. How old was Miles? On reflection, it was tough to tell, but forty-five at the most, in Eddie's estimation. So how then did Miles know about Susan?

Eddie looked intently at Miles, but by then, Miles was already slipping back to chat with other walkers. Unable to make sense of his exchange with Miles, unnerved by it too, Eddie diverted his mind by checking he still had all his group safe, well and within sight. In the meantime, Miles eased himself back alongside the chattering duo, Liz and Jenny.

Liz was strong, fit and vigorous, with the hearty enthusiasm of someone accustomed to country pursuits. Even in the first blush of youth, Liz had a chunky no-nonsense outdoorsy air rather than the slender elegance and grace of her prettier contemporaries—something she had always envied when she saw it in others. It would have been wonderful to have enjoyed their effortlessly seductive looks. In her mid-fifties, the decades had taken their toll, eroding her limited sex appeal, leaving her face and figure with the comfortable, lived-in appearance of someone later in life, about as far from a femme fatale as it was possible to be.

Her friend Jenny was altogether closer to that archetype, being younger, in her mid-forties, having kept the elegant frame of her youth, still well-preserved with the help of yoga, pilates and a sensible diet.

Liz and Jenny had been talking about the love-life of their respective children insofar as they had chosen to share it with their parents.

'My Sharon has been moody,' Jenny observed.

'Why's that, do you think?'

'She has a boyfriend, which is nice for her, but there is some difficulty between them.'

'What sort?'

'I'm not sure. She won't talk to me about it.'

'These amorous encounters at a young age,' intervened Miles, 'are more foundational in their lives than their supposedly more important college studies.'

Liz and Jenny thought for a moment and then nodded.

'Have you heard anything from James Trellwell,' Miles enquired, looking in Liz's direction, 'considering how close you were during your own college days?'

Liz was thrown off balance. She had no contact with James for over 30 years, since their acrimonious parting those years ago. She had not forgiven James his indiscretion with that salacious trollop, Lucy Greshing. In a flash, she realised why this Miles seemed familiar. He must be Andy Tillborg, James's friend from that time, who had interceded on James's behalf, begging her to relent and give his friend another chance.

There was an awkward silence. 'Your leaky roof, would you like me to put you in touch with someone to fix it?' Miles continued.

He must have overheard us talking before, Liz concluded.

'Well, I wouldn't mind,' she said. 'I've been struggling to find someone reliable.'

Miles turned towards Jenny. 'In hindsight, do you think that marrying Paddy was right for you?'

Like Liz, Jenny was thrown off kilter. With her and Paddy now divorced, it couldn't have been right. But Miles must be John Natting, her urbane wedding planner, the only one who had intimated she should rethink.

'Probably not, seeing how things have turned out.'

'Perhaps you should have kept in touch with Tracey Trubb,' said Miles.

Jenny blushed. How could he know anything about her feelings for Tracey? She hadn't shared that with anyone. This Miles, John Natting, whoever, had an uncanny mind-reading power.

Leaving the pair uncharacteristically reflective, Miles slipped back along the column of walkers to converse with others.

While observing Miles's interactions, Eddie was struck by his eerie connection with whoever he spoke with, though presumably not having met them before. Despite his lack of distinguishing features, there were things people thought they recognised. He was someone they knew or, like a human chameleon, used some mysterious agency, hypnotism or shapeshifting to fit the imagery in their minds.

Out in the open country, it was a little brighter, but without the tree canopy more exposed to the steadily streaming rain, a relentless spray trickling down people's faces and seeping around the seams of their rain gear.

After days of rainfall, the path was inundated under brown puddles and slick with cloying, slippery mud. Some tried avoiding the worst by hopping and stretching between patches of wet grass, only to find them angled at a slope, slippery as ice, tipping them over like skittles. The more experienced took the simple course, walking right through the middle, mud, puddles and all.

Over a stile encroached by brambles and hawthorn from the adjacent hedgerow was a ploughed field on a slope, a hard slog up the incline, slippery ground, suction from the clinging mud, the extra weight of the clay clods wrapped around their boots, sodden raingear and rucksacks dragging on their shoulders.

A further stile gave onto another field being grazed by cattle, slightly easier going now, downhill over the rain-soaked trampled grass interspersed with cow pats, then a gate that could only be approached through a swamp of an ankle-deep slurry of mixed mud and cow muck.

Opening onto a track leading along a valley, the going was more accessible. At some point, the geology changed from sedimentary clay to limestone. A turn off the route led up a steep climb through a field of grazing sheep. The wet chalk was slippery as glass, constantly threatening to turn an ankle.

Most walkers slow when challenged by a slope, but for those with a competitive streak, a hill climb is a challenge to flaunt superior fitness. Nobody was keener to demonstrate toughness than the ever-combative Larry and Karen.

Larry was a tough, wiry man in his mid-thirties, around six feet, his body lean and sculpted by relentless exercise.

Karen was slim and sleek, five feet seven, with a body like Larry's, optimised for endurance and every bit as tough.

As the group ascended, Larry and Karen stepped up, quickly moving to the front of the field, each determined to reach the hill's crest first and especially to be there before their detested rival. Reaching the summit in front and making it appear effortless was essential, so, with pounding hearts, they fought to dampen their laboured breathing. Miles came along, gliding like a ghost making the ascent as if he was as light as air.

Larry made the crest first, mere strides ahead of Karen, but it was a Pyrrhic testosterone-driven victory, leaving him gasping. Karen was annoyed he had been in front but contented herself that she had reached the top in better shape. Miles was the real victor, drifting behind Karen, cool, calm and relaxed.

As the remainder of the group caught up, Karen noticed something Miles said had left Larry pale and quiet, deflating his cockiness. She was pleased.

On a fine day, there would have been a splendid view from this vantage point, Eddie's selected spot for a break, but now there was nothing to see through the rain and mist. The reunited group extracted refreshments from rucksacks temporarily exposed under bright plastic rain covers. The Potterswells and Nettleberrys shared a thermos flask of hot coffee, sipping the invigorating liquid out of collapsible fold-flat cups. Karen's refreshment was a draft of a fruit smoothie out of a bright stainless-steel flask. Others chewed cereal bars and homemade flapjacks.

Batteries recharged, Eddie's flock set off with renewed vigour in the face of intensifying rain across more chalk downs, a stretch of heathland with gorse and bracken leading into a pine forest typical of the sandier areas in Surrey, a couple more fields and a path up a slope into dense mixed woodland. Coming to the top of a small hill, the course broadened, having been used by tree-felling vehicles, deep ruts churned by chunky tyres, claggy with glutinous mud under a relentless downpour, leading into the clearing Eddie had designated for their picnic lunch.

Logs from felled trees made suitable seating for the group picnic within the clearing, lying at the junction of woodland paths. On a barmy day of summer sunshine, it would have been idyllic. Under these conditions, the surrounding trees closed like dripping giants about to swallow the unsuspecting into sinister forest depths. A crumbling lichened sign identified the spot as Sorcerer's Copse.

Eddie checked the time: 12:40. Good progress, considering the conditions.

Walkers trudged around inspecting which sodden logs might be the least uncomfortable, trampling on a profusion of the same yellowy orange toadstools Eddie had noticed earlier in the car park, scattering clouds of fungal spores.

'It's wet today,' Miles pronounced as he took centre stage among the logs, his clothing glowing with renewed brightness like a lantern through the murk. 'Wouldn't it be nice if we found somewhere warm and dry?'

Several people murmured agreement.

'Somewhere with hot soup and refreshing beer,' Miles continued.

There was a collective groan at the gall of this interloper winding them up, dangling unattainable delights. Miles waved his hand to quieten the muttering.

'I'm quite serious. I know a good pub, just around the corner, not more than ten minutes away.'

Eddie was simultaneously confused and annoyed by this presumptuous intervention from someone new to the group. They were miles from anywhere, and he had reconnoitred the route encountering no habitation near this location; nothing was shown on the map. Where could Miles have in mind?

'How do you mean? There isn't a pub within miles of here. I should know.'

'Oh, but there is,' insisted Miles. 'Just over there, on the Other Side.'

'Well, I've never seen this place.'

'Honestly, it's there,' said Miles, 'not more than a ten-minute stroll.'

'We haven't got time for detours.'

'Why not?' said Larry. 'It's not as if we have a deadline.'

'Typical,' said Karen. 'Any excuse for beer and burgers.'

'Actually, why not?' said Stan Potterswell. 'It would be nice if Miles knows somewhere.'

There were murmurs of agreement.

'They'll be busy making posh Sunday lunches,' Eddie objected. 'They wouldn't welcome a group of muddy walkers.'

'It won't be a problem at the Miteby Arms,' said Miles.

'I know the landlord, and he'll be fine. Plenty of space and a lovely log fire to warm and dry ourselves.'

Eddie baulked. 'We wouldn't want our picnics to go to waste, and the pub wouldn't let us eat them inside.'

'The landlord is a personal friend,' said Miles. 'As you're with me, he'll welcome us, I promise.'

Although aggrieved by Miles's impertinence, Eddie sensed the charismatic pull Miles now had over the group, a hold over people that was as powerful as it was inexplicable. An attempt to reassert his leadership that would be a losing battle. Devoid of valid objections, he would have to humour him. Miles would end up humiliated when, after a pointless amble into the woods, this pub turned out to have been a figment of his imagination.

'Well, alright,' said Eddie. 'Who wants to give this pub a go?'

Hands went up, and Eddie could see Miles had a majority.

'Well, Miles, it looks like we're going. It had better be good.'

Sheltering from the Rain

Miles took the lead along a path that led around the gnarled ivy-strewn trunk of a majestic oak, under a sturdy arch of rugged branches and into the dense interior of the wood following a deep gully set between high earth banks densely clad with undergrowth, brambles, nettles, saplings, a tapestry of ivy tendrils and a rich assortment of seasonal fungi.

Following the rear, Eddie remained smug, confident they would soon emerge over a stile on the wood's edge into the field with a herd of cud-chewing cattle devoid of habitation for a mile in any direction. Within minutes, order would be restored as Miles was exposed for leading them on a wild goose chase.

But then he wasn't quite so sure. Instead of the gully veering around to the left, as he recalled, the bank on the right dropped, and the path followed a slope that tipped over to the right. The trees differed too. He had remembered them growing densely as a thicket, but the trees were large and dispersed. They had been in the gully, from which, to his recollection, there were no junctions or deviations from the path, yet, without seeming to branch away, they were now in open woodland.

In minutes, they hit the edge of the wood, rewarded with a vista of the surrounding countryside, unlike anywhere Eddie had anticipated in Surrey. Even the weather was different, the rain had eased, and a watery sun emerged through thinning clouds.

Fields were marked with dry stone walls and traditionally laid hedges. Sunk into the contours of the landscape and protruding slightly above the hedgerows were the thatched roofs of dwellings with wood smoke drifting from chimneys, behind which a church tower rose above the trees.

The path followed one hedgerow a couple of hundred yards, emerging onto a narrow country lane. A short way along the lane, a sign read, Welcome to Miteby. That's curious, thought Eddie, because Miteby was the surname Miles had put down on the attendee list.

Coming into the village, a hedge gave to a terrace of timber-framed cottages; some fitted out as little shops, a bakery, a greengrocer, a hardware store. They emerged before the village green, with the church set back on one side and the village pub, the Miteby Arms, on the other. Miles's surname again, Eddie pondered, does he own the place?

There was something odd about the handful of cars parked around the edge of the green, all old classics from around 50 years ago or more, yet immaculate, gleaming as if in their first flush of youth.

Eddie attempted to regain control, gesturing to the comfortable benches around the green. 'The weather's better, and these look perfect for our picnic.'

'No need to be outside,' Miles contradicted him. 'There'll be a nice fire going inside and ale for those with a thirst. Drinks are on me.'

The interior of the pub was warm, traditional and welcoming. The light from the brightly burning log fire that Miles had promised lit up the large inglenook fireplace and reflected off the well-worn flagstone floor. Brightly polished horse brasses hanging over the mantelpiece and above the bar glinted. The bar was solidly but simply constructed out of sturdy oak timber, its surface worn smooth and flat, stained to deep mahogany by spillage from countless frothing pints of dark ale. There were tall stools in front of the bar for those who liked to converse with the bar staff and chattier patrons, tables for groups to socialise, and niches with cosy benches and window seats for those who preferred a tête-à-tête.

Miles hailed the landlord, who came over, beaming a warm welcome. The landlord took orders for drinks and something warm and sustaining from the pub's menu of simple food for those who fancied more than the meagre rations they had with them in their soggy rucksacks, encouraged by the surrounding aroma of steaming broth and fresh-baked bread. The landlord told them not to worry about paying just yet. They could settle up at the end.

There were already several people spread around the bar who appeared to be best of buddies with Miles, exchanging cheerful greetings with him. Eddie's unease at having his leadership displaced was the greater knowing he was disorientated and dependent on Miles to lead the group back out of this mysterious place. Eddie scanned the pub's regulars, not expecting to know anybody but hoping to feel slightly less inadequate if there were at least someone with whom he was acquainted.

Against the odds, he caught the eye of someone familiar, confirmed when she smiled back. At least she seemed familiar. Eddie could not quite recall who she was nor when or where they had met. He ought to talk to her, but what could he say?

'Hello.' He reached to shake her hand.

'Hello, Eddie,' she replied, taking him aback as she

leaned over to kiss his cheek.

She had remembered his name and knew him on a close social or even intimate level, yet he still couldn't place her. It must be like this for people with Alzheimer's, thought Eddie, when they don't recognise people. He couldn't be getting dementia, could he?

Eddie internally cursed Miles for getting him into this hole and remembered Miles's odd remark hours earlier. Of course! The woman was Susan, the first love of his life from over forty years before. The memories flooded back, and he knew it was her beyond the slightest doubt.

'Hello again, Susan.'

Yet logically, it didn't make sense. For it to be Susan, she would have to be his age, sixty-two, but she was nowhere near that old. On the subject of age, there was something odd about the people around Miteby, Miles included. It was hard to tell their age, being somehow ageless or changing before your eyes to whatever age you imagined they might be.

Looking at Susan, Eddie was right back to when they were briefly Romeo and Juliet, with her, now sweet sixteen. Disgusting, he thought, an older man like him lusting after a teenager.

Looking again, she became an attractive, fully grown-up but still youthful woman in her thirties. Still too young for me, thought Eddie.

He blinked, and Susan was an attractive mature woman of around sixty.

He must be hallucinating. But he didn't have time to worry about that. Susan was talking to him in the familiar West Country accent he remembered, asking about what had happened to him in his life, and he was telling her about his late wife, Margot, his career in information technology, how hiking in the countryside and remote mountainous places cleared his mind. Neither of them mentioned the incident with Lucy Lansburg.

The walking party had come in expecting to sit together and chat among themselves, but the group fragmented to all corners of the pub, pairing up for intimate chats with local people they knew.

Like Eddie, Liz had made eye contact with a man who might have been a lover of hers from the past from how they interacted, withdrawing with him into a quiet niche to reminisce. He was in his early twenties, if not younger, so if he had been Liz's love interest, he would have been what the popular press refers to as a toy boy, with the sort of looks that could have earned him a place in a magazine for teenage girls. While it was none of his business, Eddie was incredulous at seeing Liz in the role of a cougar.

But then, Liz looked young, as if she had absorbed the essence of the man's youth, still recognisable as the Liz he knew, strong and vigorous rather than sleek and elegant, yet unquestionably a younger version of herself, contemporary with her companion.

Meanwhile, Liz's friend, Jenny, usually inseparable from her best friend, had herself been diverted into another corner by a woman with whom, from appearances, she had a close, almost intimate relationship, a well-formed young woman who had an air of rugged toughness, a tomboy who would fit in well in a stereotypical man's world such as lumber-jacking or fire-fighting.

From their demeanour, the friend was a contemporary

of Jenny's, although she was so young it didn't seem possible. Yet when Eddie observed the two together in this environment, Jenny, like Liz, had transmuted into a much younger version of herself. The pair could have both passed for teenagers.

To Eddie's surprise, he noticed the inscrutable strong and silent Tim deep in conversation with an eccentric young woman with a curious dress sense, hair arranged in twin plaits and round spectacles on her round face. He overheard a few snippets about some fantasy world involving the deeds of the heroic Sir Gladdifon slaying the monster Mengelfang and rescuing the damsel Princess Beatefice from the clutches of the wicked Dragellog. It didn't interest Eddie, but he remembered from somewhere that these were characters from the cult series, *Citadels of Vallborg*.

Only the two happily married couples, Stan and Mary Potterswell and Reg and Ivy Nettleberry, remained to chat happily around a table, unaffected by the uncanny surroundings.

By a miracle, the landlord kept track of the locations of his guests, bringing their orders of drinks and warm sustaining food, even managing refills as they remained absorbed, catching up with old times.

As Eddie drained his second pint of Meadow Dew ale, he came to his senses with a start. They couldn't linger here all day. There were still another 11 miles to cover, and that was after they somehow got themselves back to Sorcerer's Copse, which he wasn't sure he could manage alone. He looked for Miles. He needed to gather people and organise Miles to guide them back to what should, by rights, have been their picnic spot.

Eddie quickly scanned the pub for the members of his group, making a quick count so as not to miss anybody. Apart from the two couples, there was one other exception to the dispersion of the group. Larry and Karen were having a close tête-à-tête, surprising to Eddie because the two bitter rivals usually never had a civil word between them. It was odd in another way Eddie couldn't put his finger on.

Eddie would not have been surprised if his tally had come up short, but coming up with one more than the listed attendees was difficult to explain. He pondered for some seconds, and then the other reason for it being odd seeing Karen and Larry together became apparent. He had already seen her talking to someone else, an older man, at the other end of the bar, so he had counted her twice. Either she had a doppelgänger or moved rapidly without him noticing.

Eddie found Miles chatting with the landlord.

'Miles, we need to get going. Can we settle up?'

'Don't worry about it,' said Miles. 'I'll take care of it.'

'Are you sure? That's very generous of you.'

'Not at all. You're my guests when we're here in Miteby.'

The landlord rang up the amount on an old-fashioned mechanical cash register. It came to 2 pounds, 12 shillings, and 4 pence. Miles took out strange green pound notes, a brown ten-shilling note, a silvery florin, a twelve-sided brass threepenny bit and a giant brown-bronze old penny, which the landlord counted into the till.

Eddie watched open-mouthed. He could recall the old money from the 1960s, and this was like finding oneself in an old movie from that bygone era.

The group piled on with their appreciation of Miles's generosity. The excursion had been most enjoyable, and Miles's and the landlord's hospitality had made this a wonderful day, regardless of the dampener the weather had put on things.

Miles led them back the way they had come. Strangely, although in Miteby, the rain had stopped and the sky had looked clearer, once they had trekked up the gully through the woods and reached Sorcerer's Copse, there was the same total glowering dark grey cover as before, and the rain was cascading at full pelt.

'Darn it,' cursed Larry as he checked his recording device. 'It's stopped recording.'

'How do you mean?' enquired Eddie.

'It has our route from this morning, but the recording stopped just after we went down into that gully.'

Eddie checked his watch. It said 12:45. It didn't make sense. They must have spent almost an hour and a half in Miteby, plus 10 minutes each way to get there. That would be the best part of two hours. Yet his watch said that they had only been there 5 minutes.

Folk were a little more subdued during the second half of the walk, confused about the occurrences in Miteby, combined with an unnatural feeling, shared by all, of having been drained of energy. Eddie was simultaneously relieved to have reassumed his leadership but unnerved by his temporary loss of control and the strange events.

Everyone dug deeper into their reserves of stamina as they tackled the challenges of hill and dale, fields and woods. On the hills, Larry and Karen were still up front but less competitive, Larry even allowing Karen to emerge in the lead. Karen brusquely left him in her wake but, feeling her fatigue, felt no triumph.

Liz brought out two baking trays at the car park, one with her homemade apple and blackcurrant flans and the other a delicious carrot and greengage cake. There were also still some of the plum and gooseberry flapjacks left from the morning. By now, most walkers felt worn out, unusually so because, although it had been a reasonable distance over tough terrain covered briskly, it was well within their capabilities. It was a feeling of being mentally drained as much as physically tired. Out of politeness, most stayed to sample Liz's excellent culinary offerings and chat but did not linger, saying their goodbyes as soon as they decently could.

Miles had silently slipped into the woods before anybody could say goodbye.

Inexplicable and off Kilter

Not since recently recalled incidents from adolescence had Eddie felt so deeply unsettled as in the days after the excursion from Sorcerer's Copse.

As a man of reason, it was illogical for those experiences to have thrown him so much off-kilter. Everyone was back safe; nothing unpleasant had occurred, indeed quite the contrary. All had thoroughly enjoyed the interlude in Miteby.

Eddie stretched awkwardly on the sofa in the living room of his substantial home in West Byfleet. He had the television on, a crime drama he usually liked, but he couldn't focus on it.

He switched off the television, picked up a magazine and wandered out through the bi-fold doors into the conservatory, flopping onto an easy chair. He read a paragraph about the political situation in Mexico. He recognised the words, but they soon faded; reaching the end of the article, he realised he had absorbed no content. He flipped some pages and tried an article about investment opportunities in green energy. No good. His eyes glazed.

Perhaps a cup of tea would help. A second bifold led through what had been a dining room but had been adopted by Eddie's late wife Margot as a hobby room. Eddie had a vague intention of repurposing it now she was gone but couldn't imagine to what purpose. Being alone, it wasn't as if he needed more space.

Eddie had made an initial attempt to sort through, organise and dispose of Margot's things, but he hadn't progressed far in what was by now almost two years since she had died. He had pushed some of her craft tools and materials to one side and piled her clothes and personal effects into heaps spread about the place.

He moved on into the kitchen. There were sets of cutlery and dinner services in the drawers and cupboards, but Eddie only used one of each item from the everyday set, now chipped and scratched.

Some things needed taking care of, Eddie resolved. He took his cup of tea to his study. On his large desk was a laptop, to which a large display screen, printer, scanner and other accessories were connected. On most shelves around the wall were reference books, stacks of journals and carefully labelled box files organised into categories, apart from one where he had items of a sentimental nature, carved animals, a childhood teddy bear and a framed photo of Margot.

There were the arrangements for the FFWS Christmas event to be finalised, a notification to be sent out about next week's Halloween-themed walk—reminding people to wear suitably spooky outfits—and a problem with a walk scheduled for November because a bad knee incapacitated the walk leader. I'll probably have to step in, as usual, Eddie reflected.

Beyond that, there was next year's Munro bagging excursion to the Scottish Highlands to arrange, as well as Alpine hiking in Austria. There was so much to be done Eddie was paralysed.

This had become the pattern for Eddie since Margot passed. He coped with the loneliness by focussing on his hiking enthusiasm, leading groups on adventures, weekends in remoter parts of the English Lake District, and challenging expeditions based on the exploits of British elite forces in the Welsh mountains. Fresh air, exercise, the companionship of fellow trekkers and his administrative duties on the FFWS committee filled the yawning gaps in his life if not necessarily giving it meaning.

Eddie gazed at the photo of his dear departed Margot.

It hadn't been a marriage of passion, but a loving companionship extending more than 30 years. They hadn't had children. Eddie couldn't decide whether that good. He wouldn't have been left quite so alone if there had been children.

This home he had shared with Margot for so long was now out of scale for his needs. Most of the rooms were pleasant enough and had happy memories, but there were too many. Some rooms he hardly went into at all.

Eddie and Margot had adjusted the home to their needs, and being childless meant they had the luxury to spread out and enjoy the space, reception rooms, a conservatory and a dedicated hobby room for each of them. There was a broad expanse of the back garden and an area for shrubs and flowers at the front, next to the generous driveway and integral garage.

It was the second home they shared. Their first was a little maisonette down the road in Byfleet, too small and lacking in character for them to feel settled, but all they could then afford. This one was to have been their forever home. As for Margot, it was. After nursing her through the years of her long illness, Eddie had been with her as she passed away in their marital bed. But for Eddie, it was questionable whether it should be his forever home too.

Not only was the home too big for him, but it was

chock full of clutter. He even had bits and pieces in the garage salvaged from their place in Byfleet, untouched for over twenty years. After two years since Margot's passing, it was time to get to grips with the memories and sentimental attachment and clear the junk.

It would be sensible, Eddie acknowledged, to move somewhere more suitable, but he was torn between the recent sadness and happier memories.

It was an uncomfortable topic but kept coming back into focus because it informed every other decision. What was his purpose in life? When Margot was alive, this had been simple: to share his life with her and make her happy. Before, he had a secondary purpose with his career as an IT professional, securing their financial future. With both gone, the answer was unclear.

He could see two paths, ploughing along as always, focused on his interests such as the FFWS, or branching out afresh, a course that left Eddie, who liked to be in control, paralysed by the fear of risk and uncertainty.

The perplexing events around Sorcerer's Copse were unnerving, not least from having lost control of the situation to the mysterious Miles. The myriad of apparently unexplainable occurrences discombobulated him, the strange place of Miteby that was absent from every map, the sleight of hand with the access path.

There was only one reasonable explanation. Miles Miteby was an eccentric millionaire who had built his own 1960s-style private theme park but kept his project under wraps.

There were other oddities Eddie couldn't get his head around. The way time stood still while they were in Miteby and the lack of any trace on Larry's electronic route recorder. Also strange was that group members had taken photos during the walk, but none included Miles or Miteby.

In Miteby, it had been odd how so many of the group had been diverted by prior acquaintances. It was also peculiar how he had seen Karen twice, almost as if she had been magically in two places simultaneously.

Those had been the tangible matters. Disturbing as the unexplained technical anomalies were, meeting Susan had disturbed Eddie's equilibrium the most.

Eddie had never mentioned it to anyone, but throughout the years, he had always carried a flame for Susan and considered her the love of his life. His tenderest thoughts had been for Susan. They had both been sixteen, their first love. There had been only a minimum of intimacy, holding hands, some kissing and a little petting, but it felt like the real thing, eternal love.

It was not to last. All was shattered by the arrival of the sexually precocious Lucy Lansburg. With puberty, Lucy quickly discovered the power she could exercise over boys and men alike, including Eddie. While more timid girls would have been intimidated or repelled by such male attention, Lucy revelled in it.

Lucy had a sexual magnetism impossible to ignore, particularly for pubescent boys like Eddie and his schoolmates. Fond as he was of Susan when Lucy was in the vicinity, his attention inevitably swung in her direction, attention Lucy not only noticed but encouraged.

'Do you like what you see?' she enquired.

Eddie nodded.

'Would you like to see more?'

Eddie could only blush and stare at the floor.

'Come now, don't be bashful. What kind of a man do you think you are if you can't respond to a real woman?'

'Of course, I can deal with a real woman,' Eddie stammered.

'In that case,' said Lucy, tickling him under his chin with her finger, 'come around the back of the scout hut after school.'

All a-tremble Eddie did as he was bid. Lucy was there as promised, but she was not alone. With her was Duncan McTaggetty, the huge star member of the school football team and a notorious schoolyard bully.

'He's the one who has been leering at me and making disgusting suggestions,' said Lucy, pointing at Eddie.

Eddie received a rapid succession of crushing blows from Duncan's fists. First hurled against the wall of the scout hut, Duncan continued pummelling until Eddie slid down onto the floor, where Duncan finished off the brutal beating with a kicking with his heavy Doc Marten boots.

Lucy's story around the schoolyard was that a lecherous Eddie had enticed her around the back of the scout hut, where he had tried to take advantage, her virtue only saved by Duncan's heroic intervention. For a time, Eddie had been a pariah among his contemporaries. Susan quickly dropped him, backing away as if he was diseased.

From then on, Eddie had felt deep guilt, shame and regret about his sexuality, disgusted about where his urges and fascination for the comely female form had led, and especially regretful about the shattering of what had seemed a made-in-heaven relationship with Susan. Susan would always be his idealised vision of love.

It was years later that he met Margot. Theirs had been a delightful friendship built on shared interests and a compatible humour. The friendship had probably only developed precisely because Eddie did not initially have carnal desire for her. Had he done so, he would have been nervous, either backing away or ruining everything with a clumsy pass, as happened on many of Eddie's previous encounters. He may not have seen the relationship in a romantic light, at least not early on, but Margot had other ideas, and Eddie had coasted along.

Eddie certainly loved Margot, if only platonically, and throughout their many years together, they had always endeavoured to be the best and most devoted husband. But deep down, it was not carnal love. That was reserved for Susan, which hardened Eddie's resolve to track down Miteby and uncover its mysteries.

Back to Miteby

Eddie's plan to locate Miteby was a systematic survey of paths fanning out from Sorcerer's Copse, focussing especially where Miles had led the group to Miteby and back.

Recollecting this path down to a grazing cow field, Eddie planned to follow it up towards Sorcerer's Copse, checking for previously unnoticed deviations.

Setting off at around 8:30 am the following Friday, Eddie quickly covered the ground from the nearest parking place about a mile away. Checking en route for signs of unmapped habitation that could have been Miteby, he struck off from the footpath, crossed a field to investigate buildings hidden in a dip that he had previously swept past without interest, to find only two barns, an older one with its roof caved in and a larger intact modern replacement.

The cows in their field and the path towards Sorcerer's Copse were, as Eddie remembered, leading up through the wood along a gully between two high banks covered in brambles, ivy and saplings.

As the path flattened at the top of the hill, Eddie saw the distinctive large oak tree where it emerged onto Sorcerer's Copse. Looking from within the clearing, there was no doubt this was the path along which Miles had led the group to Miteby, perplexing because his meticulous examination of the route hadn't revealed the slightest indication of any other path crossing or branching off.

The time on Eddie's watch was coming up to 9:15.

Baffled, he wandered between the fallen logs, kicking

and trampling on the clumps of yellow and orange toadstools. Frustrated, he shouted, 'Miles, I don't get it. Where is this Miteby of yours?'

A voice replied, 'It's not far, just over on the Other Side.'

He swung around to see Miles, glowing in his bright yellow and orange outfit, standing beside the oak tree, emerging from the same path Eddie had arrived from.

Although momentarily startling, Miles's appearance wasn't a surprise. Eddie acknowledged everything about Miles was odd, but who exactly was this Miles character? A second later, it was clear, not a logical deduction, simply a revelation. He was Jez, his schoolmate from years ago.

'You're Jez, aren't you?' said Eddie.

'Yes, that be me. Remember how we went round Langport together? We had some larks, didn't we?' replied Miles, or rather Jez.

Miles, as himself, had no discernible accent, but his voice shared the same chameleon quality as his appearance, seamlessly matching whoever he was conversing with or represented. As Jez, a West Country burr came through, reflecting his and Eddie's shared upbringing in the Somerset town of Langport.

'Yes, I remember now,' replied Eddie, his own West Country tones reasserting themselves over his acquired bland home counties middle class received pronunciation.

'It'll all be flooding back. You'll see once we're over on the Other Side,' assured Miles in his guise as Jez.

'I don't know what you mean,' said Eddie, more puzzled than ever.

'You did ask me about Miteby, didn't you? You want to go over there or not?'

'What, you mean now?'

'Yes, why not?'

Eddie hesitated for only a second or so. 'Alright then,' he replied, for once throwing caution to the winds.

'Well, let's go.'

Like an excited little boy Miles bounded back along the path under and around the sizeable spreading oak tree, beckoning Eddie to follow.

The path was familiar as it led down the gully between the high overgrown earth banks. Yet, they were somewhere else within a minute, seamlessly without any transition.

As on their previous visit to Miteby, they emerged from the wood, but the season had changed from a grey, wet autumn to a warm and bright summer's day, probably July or August. As before, the surroundings were pretty and inviting, and now in the sunshine of high summer, it was idyllic, full of the buzzing of bees, birdsong and the myriad scents of the countryside.

It wasn't only the season that had altered. There was a difference in scale. Everything, the trees, hedgerows, fences and gates, appeared bigger. Miles had transmuted into the guise of Jez, but not any Jez; he was a young boy of around eight or nine years old. Looking at himself, Eddie could see himself also regressing to the same age.

Their clothing was different too. They were now wearing frayed grey flannel shorts, short-sleeved cotton shirts with a check pattern and leather sandals over grey woollen socks.

Jez ran on ahead, skipping and scampering.

'Come on, race you to the village.'

Eddie ran along behind in a childish bounding gait.

'Let's go to your auntie's,' suggested Jez. 'She might give us lemonade.'

Eddie was puzzled. 'My auntie? Where's she then?'

'At her house, silly.'

Eddie followed Jez, who skipped ahead, taking them past the Welcome to Miteby sign, then dashing along the garden path of one of the little cottages on the village outskirts. The door opened, and his Auntie Jane stood as Eddie remembered her from all those years ago.

'Oh, hello boys, what have you been up to? Mischief, no doubt,' said Auntie Jane in her thick West Country burr.

Jez scuttled past her through the front door, with Eddie skipping behind. Auntie Jane followed on through to the kitchen. There was a smell of cooking. Auntie Jane opened the oven and slid out a tray of freshly baked pasties, still piping hot.

On the sturdy timber kitchen table stood a jug wrapped by a circular net cover with ceramic beads sewn around the sides to weigh it down over the rim.

Auntie Jane let the boys share one of the pasties and wash it down with a mug each of lemonade from the jug. No sooner had they gulped their refreshment than Jez had them dash off for further fun.

'Could we see Susan?' Eddie asked as they approached the village green.

'Yes, we might,' Jez concurred.

'She might be in there,' said Eddie, beckoning towards the Miteby Arms.

'Shouldn't think so,' said Jez. 'There's only grown-ups in there, and they wouldn't let us in any way.'

'Oh, no, I suppose they wouldn't.'

47

'Let's go and see the trains,' urged Jez.

Jez skipped out through the other side of the village and then turned abruptly off to dash across a field with Eddie following close behind. Their route sloped down into a valley with a railway line marking its route. A little way along the track was a short rough platform on its own without accompanying buildings, a sign announcing it as Miteby Halt. Despite approaching puffs of smoke, clickety vibrations on the rails, and chuffing and clanking, Jez and Eddie scurried across the track, ignoring the signs threatening a forty-shilling penalty for trespassing onto the trackway, running up onto the platform.

As they arrived, a short passenger train hauled by a smoking, clattering steam locomotive emerged around a bend in the track, trundling into the little station.

'Can we have a ride?' Jez called out to the driver. 'On the engine.'

'Not allowed,' the driver called back.

'Go on,' said Jez. 'Just this once. We won't tell.'

'Alright, just this once.'

Jez and Eddie ran up beside the engine.

'Jump on, quick now,' urged the driver.

Each in turn, the fireman grabbed them by the arm to haul them aboard.

'You'll have to get off at Hollingsby, mind, next stop,' said the driver. 'And make sure nobody sees you and all.'

Excitedly the boys asked the driver and fireman what all the wheels and levers did as they rattled and rocked along the track. In turn, the driver held them up to let them each pull the cord, operating the engine's whistle as they approached the small town of Hollingsby.

The driver held the young lads back while looking

around for the station master and guard, choosing his moment when both were preoccupied.

'Quick boys, off you go,' he urged, hustling them quickly onto the platform.

'Round here,' said Jez, nodding his head to a train shed at the far end of the platform, well away from inquisitive ticket inspectors.

Eddie followed Jez in, squeezing through a tight gap behind the train shed and then through a hole in the dilapidated fence, letting them out onto a road climbing up through the town, whose stone and slate dwellings clung onto a hillside.

'Let's go up there,' suggested Jez, indicating granite outcrops above the town.

He led the way onto a rocky path, zigzagging uphill until they reached a wire fence overlooking a rock quarry. A sign said Danger Keep Out.

'Let's pretend we're prisoners of war escaping from the Nazis,' said Jez as he lifted the wire mesh to make a gap at the bottom.

He squirmed through on his belly with Eddie close behind.

'Better be quick; they've got SS and Gestapo after us, with bloody great hounds on our scent,' Jez said.

They hurriedly clambered down the steep slope, sending cascades of loose stones over the rock face.

At the bottom, a large opening led into a tunnel sloping deep underground into an inky blackness out of which wisps of foul sulphurous fumes emanated from unfathomable depths. The rocks vibrated from distant low rumbling, heavy machinery clanking, thudding, reverberating deep below.

Eddie made to investigate, but Jez held him back.

'Better not go in there. It leads to the Underside, a perilous place. There's Underhexes down there.'

'What are Underhexes?'

'Them's that lives down there. You wouldn't want to meet them.'

Eddie peered down into the abyss with awe.

'Better get back now,' said Jez. 'We can get the bus.'

'How are we going to buy tickets?'

Jez checked his pockets. He had half a crown.

'It's ninepence, child fare,' Jez figured. 'So that's one and six for the two of us. Shilling change'

They took seats on the back of the bus, which was raised, giving them a good view of the typically English landscape of rolling hills and meadows.

Back in Miteby, they came across two children, a boy and a girl. Eddie didn't know them, although the boy looked familiar.

'Who are they?' Eddie whispered.

'Tim and Tina,' said Jez. 'They're friends. Always together.'

Jez and Eddie sat on the grass a little distance away, far enough not to intrude but close enough to hear their conversation, from which Eddie could tell that they were lost in some strange pretend world discussing the minutiae of how the wizard Tennmer called upon the powers of the mighty spirit Odel to defeat the demon Doomengel. Eddie didn't know much about it but vaguely remembered it concerning the *Citadels of Vallborg* series.

They passed the pub again, the Miteby Arms, but Eddie's attention was drawn towards the little village shop. The recent rushing around had created a hunger and thirst for something sweet and refreshing.

The establishment sold nearly everything for the household, but the sweets and other children's treats excited Eddie and Jez. It was a hot day, and the ice creams the shop sold at 6d a time were particularly enticing.

'I paid for the bus,' said Jez, 'so now it's your turn.'

Eddie checked his pockets and found a shilling and a couple of threepenny bits. He couldn't imagine how they had got there, but it would cover the ice creams.

They were leaving the shop when a cheeky little girl, young Susan Sensberry, came in. She looked at their ice creams.

'Do you want one?' asked Eddie.

She nodded eagerly. 'Oh, yes, please.'

The two threepences covered it, leaving Eddie's pockets empty. The three of them sat on one of the benches on the village green, eating their ice creams.

'Better get you back home,' said Jez.

They took the now familiar path back to Sorcerer's Copse. Jez slipped away, and Eddie found himself alone, fully clothed in his practical hiking gear on a damp day in late October and feeling every one of his sixty-two years.

He checked his watch, 09:22. Somehow, he had spent all day on the Other Side, and here he was with his watch telling him it had taken almost no time.

It may not have taken time, but it had taken its toll on his energy. He couldn't remember feeling so drained. Somehow, on autopilot, he trudged back to his car. He took the same path as he had approached Sorcerer's Copse initially, the same path as Miles or Jez, whoever he was, had taken him over to the Other Side and back, which this time led him back to the field of grazing cows, just as the map said it should. Eddie was too tired now to be perplexed, too weary of doing anything except get himself home, too drained to even think about what could have happened, to do more than collapse into bed, exhausted.

Rekindled Passion from Long Ago

The first hint of morning light glowing in the windows wasn't sufficient to see by, so Liz turned on the light as she came down into her kitchen for breakfast.

Stepping into her larder, a lean-to construction on the side of the house, she sighed as she noticed the spreading brownish-black stain on her ceiling, sagging and split with an expanding crack, dripping water onto the floor.

Carefully avoiding the expanding puddle, she surveyed what she might blend in with her porridge. Rows of shelves lined all three walls of the little room, groaning under the weight of produce, some still raw from the garden, others preserved in jam jars, Kilner jars, sealable plastic containers and storage barrels.

Liz's diet, daily work in the garden, and regular long-distance walking contributed to her overall fitness, robust constitution and sturdy figure.

Selecting a couple of figs and a pear, she came back into the farmhouse-style kitchen with rustic beams and a flagstone floor. Liz put her pot of coffee substitute, a blend of dandelion root, chicory and cinnamon, onto the range to heat. She rummaged among the miscellaneous saucepans, mixing basins and earthenware pots for a pan to pour a cupful of organic oats for her porridge.

After breakfast, with the day's first rays of sunlight, she wandered out to survey her substantial garden spread around the cottage, extending to about an acre. Apart from a token piece of lawn and flower borders at the front of the property, almost the whole plot was devoted to fruit and vegetables, raised beds for carrots, onions, potatoes, beans and cabbages, a tract of orchard with assorted varieties of apples, pears and plums, trained raspberry and blackberry canes, pumpkins and two greenhouses, one dedicated to propagating seeds, the other for tender crops such as tomatoes, radishes and lettuce.

As always, Liz carried a trug with her to gather ripened crops. The blackberries were finished, but there were plenty of pumpkins, some remaining apples and aubergines from the greenhouse.

Liz's life revolved around coping with her ever-bountiful harvest, in one sense, a joy. Abundant apples, pears, onions, lettuces, courgettes, potatoes, raspberries, carrots, parsnips, radishes and various herbs greatly exceeded her needs, giving her a constant worry about how to distribute them and guilt as beautiful, wholesome food inevitably shrivelled and rotted when it could not be consumed in time.

Her chocolate box cottage-style home, in its picturesque setting on the outskirts of the charming village of Brocklehirst, in the Surrey hills not far from Dorking, drew gasps of admiration from passers-by. At its core, the cottage dated from the 18th century, extended in the 19th century, again in the mid-20th century and finally by the Lenburys themselves in the 1990s to accommodate their growing family, resulting in a substantial home with four charming bedrooms, three downstairs reception rooms, a generous hall and kitchen diner that was the heart of the home. She had shared the comfortable and cosy family home with her late husband Trevor and two daughters, Nancy and Amy, but these days, living there alone, Liz sometimes wondered whether it had become too much for her.

Some years ago, Liz's daughters, Nancy and Amy, had flown the nest intermittently during university term time and then permanently as they pursued careers. They eventually married and established their own households. Even now, with Trevor gone, Liz preserved the girls' childhood bedrooms ready for their return at any time, their original single beds exchanged with doubles after they were married.

When the girls had first left home, Liz and Trevor had welcomed their quieter, more relaxed lifestyle, but for Liz, the place only really came to life with a family atmosphere on the rare occasions the girls briefly stayed.

Trevor had enjoyed a lucrative career working in the Lloyds insurance market in the City of London, providing amply for them as a family. Liz had also had her own career as an office manager, despite not needing the income, which was only a fraction of what Trevor earned anyway. When, about five years ago, Liz's firm closed down its Dorking operation, making her redundant, they had agreed that getting another job, especially one that involved a stressful commute into London, was not something she needed to do, giving her more time to spend on her horticultural passion.

Just two years ago, while Liz busily cooked and bottled their excess fruit harvest, Trevor had gone to tend to cuttings in their greenhouse. Later, concerned by his prolonged absence after dark, Liz had found him stretched out cold on the greenhouse's rough flagstones, dead from a heart attack.

With their two daughters rallying round, briefly, they were a family again, saddened and diminished, but still a family, until the girls, grown women now of course, but still in Liz's mind her little girls, had returned to their own lives, Nancy in Zurich with her husband, a Swiss banker, and Amy resuming her career as an ecologist in the Philippines.

Telling herself there was no time to mope, Liz briskly walked back into the house. Apart from getting that confounded roof fixed, she needed things for the fête in aid of the church restoration fund, cakes to hand out at the next FFWS walk, and the food bank in Dorking was always grateful for fresh vegetables. Today there was fruit to be bottled, and she would make jam and bake cakes if she had time.

It was a struggle at this time of year, harvest, because she couldn't always cope with everything. The food bank had more than they needed, and the vegetables only lasted so long, even in the larder. It was always a shame when good food went to waste, though it wouldn't go completely to waste because she would fork the mouldering excess into the compost heap from where it would be recycled to produce even more the following year.

Liz collected apples from the larder for bottling. She picked up her little knife to start peeling and coring the fruit, cutting around emerging brown patches of rot.

It was no good. She couldn't focus. The vivid image of James Trellwell, young and glamorous, never far below the surface since her visit to Miteby, inveigled into her consciousness, front and centre, jostling aside other thoughts. She laid her knife down.

She knew it was foolish and unrealistic, but the gorgeous sexy likeness of him would not depart. She could do nothing to suppress her reaction to his phantom presence. Her face flushed, her nipples swelled and hardened against her blouse, and her knees flopped apart in response to the woosy wetness. Her imaginary James had become her ardent lover, urgently wanting to have his wicked way with her, here and now. Liz slid her fingers between her legs, slipping inside, pressing and stroking, her fingertips representing James's hard male member. Her fingers did their work for a brief few minutes, bringing her urgently to a moaning climax.

She flopped back, her racing heart and rapid breathing gradually subsiding. Damn, she thought. Sitting in a slippery mess, she knew she would have to go to the bathroom to clean herself and change her soggy pants. This was now the third occasion that this had happened in the brief time since she had been reacquainted with James in the Miteby Arms.

She could not resolve the situation like this, Liz realised. Masturbation gave her only temporary release, but in the process, it raised James's presence in her psyche. I don't know what has come over me. I'm generally not like this at all. Before the Miteby episode, I went for months with barely a carnal thought.

Her dear departed Trevor had ignited little more than a glow of cosy togetherness, but he was a pleasant, kind, companionable man and a good provider. Once they had met, Liz had already abandoned expectations of ardent passion.

It had only ever been James who invoked those feelings. All had been well until the intervention of that hussy, Lucy Greshing, who, in the full knowledge that she and James were an item, had unscrupulously seduced him. It wasn't as if Lucy mainly wanted him because, within a short time, she had cast him aside like an old item of clothing. She did it out of sheer devilment because she could and for the power it gave her. Liz had hated Lucy more than she had detested anyone.

At that time, Liz had been so deeply hurt by what James had done she could not forgive him. In hindsight, that had been the biggest mistake of her life. Never again would she meet anyone who could affect her as he did.

And then, in Miteby, James had reappeared. Liz's feelings were more than sheer lust; they were the joy of first love rekindled.

For decades I may as well have lived in a nunnery, Liz mused, but now, having tasted the passion I could have had, I can't let it go.

But what could she do? There were mysteries on top of mysteries about their visit to the Miteby Arms, as if it was a dream and hadn't happened at all. Absent from an online search and not on any map, Miteby seemed not to exist. Miles was mysterious too. He had appeared to be Andy Tillborg, James's friend. How could that be? All a figment of her imagination, perhaps. It had felt real, though. Liz felt compelled to figure it out, but she would need help.

Sponged down and with fresh underwear, Liz phoned her friend Jenny.

'It's Liz. How are you?'

'Good, thanks, completing on the new flat today,' Jenny announced.

'So, you're moving out then?'

'Yes, boxes all packed, all ready to go.'

'I'm sorry, it must be a wrench, losing your home like that.'

'Not to worry, new start. I'll be fine.'

'Is Paddy around?'

'No, he moved out a couple of months back, with all his stuff. No need for him to be here.'

'But it's all his doing, this business of you splitting up and losing the house and everything. The least he could do is to be there to give you a hand.'

'Better off doing it on my own, to be honest,' said Liz. 'Paddy would just be in the way.'

'But it's a lot to cope with. He should be there for moral support if nothing else.'

'My morals are holding up alright. Can't imagine he would improve them much.'

'I'd say not, after what he's done, the swine.'

'It's not all his doing, us breaking up. I don't want to make him the villain. Best if we don't fall out.'

'You're a saint, the way you always see the best in him, despite what's happened.'

'Listen, Liz, I've got to go now. Removal men are here, and they're demanding mugs of tea.'

'We should get together for a natter, when you've got a chance.'

'Yes, that'd be nice.'

'When would suit you?'

'Well, I'm off work for the rest of the week to move in, but I'll be busy.'

'Yes, of course, you will. Suppose I come over to you for a quick coffee.'

'Well, okay, but not in the flat. It'll be chaos in there.'

'How about that café in Dorking, where we were before? The Muddy Duck.'

'Great, tomorrow at about 11?'

A New Home

'Just waiting for my friend. Okay if we sit over there?' said Liz, indicating a table in the window, well placed to see people coming and going, in the street and within the café.

Well-practised at baking, Liz observed the cakes and scones on offer with a professional interest. Too much sugar and cream, not as healthy as her cakes, which used more wholesome organic vegetables and fruit.

A corpulent woman heaved across the threshold, stood breathing heavily for a moment before dragging herself to the till, and gasped a couple of seconds before treating herself to a large slice of chocolate gateau laden with whipped cream. Liz smiled with grim satisfaction.

Jenny sprang lithely across the threshold and glanced around the shop. Spotting Liz, she smiled and waved, then swiftly glided over as gracefully as a ballet dancer.

'What can I get you?'

'A flapjack and an Americano coffee would be lovely,' replied Liz.

Jenny shimmied across to the till and placed her order before striding back to take her place next to Liz. Moments later, the waitress came over with a tray, setting down one austerely black Americano and a flapjack for Liz alongside a frothed creamy Cappuccino topped with powdered chocolate and a monster slice of the cream-laden chocolate gateau for Jenny.

'How do you stay so slim?' enquired Liz, wrinkling her nose.

'I'll have you know I've burned off a load of calories

getting my stuff set out in the new flat.'

'Alright, I suppose you have,' Liz conceded. 'How's it going?'

'Still chaos at the moment. Boxes stacked up everywhere.'

'Sorry to have dragged you away when you're so busy.'

'Not at all. It's good to take a break from it.'

'It's such a shame that Paddy is putting you through all this.'

'To be fair, it's not just about Paddy.'

'Well, he ran off with that floosy from his office.'

'He did. But things hadn't been very close between us for some time,' explained Jenny, glancing downwards.

'You mean he lost interest in you, more interested in that floosy of his?'

'To be honest,' said Jenny, screwing up her face, 'it was more me who lost interest.'

'Typical bloody man, just after getting his kicks without a care for your needs.'

Jenny squirmed. 'Look enough about me. What's happened about your roof?'

'Nothing. Still leaking.'

Jenny waited for more details, but Liz's eyes had strayed towards the door of the café. Jenny followed her gaze to a well-put-together young man as he went to the till. The words 'Miteby Roofing Services' were sewn across his workman's overalls.

For a moment, as the young man came in, Liz thought she was seeing her James, not as he would be now, but as she remembered him all those years ago and bizarrely as she had seen him again recently in the Miteby Arms: a trim athletic body and smooth, youthful face with hair in blonde curls. A closer look told her it wasn't James, but someone who could have been his brother.

'I know he's nice, but you needn't drool quite so blatantly,' said Jenny.

'My boss, name of Miles, called earlier about a couple of bacon butties,' said the young man to the woman behind the display of cakes.

'Excuse me a moment,' said Liz as she leapt up abruptly from her seat. Jenny watched wide-eyed as she dashed over towards the till.

'Excuse me,' she said to the young man. 'But did you say Miles called to order the butties?'

'Yes. Do you know Miles?'

'Well, sort of,' said Liz. 'He told me he would send someone to look at my roof.'

'Roofs are what we do. When did he say that?'

'A few days ago. Anyway, here you are, so I thought I'd mention it.'

'Oh, right. When did Miles say we'd come over?'

'He didn't say exactly. It was all a bit vague.'

'Give me your details, and I'll remind him.'

Liz jotted down her phone number and address on a paper napkin.

'You're a one,' said Jenny, once Liz was back in her seat.

'What do you mean?'

'I mean a cougar, preying on innocent young men.'

'I wasn't preying on him.'

'Come off it. The way you pounced on him, giving him your number and everything. I've never seen anything like it.'

'It was about my roof.'

'If you say so,' said Jenny, her face contorted with

scepticism.

The location of Jenny's new flat, a conversion from what had once been offices above a branch of the Midshires Bank, situated on Dorking's busy shopping thoroughfare alongside local pubs and restaurants, was a mixed blessing, great if you enjoyed being in the thick of things, less appealing if you weren't keen on noise and traffic.

Jenny returned to the chaos, squeezing past unopened boxes in the hallway. Further boxes were stacked against the wall in her bedroom, several already open, their contents spread over the bed and drawers competing for space on an easy chair with a pile of assorted clothing. She had set herself the objective of at least making the bedroom and bathroom reasonably tidy by bedtime, even if it meant shoving some stuff onto the untidy heap in the living room.

Ultimately, she reflected that some things would simply have to be dumped. She had tried to get rid of belongings before she left the marital home, but she hadn't turned out nearly enough. The new flat wasn't big enough to take it all. More space would have been nice, but the harsh truth was that this was all she could afford on half the proceeds from selling up the home she had shared with Paddy. With Paddy's career as a carpenter and joiner and Jenny's job in the travel agency, they had earned enough to afford the mortgage on their modest three-bedroom semi, pay the bills and enjoy small luxuries, but that had left them nothing to spare or save for a rainy day.

There was a box on the floor she had been putting off opening, where she had packed items she didn't need but were sentimental. On the top was a decorative cardboard box adorned with a Swiss scene of snow-covered peaks and a chalet set out with Christmas lights. It was a box of chocolates Paddy had bought her. The contents had long since been consumed, but she had kept the box. Inside were other small gifts from him: costume jewellery, a joke keyring and little cards with messages telling her how much she meant to him.

Tears welled. He had undoubtedly loved her, that was clear, and he had been patient too. Such a pity she couldn't feel for him the way he had felt for her.

She had tried. On their wedding night, he had been ardent to consummate their marriage. She had gone along for the ride, but in truth, she had not felt much excitement. Not to worry, she had thought, the passion would grow. Plenty of time. But it didn't. She pretended as best she could so as not to hurt Paddy's feelings, but she never felt desire for him. Ultimately, she couldn't even make herself pretend, resorting to excuses to avoid intimacy. Paddy, to his credit, had made every effort to bring romance between them, as demonstrated by all these little gifts, but to no avail.

It had been meeting Tracey again at the Miteby Arms that had compelled her to face the truth she had been denying all her life. It wasn't only Paddy that failed to get her love juices flowing; the same would have applied to any man.

Jenny had been sixteen when she first became close to her schoolmate Tracey.

'You're not like the others,' observed Tracey one day.

'How do you mean?'

'They're all going on about boys. You don't do that.'

'How do you know?'

'I've seen you. When they start whispering to each other about it, you keep out of it.'

'Well, I haven't done anything with boys to talk about.'

'Neither have most of them. Doesn't stop them sniggering and giggling about it, almost non-stop.'

'Well, so what if I don't? You don't either.'

'I know. We've got that in common. I think we should be friends.'

So they became friends, going everywhere together, forming an ever-closer bond. Initially, it had been nothing more than that. In her naïvety, it had never occurred to Jenny that their friendship was anything more until Lucy Fanshow, one of the nastier bullies at her school, intervened.

'I think it's disgusting what you do,' said Lucy one school dinner time.

'What do you mean?'

'What you do with Tracey? I've seen you. You're a right pair of dirty dykes.'

Jenny blushed. She didn't know anything about lesbianism, except that it was not talked about. At home, she had heard disparaging things about the activities of gay men, implicitly assuming that women, being inherently nicer and purer, would never do anything like that. Being not even mentioned must make it even worse for a girl to do such a thing.

'We're nothing of the sort,' Jenny insisted hotly. 'Just friends, that's all.'

'Friends with benefits, I'd say,' sneered Lucy.

Although shocked by Lucy's accusation, Jenny did not take it too seriously then, accustomed to Lucy saying nasty things.

A physical dimension developed slowly. As they hung out after school, Tracey found reasons to put her arm around Jenny's shoulders, hug her, and grip her arm or hand, initiating playful rough and tumble. Jenny didn't mind; it felt right, what best mates would do. Such little physical intimacies were not disagreeable.

The traumatic crisis came on a summer evening in the local park. While sitting outside the sports pavilion, Tracey attempted to take matters to the next stage. They were sharing a bottle of wine Tracey had raided from her parents' drinks cabinet, drinking out of plastic cups.

'You do like me, Jenny, don't you?'

'Yes, I do. You're my best friend.'

'We could be more than friends, you know.'

'I don't know what you mean.'

'I mean this.'

Tracey leaned across to kiss Jenny on the lips, and Jenny jerked her head away. While she was still in shock, Tracey reached across and fondled her breast. Jenny pushed her arm up to push Tracey's hand away, whereupon Tracey reached down and stroked her thigh.

Jenny leapt to her feet and screamed.

'What's the matter?'

'I don't want to do this,' said Jenny emphatically, hurrying back home as fast as she could.

Most shocking for Jenny was that afterwards, once she had reached home, she was convulsed with an unfamiliar sexual response. She felt revulsion at herself, and Lucy had been right. She was disgusting.

From that moment, she cut Tracey dead, refusing to acknowledge or talk to her. Tracey tried vainly to ask what was wrong, but Jenny refused to engage.

Later, Jenny tried to do what she considered right, forming relationships with men. Eventually, she found Paddy, who was nice enough: considerate, always trying to please her. She drifted into marriage with him.

Family and friends were delighted, rallying around for the wedding. Only one person, John Natting, their wedding planner, had expressed misgivings.

'These weddings take on a life of their own,' John had observed.

'Yes, I suppose they do,' Jenny concurred.

'With everything arranged, it can be difficult to back out if things aren't right.'

'Why wouldn't they be right?'

'Could be anything. Much worse later, though, if things aren't right, but the wedding has gone ahead to keep the families happy. I've seen it happen.'

'Why are you mentioning this?'

'Just making sure. Not too late to back out if it doesn't feel right. That's all.'

Perhaps, as a gay man, he had a sixth sense, a gaydar.

Jenny had a guilty secret, shared with nobody, that her recollection of that incident with Tracey continued to excite her throughout the years. When she recalled it, she yearned to relive the occasion, but this time embracing Tracey.

'Here's the blackberry and apple jam, the pumpkin and the onions for you,' said Liz as she showed Jenny into her cottage's rustic kitchen.

'Thanks, that's brilliant,' Jenny acknowledged.

'Not at all, you're absolutely welcome.'

'Looks like you've got more on the go,' said Jenny, indicating the pot simmering on the large range cooker containing cored and sliced apples mixed in with the remains of the season's blackberries.

Besides being a functional working area for Liz's industrial-scale food processing activities, with its handmade cupboards in rustic timber, granite worktops and antique Welsh dresser, it was also a convivial entertainment space for guests. They took their places at the rough-hewn farmhouse kitchen table. Liz set out one of her spiced pumpkin and carrot cakes and put the kettle on for tea.

'How is your leaky roof?' Jenny enquired.

'All fixed,' said Liz.

'That was quick.'

'It was that young man who we saw in the café. Did a great job.'

'And that's all he did for you, just fix the roof.'

'Yes, that's all. What else did you have in mind?'

'From the way you chatted him up, I was wondering.'

'Cheeky.'

'Sorry, just pulling your leg. He was nice, though. I wouldn't blame you if you did.'

'Enough about me,' said Liz. 'You need to be looking for someone too; now you're on your own.'

'No, I'm not really looking now. Not sure about men at the moment.'

'Don't let Paddy's behaviour put you off. Not all men are like him.'

'It's not Paddy. I need time now to find myself and figure out what I really need.'

'Don't take too long. We're none of us getting any younger.'

'I'm not sure now that there is a man for me anymore.'

'Of course there is. You're gorgeous looking. So gorgeous, I'm envious. Men would fall over themselves chasing you if you gave them half a chance.'

'Well, what about you then? Besides cradle-snatching young men, have you got anything on the go at the moment?'

'No, more's the pity.'

'But you'd like to find someone, though?'

'Yes, but there isn't much interest in a plain Jane like me.'

'There'll be someone, I'm sure,' reassured Jenny.

Liz nodded. She had a wistful expression as she poured out the tea.

'What did you make of our lunchtime visit on our last walk?' Liz enquired.

'Very strange. The pub was nice, cosy and hospitable, but very odd.'

'The place doesn't seem to exist, yet we were there.'

'I know. I looked it up, and there seems to be no such place. It was called Miteby, wasn't it?'

'Yes, that's right,' Liz concurred. 'I was beginning to think that I'd imagined it.'

'We couldn't both have imagined it.'

'No, so it must be there.'

'That man, Miles,' said Jenny. 'He seemed to be in charge somehow, treating us to our lunch, friends with the landlord.'

'Yes, he was. Funny that.'

'I was thinking, perhaps he owns it, like it's his private

place, so it's not on the map.'

'Could be,' Liz agreed. 'There were all those classic cars and other old-fashioned things. Makes sense.'

'He was odd, though, wasn't he? Seemed to know things about us.'

'Yes, that was creepy. Also, there was someone I met when we were there.'

'You mean someone you knew from way back?'

'Yes, that's right.'

'Happened to me too.'

'Did it?' said Liz, relieved it wasn't just her. 'For me, it was someone from years ago, when I was really young. Strange thing was, he still looked young. I don't understand how that can be.'

'Same here. Very strange.'

'It's almost as if we had gone back in time.'

'Yes, it did feel like that, especially with the old cars and other stuff.'

'But that's impossible, isn't it?'

'Well, until recently, I'd have said it was,' said Jenny. 'But I'm not so sure now.'

'It was a man called James I met there. I'd known him way back. We were very close at the time.'

'I met Tracey, I'd been close with her too, a long time ago. Back at school.'

'Perhaps not as close as I'd been with James.'

Jenny pondered and looked away. 'Oh, I don't know. As you say, perhaps not.'

'Fancy us both meeting someone like that,' mused Liz.

'Actually, it wasn't just us. Did you notice? Nearly everyone seemed to have connected with someone they knew.'

'Now you mention it, yes, they did, didn't they?'

'Almost as if it had all been set up for us.'

'Now that is weird,' said Liz. 'But why would anybody want to do that?'

'Couldn't say, but you've got to admit, it looks like it, the way that Miles knew so much about us, for example.'

'If it were arranged, it would have been Miles. Can't see how it could have been anybody else.'

'He was very persuasive about getting us to follow him to Miteby.'

'A sort of a pied piper,' Liz observed.

'It's getting extra strange, Grimm's fairy tales. Like it's Halloween or something.'

'Eddie didn't like it when he did that. He was quite put out.'

'Eddie likes to be in control. It upsets him when things are uncertain, and people don't do what's expected.'

'So, if this man Miles arranged it all, who is Miles? What does he want?' Liz wondered.

'He reminded me of someone I knew when I was getting married to Paddy.'

'That's funny,' said Liz, 'he reminded me of someone from my college days too.'

'Almost as if Miles is all things to all men.'

'It's been preying on my mind,' Liz confessed. 'I really want to see James again. I don't care if it is strange. I want to go back there. Somehow. Don't know how.'

'Yes, I would too,' Jenny agreed. 'But how exactly?'

'We should talk to Eddie about it,' suggested Liz. 'I could see that he had been disturbed and must be wondering about it all, just like us.'

'Good idea.'

The Expedition

A few days later, Liz, Jenny and Eddie were at the Queen Alexandra pub near Guildford, where the regular Surrey FFWS committee meeting was held.

Larry and Karen, the Lycra-clad rivals, were present too. Having both on the committee could be awkward. The pair could hardly say a civil word between themselves and sat on opposite sides of the group glaring at each other.

The committee members dressed informally, which for some was as if they had just emerged from tending their allotment, but for Larry and Karen, it was what is often referred to as smart casual, the designer label version of informal, immaculately laundered and pressed attire, carefully colour coordinated and tailored to show their sleek figures off in the best light. It intended to suggest that if they *had* arrived from a previous activity, it would have been a gym workout, but without the sweat stains and signs of stretch and wear, rather like James Bond appearing immaculately in a tuxedo supposedly having moments before been in a life and death struggle with enemy agents.

On this occasion, Larry put on his most friendly smile. 'You look really stunning in that outfit, Karen. It really suits you.'

What he said was true. She was beautifully turned out, which admittedly wasn't hard considering the faultless raw material she had to work with.

Eddie's hopes of them having reached some rapprochement in Miteby were soon dashed.

'Keep your pathetic misogynist chat up lines to yourself,' she spat back, publicly and crushingly rejecting his small overture, her face contorted with distaste and mistrust.

Eddie reflected that it took a particularly paranoid interpretation of radical feminism to perceive what seemed to him an honest compliment as a sexist attack.

Larry and Karen sat silently for the rest of the meeting, pointedly avoiding eye contact between them.

Liz and Jenny persuaded Eddie to stay when the sometimes tense and uncomfortable meeting ended.

'Have you had thoughts about that last social walk when we all ended up in that pub?' enquired Liz.

'Yes, I have. It was all very strange.'

'We thought it was strange too,' said Liz.

'There is quite a bit about it that I don't understand.'

'We were confused too,' said Jenny.

Eddie pondered sharing his second visit to Sorcerer's Copse and subsequent even stranger experience but concluded it was too personal and far-fetched.

'What do you think we might do about bottoming out the mystery of this strange place, Miteby?' Eddie mused.

'We don't really know,' admitted Liz, 'which is why we thought we might talk to you about it.'

'Have you got any ideas of your own?'

'It might be useful to return to that place, Sorcerer's Copse, and take a look around,' Liz suggested.

'Good plan.'

'Should we, the three of us, go together, do you think?' Jenny suggested.

'Yes, I think we should,' Eddie agreed.

'How are we going to get there?' enquired Jenny.

'We should come in from a different direction,' said Liz.

'That's right,' agreed Jenny. 'No point coming in the way we did before.'

'I know,' said Liz. 'Suppose we approach from the other end of the path Miles led us down, so we're going up instead. For instance, we might spot something we missed, like a path branching off.'

Eddie frowned. 'Bear with me.' He pulled out his mobile phone, selected his map application and zoomed in on Sorcerer's Copse. 'Here, look, there's another path in we haven't been on yet. Let's come in on that one.'

'Let's have a look,' said Liz, reaching for the phone. She zoomed out the display. 'It comes in from Gettlesdon. Not my favourite place.'

'We're trying to figure out what's going on,' Eddie retorted. 'We can't just look where we like the scenery.'

Taking Eddie's lead, the intrepid explorers, Liz and Jenny, followed this new access route. There was perhaps a reason none of them had explored this path. It was unpleasant.

The team parked on a side road in a down-at-heel suburb in Gettlesdon, one of Surrey's smaller and least prosperous towns. Not being remotely picturesque, Gettlesdon attracted neither tourists nor well-heeled London commuters. The town principally earned its living from the light industry within the Gettlesdon Trading Estate and nearby Mid-Surrey Waste Recycling Plant.

Greeting his companions, Eddie looked at his classic Jaguar and then around the scruffy graffiti-ridden surroundings. 'I suppose the cars will be safe here.'

'As safe as anywhere around here, I'd have thought,' said Liz.

They took the footpath from the end of the street they were parked in, a narrow access between two tall wooden fences, spray painted with graffiti.

'Careful where you walk,' said Jenny, picking between the randomly strewn debris of empty cans, bottles, used needles, cigarette ends and dog mess.

A couple hundred yards on, one of the wooden fences gave way to a rusty chain link fence separating the path from sad-looking allotments, dilapidated wooden sheds, their contents protected by padlocks, dotted amidst muddy strips of land given to vegetables arranged in neat rows.

Eventually, clear of the town, the path widened out alongside a field of turnips.

Their slow trudging through the field's cloying mud became easier as they came out onto a concrete driveway. Still, now at intervals, they were obliged to stop and flatten against the bordering, clothes-snagging barbed wire fence to allow immense tractors towing industrial-scale trailers to pass by.

They became increasingly aware of a foul smell from a gigantic barn-like building looming before them, which did not identify its purpose other than from its unpleasant stench.

'What do you think goes on in there?' said Jenny.

'From the look of it, I'd say it's chickens,' said Liz.

'Thousands of them,' said Eddie. 'Battery hens.'

Having passed the avian gulag, the stink mercifully fading, they walked alongside more fields of various crops to reach the wooded hill topped by Sorcerer's Copse.

From this side, the foliage was untended scrub rather than mature trees. The copious brambles and gorse tore at them as they struggled uphill, following the untended, overgrown and barely used path, leaving them bruised and scratched by the time they approached the crest of the slope, their feet slithering on leathery fungus topped with a dark ruby red toadstool as they emerged into the clearing.

The hairs on Eddie's neck stood up. For a moment, he made out a woman clad in a burgundy jacket rising amongst the surrounding bracken, not just any woman but one with a strange, alluring attraction who had a familiarity about her. He turned to look properly, but she was gone.

'What's the matter?' said Liz, seeing Eddie's anxious look.

'Nothing. I thought I saw someone for a moment.'

Fortunately, it wasn't raining, but the air was chilly, and the sky grey and autumnal. Sorcerer's Copse was very much as they remembered. The broad access path for the forestry machinery was there, as was the path they had followed Miles towards Miteby. The damp logs Eddie considered suitable seating for a picnic remained strewn around.

Having arrived, the trio weren't sure what they should do next. Eddie checked the time on his watch. 10:22. They wandered around for a minute or two, taking it all in, trying to figure out what might enlighten them about the mysterious Miteby.

As she shimmied between logs, Jenny scuffed her boots against a clump of bright yellow and orange mushrooms.

Our explorers became conscious of another presence, a

slight shuffling of fallen leaves, the misty forest gloom lit by a hint of warm colour shimmying like a lantern betraying movement between the trees, revealing itself as Miles emerging from behind the gnarled trunk of the majestic oak tree, marking the path they had previously taken towards Miteby.

While Miles was instantly recognisable, strangely, the people who knew him would have struggled to describe him, and even had they done so, their descriptions would have differed. There was little or nothing about his distinctive appearance, and what features he did show varied depending upon who he was with and the circumstances. An indefinable yet unique aura made Miles recognisable, a ghostly light different from that emitted by familiar material light sources, a spiritual light that could shine into souls.

Miles was followed by three more familiar figures, the trio's ghosts from their distant pasts: Susan from Eddie's, James from Liz's and Tracey from Jenny's.

'It's so nice to see you all. We were so hoping we would meet you here. We'd love you to join us for the Miteby Festival,' said Miles, radiating welcoming happiness.

'The Miteby Festival? We didn't know about that,' admitted Eddie.

'It's on today. We're just in time,' said Miles.

Eddie looked around at the others to assess what they were thinking, then gazed across at Susan, a gorgeous vision of teenage perfection, who looked back with fondness.

'Susan, James, and Tracey were hoping you would join them for the festival as their guests,' added Miles.

Susan, James and Tracey nodded vigorously and

looked at their prospective partners imploringly.

Eddie's heart pounded, his hands shook slightly. He saw Liz and Jenny pale and tense, no doubt beset by the same nervousness at stepping into the unknown.

'What do you think? Should we go?' Eddie asked his companions.

Liz and Jenny glanced at each other, reinforcing their resolve. Their hands bunched into fists, they nodded.

The decision made, they quickly paired off into their three couples, following Miles along the now familiar path past the grand oak tree.

So intent were they on catching up with their long-lost love icons they paid little attention to the path they took through the wood. As they emerged into the countryside surrounding Miteby, the lightning-fast transition from mid-morning to late evening or the instant progression of the seasons from autumn to high summer might have puzzled them, were they not so absorbed with their respective festival partners.

Flickering lights and distant sounds of gaiety were already in evidence as they emerged from the wood, coming over above Miteby's thatched roofs and lighting up the church tower.

As they emerged through the fading light onto the lane that led on into the village, there was a large straw effigy tied onto one of the fence posts, dressed up in old clothes and a garishly decorated face with gnashing teeth, staring eyes and a prominent nose fashioned out of a carrot.

'That's an impressive-looking scarecrow,' observed Eddie.

'Not a scarecrow, that's an Underhex,' replied Miles.

'What's an Underhex?' asked Jenny.

'Not an actual Underhex,' explained Tracey, 'It's an effigy. Later we'll burn them.'

As they walked along the lane, they saw two more Underhex effigies hung on either side of the Welcome to Miteby sign; then, as they went through the village, each of the cottages had its own Underhex effigy hung on its front door or garden gate. The effigies came in all shapes and sizes, with both sexes represented.

As they emerged into the centre of the village, they could see an enormous and ornate Underhex effigy propped up outside of the Miteby Arms.

The village green was strung with lights, assorted stalls and amusements, a steam-powered merry-go-round with ornately painted horses, stalls offering tasty snacks, ale and mead, a maypole strewn with coloured ribbons and a platform on which the village band played and sang raucous songs in a thick West Country accent about combine harvesters, mangold wurzels and buxom maids rolling in the haylofts with farmer's boys. A large heap of assorted timber offcuts and kindling was at the far end of the green, separated from the main activities.

The group dispersed into three couples, Eddie with Susan, Liz with James and Jenny with Tracey.

Miles faded into the background. Usually, when people depart, they do so by physically removing their presence from the scene. But Miles had a different quality, the ability to blend himself into the background as an octopus does against sand and coral, making himself an ever closer match until he vanishes altogether.

As Eddie had been walking into Miteby, he had sensed

the years peeling away to reveal a younger version of himself. A knowledge and recollection of his later years remained, but not as a memory of his past life, instead as a narrative about someone else who shared his name but he hadn't yet become.

Eddie gazed at the lovely Susan. Seeing her now, still aged sixteen, as they had both been all those years ago, he could not conceive of how he could feel desire for anybody else. Susan was perfection itself. Perfectly formed, not yet with the full roundness of a more mature woman, yet more than sufficiently curved to be delightfully sexy, seductively proportioned with the promise of blossoming out into an even lovelier bloom, lovely blue eyes shining out of her round youthful face, her skin smooth as ivory, framed by her shiny blonde plaited hair.

There was a story in Eddie's head of someone else who resembled him being diverted by the temptress Lucy Lansberg, as yet no more than a vague premonition.

Eddie, in his mature form, would have felt there was something indecent about his attraction to Susan. But in this setting, he was again a fresh-faced sixteen-year-old, their togetherness wholesome.

Then the memory of those events all those years ago in Langport came crashing into his head. He felt Lucy's compelling sexuality, altogether more striking than Susan's subtle allure, her sexiness fully formed, instantly eye-catching, the waft of her fragrance as she passed not only promising but demanding animalistic, insatiable passion. It must have been the naivety of youth, falling for the promise of instant gratification.

'Forgive me, Susan, for what happened with Lucy,' said Eddie as soon as they were alone.

'How could you do it?'

'I didn't actually do anything.'

'What, nothing at all? I don't believe it.'

'Honestly, nothing at all,' Eddie insisted. 'I would have done, though.'

'So, what did happen?'

'She invited me to go with her behind the scout hut. I did go, that's true.'

'So, what happened then?'

'Nothing. As soon as I was there, Duncan McTaggetty was there too. He beat the crap out of me, and then she put it around that he had rescued her from me.'

'And that's what happened?'

'Yes, honestly.'

Susan looked Eddie in the eyes.

'Alright, I believe you. I know what Lucy was like. I can believe she would do that.'

'Thank goodness. I thought I'd lost you for ever.'

'It was a long time ago. We can be together now if you want.'

'Yes, I definitely want us to be together, as we should have been all along.'

James was everything Liz remembered. He had an understated masculinity. Not ostentatiously tall, large or muscular, he was only fractionally above average in stature. His body was strong and lithe, compact but with enough breadth in his shoulders and firmness in his arms to feel confident in him for protection, his face smooth and youthful but with sufficient firmness to his brow and jawline to make a woman feel he could be her gallant knight.

Liz, now as herself in her early twenties, contemporary with James, had the advantage of her youth, but no amount of artful presentation would ever have put her in the dolly bird category. Never likely to be selected for dancing in the ballet or a chorus line, she was powerfully built, chunkily athletic and moved with the purposeful air of a workman accustomed to heaving gravel. She was, however, cheerful and witty, fun to be around with an earthy humour.

Taking stock of herself, dejectedly Liz had to admit that as a seductress, she could come nowhere close to competing with that unscrupulous trollop Lucy Greshing, who seduced any man with a single flicker of her outrageously long eyelashes, and often doing so for no better reason than she could and it amused her, the unscrupulous cow.

'Whatever happened between you and Lucy, I don't care anymore,' Liz assured him. 'I have never felt about anyone else the way I feel about you.'

'Thank goodness for that,' said James. 'I curse the day I ever set eyes on Lucy. I have regretted ever since not remaining true to you.'

Tracey, though clearly and delightfully feminine, lacked the fluffiness and vulnerability some women have. Perhaps fluffiness and vulnerability are useful to women by inspiring men to come to their aid and provide protection, but such characteristics were useless to Tracey.

Tracey had the shapeliness and pleasing curves of the female form combined with the confident athleticism and strength typical a well-formed young man in his teenage years, combining within her the best characteristics of both sexes. Her blonde hair was cut short, setting off her blue eyes and round fresh face.

Jenny was also svelte and athletic but slenderer and more delicate than Tracey. They complemented each other beautifully. They were like dance partners, but a partnership where Tracey would inevitably take the lead.

'I'm sorry I was the way I was back then when you wanted to kiss me,' said Jenny.

'I thought you liked me,' said Tracey.

'I did. That was the problem.'

'How do you mean?'

'The way I was brought up, girls weren't supposed to like each other that way.'

'What way?'

'You know, sexy.'

'So, it did make you feel sexy?'

'Yes, but everyone went all, you know, yuk, about being sexy with another girl. I felt I was disgusting.'

'Most natural thing in the world.'

'I realise that now, but it's not how it felt then.'

'I see,' said Tracey. 'I get that. Things were different then.'

'They were. They used to make all kinds of faces about men doing things together, but at least they talked about it. They didn't even say anything about women, you know, doing things like it was so bad it couldn't even be mentioned.'

'How do you feel about it now, us being together, I mean?'

'I feel good about it,' assured Jenny. 'I know that it would be right between us.'

'You really feel that?'

'Yes, totally. Could we perhaps, you know, try again?'

Tracey smiled and wrapped Jenny in a close, affectionate hug. Their lips met, and they kissed passionately with urgent waves of lust swelling through them.

Wrapped up in themselves, the couples spent an idyllic evening getting to know each other again, generously stuffing on the available food and drink and trying various amusements.

As midnight approached, the villagers emanated towards the heap of brushwood at the end of the green. Most were carrying the effigies of Underhexes seen earlier around the village. The pile was set alight, and within minutes huge flames were reaching into the night. The effigies were hurled into the conflagration accompanied by shouts of 'Away with Underhexes' and 'Go back to the Underside, witches.' There were thunderous cheers as the gigantic effigy that had been propped outside the Miteby Arms was hurled on by six of the pub's burliest patrons.

The couples held hands as they watched the effigies flare up and dance in the inferno before crumbling into ash and vanishing. With the fire dying, they had to consider what they might do.

Miles was nowhere; besides it was too late for them to return to Sorcerer's Copse, which now felt like another world.

Eddie and Susan spent the night at his Auntie Jane's. Rekindled as their romance was, Auntie Jane would not allow them to sleep together, so Susan slept in her spare room while Eddie slept downstairs on the sofa.

Liz went to stay at James's parents, where proprieties

were preserved as with Eddie and Susan, and Liz slept separately in the spare room.

Jenny slept on a foldup bed in Tracey's room at Tracey's parents', a sleepover with a school friend considered innocent enough. By now, tired and inebriated from the mead and ale, no more took place beyond holding hands and a little kissing, but taking matters further was in the mind of each of them.

Miles reappeared that morning, calling in at each home where they had lodged. Miles was never seen to arrive. Instead, he would be there without a sound or hint that he was coming. Even out of sight and silent, one would know because his aura would be there too, the disturbing magical light penetrating within, illuminating one's innermost thoughts.

He informed them it was time to return to what he called the Material World, presumably their everyday existence. But not to worry, they could come back another time. Nobody argued. Miles's aura gave him an air of power and authority that inspired confidence and quietened dissent.

They were hungover from the previous night's festivities. The return trudge and their arrival at Sorcerer's Copse was an anti-climax after the elation of the last evening in Miteby. The summer warmth was gone, replaced by the damp morning chill of late autumn.

Eddie checked the time: 10:27. He checked the date too. The same day as they had arrived. Barely five minutes had elapsed while they had been in Miteby. By now, he was beyond surprised. The strangeness was so prevalent as to be expected. Besides, he was so exhausted it had become an effort to think about anything. It wasn't just

Eddie who felt this way. Liz and Jenny were equally shattered.

They sat on the logs in Sorcerer's Copse for a few minutes staring into space. Eventually, Eddie forced himself to his feet, urging the others to gather themselves—time to go home.

Barely a word was exchanged between them as they painstakingly edged down the steep overgrown path infested with gorse and brambles, along the edges of the fields, past the enormous grim shed of incarcerated chickens, emerging into the untidy suburb of Gettlesdon.

It was not only tiredness suppressing conversation on the return journey. Each now had their own private and personal connection with someone in Miteby, a connection each was already plotting to maintain on further visits, but in future alone, these not being matters they were inclined to share between them.

Without lingering, they found their respective cars, fortunately still unmolested, waved quick goodbyes and drove off on their separate ways.

Love in the Summer Time

As morning came, waking late, Liz was in a daze, elated, yet lacking energy. She neither tended her garden, cooked, nor even let her mind do more than drift.

It took a day or so for her euphoria to subside and to regain her need to be on the move, but that need was like an addict's, in one direction, to see her James again as quickly as possible.

Strange and inexplicable as her experiences in Miteby had been, her recollection was clear and detailed, feeling real and fantastic, which is what mattered. Rekindling her relationship with James put her on a high beyond description.

What could she say to Eddie and Jenny about it, she wondered?

Talking to Eddie did not appeal to her. He would get pernickety, examining the inconsistencies, finding a hundred objections to prove that what they had experienced were figments of their imagination.

If she talked to Jenny, she would only remark about cradle snatching. The annoying thing was, Jenny was right; her lust for James had an earthy rapture about it, an obsession she was ready to share with no one except James.

Having made her way to Sorcerer's Copse alone and surreptitiously, stomping around for fifteen minutes, her eyes scanning surrounding trees and shrubbery, she saw nothing remarkable about it all, just the stillness of a damp clearing in a wood.

Then there was a rustling and swishing. Liz's heart

pounded, her heart rate surging like a racing car engine leaping from a tick over to maximum revs instantly. She swung around towards the sound. A large stag emerged from the wood into the clearing and trotted sedately along the tyre-churned muddy track used for timber extraction before disappearing under the forest canopy.

Liz breathed out, unclenched her fists, annoyed at herself for getting spooked by such a harmless everyday happening in the forest. She wandered towards the fallen logs that remained scattered, her boots squelching in the damp mulch that had built up between them, kicking over a yellowy orange toadstool. A dust of spores puffed into the air from the underside of the mushroom's flat top.

'Hello Liz,' said a voice. She turned in its direction, and Miles stood beside the trunk of the giant oak tree dominating the setting. Miles emanated an aura, a reassuring beacon, a light, but not light in a physical sense, a spiritual light shining within, illuminating a person's inner character.

'James would love to see you. He's been waiting for you to come back.'

'Oh Miles,' said Liz, tears of joy in her eyes. 'Yes, I'd love to see him too.'

On the Other Side, it was still summer. James was waiting for her in the Miteby Arms. A feeling of mutual bliss consumed them as they fell into each other's arms, hugging each other so hard they could hardly breathe.

Despite the bits and pieces in Jenny's new flat that still needed attending to since returning from Miteby, all she could do was sleep and then, having slept, even after a mug of strong coffee, doze off again on the sofa.

As her energy levels rose, so did a surge of the sexual response of an intensity she hadn't felt for many years. It didn't matter what she tried to focus her mind on. Whatever it was would be swept aside by an image of Tracey wanting her and herself yearning for Tracey's passion in return.

She fought to suppress it. It didn't make sense. Surely Tracey would be well into middle age by now, not the sweet sixteen-year-old she met in Miteby. It could be no more than a dream, yet, it felt real enough.

Days went by. Jenny went back to her routine, working in the travel agency. At work, she kept herself together, but in the evening, the vividly sexual, passionate dreams of Tracey returned, haunting her.

She resolved that however improbable this vision of Tracey was, she must go back in case this spectral lover might actually be there.

She backed away from sharing her thoughts with Liz or Eddie, unready to share her sexual proclivities with anyone, not even close friends.

Back in Sorcerer's Copse, uncertain what might enable access to Miteby, Jenny hovered around the path leading into the woods beside the ancient oak tree, stepping over and around fallen logs, crunching on the prevalent fungal growth.

Miles appeared, glowing in the grey autumnal gloom, commanding her attention and confidence with his unique radiance.

'Tracey is waiting for you, Jenny,' he informed her.

She followed along eagerly, in a short time to be joyously reunited with her Tracey in the summer sunshine lighting up the Other Side.

After being in Miteby three times, Eddie was almost used to visiting this strange place. It was exhausting, though, not physically but mentally; he was prone to drifting off into a slumber, unable to think.

After a day or two of rest, the thoughts returned.

The whole business made no sense. They had visited a place that did not exist on the map, to find they were in an entirely different season in an undefined bygone age where people's own ages were fluid but generally youthful, able to spend an entire night there while back in the ordinary everyday world no time elapsed. Yet, this experience felt vivid and real, as if his mind was playing tricks on him. There had to be a logical explanation.

The dependency on Miles was irritating. Having anybody else take away control would have been annoying, but this person being some magician conjuring weird visions, made it only more frustrating.

Underneath it all, there was his beloved Susan. Even though it didn't make sense, finding her again was wonderful.

No harm in going back to Sorcerer's Copse, Eddie thought. He would do so on his own, lest he gave the impression to others of lending credence to these supposed happenings.

Arriving in the clearing, Eddie made straight for the path beside the oak tree, walking down confidently between the high earth banks to emerge five minutes later into the field of cows that his own experience and the map had told him he should find there. He walked up and down the path repeatedly, slowly and methodically, checking for a turning leading somewhere else. Two hours of painstaking checking and searching did nothing except prove beyond doubt that the only two places linked up by that particular path were Sorcerer's Copse and a field of cows.

Emerging one last time from behind the oak tree into Sorcerer's Copse, Eddie stamped his feet in annoyance as he made his way into the centre of the clearing, trampling on the fungal growth surrounding the scattered logs.

'Hello Eddie,' said Miles as he emerged beside the oak tree, giving off his signature reassuring glow of spiritual energy.

'Oh, it's you, Miles,' replied Eddie.

'You'd like to see Susan, I expect. I know she'd like to see you.'

'Yes, I'd like to see her very much.'

Within minutes, defying reason, guided by Miles, Eddie and Susan were embracing under the summer sun in Miteby.

For Eddie, Liz and Jenny, having tasted the sweetness of their newfound love in Miteby, addictive as the most potent narcotic drug, they could not get enough. No sooner had they regained the energy inexplicably sapped from them by each visit to Miteby, they were compelled to return to Sorcerer's Copse, waiting eagerly and anxiously for Miles to serve as a courier.

Miles controlled his flock like a diligent Border collie. The three young couples might gladly have stayed in Miteby indefinitely, but Miles would not allow it for an unexplained reason.

Young may have been a strange way to describe Eddie, Liz and Jenny, three people in late middle age, but on the Other Side, they were all young, taken back to when love had first blossomed. It was only after having returned to an everyday reality that the physical limitations of their chronological age caught up, including the nervous exhaustion they experienced after each visit to the Other Side.

Like children on their holiday beach who see no reason for the afternoon's fun to end, the visitors' time in Miteby felt as if it should endure forever in the present moment. Like their parents coming to gather their children for tea, Miles would round them up for their return after a brief few hours of delight.

Children might complain and plead for a few more minutes of playtime but eventually submit to parental control. Miles carried with him an authority the visitors instinctively respected. If he said, it was time to go, their time in Miteby was up. There was an instinctive trust among them that Miles knew best.

For each of the couples, the inevitable happened. They became lovers, enjoying the passion and closeness they could have had all those years ago before their futures had been shattered.

One day, the young sixteen-year-olds Eddie and Susan, elated and full of the joys of the new elixir they had discovered, walked hand-in-hand through the summer meadows around Miteby, adorned with multi-coloured wildflowers, glowing like bright jewels: red poppies, deep blue cornflowers, bright yellow dandelions and buttercups, set against the mingled lush green leaves and pale amber stalks of the long grass.

For Eddie, it wasn't only the flowers that were like jewels. In her fresh-faced perfection, Susan was the brightest and best of all the jewels in that delightful setting. Not quite blossomed into full womanhood, the teenage Susan was like a perfect rosebud, opened up enough to reveal all its features but still tight and unblemished, her petals yet to expand to their fullest extent.

Now reverted to his teenage self, a still growing lad, Eddie had almost stretched to his full height as a man, but gangly, his flesh not yet expanded to fill the space, leaving muscles, skin, and sinews stretched taut and spindly, like over-tightened violin strings, trying to move with the dash and energy of a child, his heavier frame made his movement clumsy and jerky.

Eddie's mind was also that of a teenager: impulsive, careless of long-term consequences, the memories of his subsequent life present only as dusty facts about another person he was yet to become, the hazards from succumbing to the glitzy glamour of Lucy Lansburg unreal, a mere abstraction.

Hormones flooding through their veins, Eddie and Susan felt a closeness and deep attraction, a new, joyous, fresh and unfamiliar sensation for both of them, free of the cynicism and suspicion arising from unrequited love, betrayal and disappointment that might have marred the occasion later in life.

The evening drawing in, the sun slipping towards the horizon, they came across an old barn, sturdily built of stout timbers, leaning slightly but structurally sound. Nobody was about, so Eddie opened the creaky old double doors and peered in.

There was old farming machinery, rusty and dilapidated, straw bales stacked to one side and a ladder leading up to a hayloft.

Eddie and Susan looked around, glancing at the ladder and where it led, thinking it might be a cosy and intimate place, each feeling too shy to mention it.

They looked around the downstairs area of the barn. Eddie glanced up again towards the loft, thinking carnal thoughts. Glancing back towards Susan, he realised she had seen his gaze. Surmising that she had read his thoughts, he blushed crimson and looked away, unconvincingly pretending to be fascinated by the intricacies of a mechanical seed drill.

The sun had gone down, and it was getting chilly. Susan shivered. Eddie put his arm protectively around her shoulders.

Susan was the first to mention it. 'It looks like it might be cosy up there,' she remarked, nodding towards the hayloft.

'Yes, it probably would be,' Eddie agreed. But he didn't do anything. Susan looked at him expectantly.

'Shall I go up and take a look?'

Susan nodded, so Eddie climbed the conveniently placed ladder. It looked warm and inviting. Soft hay spread around conveniently to form a cosy nest. He leaned over to report back. 'Yes, it looks nice.'

Susan climbed up to join him.

The two stretched side by side in the hay. They cuddled down in each other's arms to keep warm. Feeling calm and peaceful in their eyrie, they soon lost themselves in a deep kiss.

Tentatively their hands wandered, gently and exploratively caressing each other's bodies. For a while, anxious lest he would touch Susan in ways she didn't want, Eddie held back from straying onto her more intimate areas. He tried a fleeting, almost accidental touch on her breast, and she didn't seem to mind. Emboldened, he stroked her thigh. She encouraged his hand to reach further while approaching Eddie's private places.

They paused to loosen and remove their clothing to expose each other better. All modesty gone, their bodies entwined, this tryst could only end one way, passionately and in an explosion of sexuality that far exceeded anything Eddie had ever had in all his years of married life with Margot in the Material World.

Jenny and Tracey were enjoying a walk along the banks of a gentle River Maevon flowing near Miteby.

The years had fallen away, and they were now sixteen again. Jenny was fresh-faced and naïve. Tracey had a laddish manner that didn't quite match the developing curves of her female form.

The intervening years were almost erased, but somewhere in the distance, the teenage Jenny had a vague premonition of her subsequent existence as a woman in her forties, hazy and indistinct like a memory of a past life.

Tracey wanted more than what they had, ostensibly best friends, schoolmates who hung out together, but was Jenny, perhaps still content with platonic friendship, ready to take it further? If she were to test the water, Jenny might be spooked, appalled by what right-thinking folk considered unnatural, immoral and reprehensible. Jenny was generally content to let the more adventurous Tracey take the lead, so there was a good chance she would be amenable.

'Do you think much about boys?' Tracey enquired.

'Well, sometimes,' replied Jenny.

'All the other girls are talking about nothing else, but you don't have much to say about them.'

Jenny paused. Was Tracey hinting that Jenny was unnatural because she didn't talk about boys? She wondered that herself. Other girls were obsessed with boys, but she didn't care for them much. She would have to be careful what she said.

On the other hand, Tracey didn't talk about boys either, so if she was unnatural like that, then perhaps Tracey was too.

Resident in her sixteen-year-old head like a wise auntie offering advice, Jenny's adult persona intervened. What was she thinking of? Those thoughts were from her sixteen-year-old self; she had lived her whole life since and now knew what Tracey's and her own proclivities were.

'I haven't got much to say about boys, to be honest,' Jenny responded, eventually.

'I don't think that most of the others do either. At least they haven't actually done anything much in reality, but it doesn't stop them talking about them.'

'I know. They never stop. What some boy said to them. What someone told them about some boy. How they had to fend some boy off when he got fresh. Blah, blah, blah.'

'It must be because they are thinking about boys a lot, even if, in reality, they don't actually do much.'

'What about you? Do you think about boys, you know, in that way?'

'I don't think about them much. If I do, it's mostly about how to keep them away. I don't really fancy them coming on to me at all,' said Tracey.

'Me neither.'

Tracey let the implications of the conversation sink in. It had gone better than expected. Much better. She was tempted to explore the next stage, to ask whether Jenny fancied girls more than boys, but she decided not to push her luck.

They walked along without saying much until they encountered a watchtower set up on a grassy bank. Tracey suggested they go to the top and look at the view, and they could make it a race to see who could get up there first.

Jenny reached the bottom of the tower first, with Tracey on her heels. There was a narrow spiral staircase the width of only one person, but Tracey tried to jostle past. They reached the top, scuffling to be first, and landed in a heap on the floor of the viewing platform.

Tracey rolled over Jenny, holding her down on the rough flagstones. For a few moments, they wrestled, then, tiring, they stood to get their breath back.

Flushed and sweating, Tracey felt as passionate as a rutting stag, but she could not share that with Jenny yet. Jenny had an unconscious sense of sexual energy, but it was not something she could admit to, even to herself.

They stood and surveyed the view while they recovered their breath.

Tracey had been going to let things rest for the time being, but now, charged up with her aroused feelings, she felt compelled to continue with their earlier conversation.

'You know you said that you didn't really fancy doing stuff, you know, with boys?'

'Well, yes.'

'I mean sexual stuff, shagging, that sort of thing,'

explained Tracey unnecessarily.

'Yes, I knew you meant that.' For Jenny, it was something that, although they were only stating what was understood, was disquieting.

'Well, do you really not fancy that sort of thing with boys?' Tracey asked, piling on the discomfort.

Wasn't everybody supposed to want that sort of thing? Jenny thought. She wouldn't be normal if she didn't. Tracey was putting her under pressure, making her say things she would have been more comfortable leaving unsaid. What could she say? Dare she admit to not fancying that sort of thing with boys? Her adult self stepped in. Don't be silly, of course, she dared. She was reliving this now with the benefit of hindsight. Or was that foresight? Her sixteen-year-old self benefited from her adult experiences and wisdom.

'Well, no, I don't fancy it much, to be honest,' Jenny admitted.

'But you must have, you know, sexy feelings. You're old enough for that.'

This was getting into uncomfortable territory. 'I don't know what you mean.'

'Come on, you do. You must think stuff and then, you know, get wet and that, down there,' insisted Tracey as she daringly cast her eyes towards that part of Jenny's anatomy.

As her original sixteen-year-old self, Jenny would have been spooked out of her mind. Now replayed in Miteby, Jenny relived the pressure towards an intimacy she wasn't quite ready for, but her adult self steadied her enough to overcome her unease. 'Alright then, yes, I do.' Jenny blushed, squirming.

'No need to be embarrassed. We all do. It's normal,' reassured Tracey.

During her teenage years, Jenny would have left the conversation there, but by reliving it, the adult in her overcame her hesitancy. 'You mean, you do too?'

'You bet I do.'

'Oh, right.'

Tracey decided she had pressed the conversation as far as she dared, so they stood silently for a minute before descending the tower.

As they moved on, grey clouds were gathering and spreading. They walked along the river path for about half an hour. The light was fading, with the sky becoming increasingly dark and threatening by the minute.

In a short while, they reached the old Maevon mill. The two girls clambered onto the stonework to examine the workings of the water wheel.

It rained in a torrent, not a drizzle or gentle rain. Next to the mill was a timber cabin. They huddled under its eaves, but it was not much help. There was nobody around, so Tracey tried the door. When it swung open, they ducked inside.

The rain rattled onto the cabin roof, but at least it wasn't falling on them anymore. At the far end, there were sacks of grain. They settled, half lying, half sitting on the sacks, listening to the rainfall drumming above.

It was chilly. Jenny shivered and hugged herself to keep warm. Tracey used this pretext to snuggle up to her and put her arm around her shoulders. Jenny, defensive for a moment, relented and reciprocated.

Tracey, bursting with uncontainable lust, suppressing her apprehension about how Jenny might react, leant across, stretching her lips towards Jenny's. All those years ago, this had freaked her out, but this time Jenny, overcoming her unease, allowed their lips to meet, passive at first and then kissing back.

They remained locked in a passionate kissing embrace for what must have been minutes. Tracey's lust got the better of her again as she reached to caress Jenny's still-forming, dainty young breasts. Jenny quivered as Tracey's hands massaged her tender, sensitive nipples. It felt like an intrusion, but she did not attempt to fend Tracey off.

Emboldened, Tracey took Jenny's hand and guided it towards her own slightly more mature, rounded breasts, encouraging her to reciprocate. Tentatively and then gradually with more confidence, Jenny stroked and massaged Tracey's boobs.

Tracey took matters further, her fingers gently stroking Jenny's thighs, creeping up a tentative step at a time. Jenny's arousal was taking precedence. It was becoming easier for her to allow Tracey to take charge.

There was no rush. The rain continued to bucket down. There was nowhere they must go. For now, they were best remaining undercover. Tracey reined back her ardour, allowing Jenny to relax. The sexual tension built. Their skin was flushed, legs spread, pussies wet, and ever more urgently craving to be consumed; it felt urgent their lust be slaked.

Tracey relieved Jenny first, massaging her to a moaning climax, making little gasping squeaks in time with the pulsating contractions in her pussy, sighing and letting the feelings of satisfied bliss envelope her as her climax subsided. She had mixed feelings about what had just happened. Tracey had dragged her to something she felt barely ready for, yet she had to admit it felt good.

Despite her misgivings about the robbery of her innocence, Jenny simultaneously felt deep love and gratitude for Tracey for having unleashed her budding sexuality. She needed to return the favour. Now taking the lead, Jenny brought Tracey to her own peak of ecstasy.

Both relieved, they settled into each other's arms, pleasantly dirty as their bodies slid against each other, lubricated by their mingled wetness.

Liz and James were enjoying a convivial tête-à-tête romantic dinner for two at the Miteby Arms.

While her robust frame, forcefully energetic style and hearty manner might have lacked overt feminine charm, Liz made up for this with her enthusiasm, intelligence and wit.

Looking younger than his 20 years, James was not a man who naturally projected himself as a hero or stud. While of slight build for a man, not particularly tall and lacking macho features, there was nothing about his looks that he needed to have been ashamed of; indeed, Liz saw him as ideal, his body slim yet solid, his movements had the elegance and subtlety of a dancer, something she could never aspire to. With nothing more than confidence and chutzpah, other more outgoing, competitive men would have had plenty of success with his attributes on the meat market of the college social scene. But James was no alpha male. Thoughtful and retiring, he tended to fade into the background.

A shared fascination with ideas and intellectual debate brought them together, continuing discussion after class in a small group that dwindled to just them two.

In their quiet corner, fortified by steak and kidney pie, spotted dick and custard washed down by copious quantities of the Miteby Arms's excellent ale, they had shared their thoughts on existentialism. Does something truly exist if it cannot be observed? Does what is observed exist, or might it exist only in the imagination?

The warmth and cosiness of the room, the friendly companionship of their shared exploration of the meaning of life and the love hormones released by their mutual attraction contributed to a feeling of bliss.

Liz thought James had buttoned up his shirt too high. She considered it would look better if it were more open at the neck. She reached to make the adjustment.

James's hand skimmed momentarily against Liz's knee under the table. He was making to move his hand away as if he had merely brushed against her by accident, but Liz would not let him. She took hold of the back of his hand as it retreated, guided it right to her knee and pressed it back in place.

Emboldened hands wandered under the table, pressing and stroking thighs. The conversation about existentialism dried up. No longer being used for talking, their mouths were put to use in another way, reaching out to kiss, gently and tentatively at first, but quickly escalating into something deeper and more passionate.

One of the other Miteby Arms's patrons wandered past. Nudging and looking meaningfully at his companion, he said, 'You two should get a room!'

James broke from their kiss. He hesitated, but then, for once, he was bold. He whispered into Liz's ear, 'He might be right. Perhaps we should.'

Liz hesitated, but not for long. She had let James get

away once before. She wasn't going to let it happen again. 'Yes, perhaps we should.'

James hadn't expected such instant acquiescence. He thought that he had better check. 'Really? They have rooms here. I could see if there is one. Shall I?'

Liz nodded. 'Yes, do it.'

James slipped away to have a word with the landlord. He returned minutes later holding a room key attached to a large wooden key fob decorated with the Miteby Arms logo and the name 'Room at the Top' engraved in gothic script.

They went up the two flights to the attic room in the eaves of the building. It was cosy and romantic, set into the roof with dormer windows on either side, decorated in the style of a bridal boudoir.

The two stood there looking around, taking in the scene. Downstairs the prospect had just felt like carefree fun, but now, in this almost matrimonial setting, it had a greater significance, as if they were embarking on a course that would set a new direction for their lives.

For a moment, they were hesitant, unsure yet where to take things.

Liz broke the spell, leaning towards James, letting her head rest on his chest. James responded, putting his arms around her and giving her a long, tender kiss.

After a minute or so, they paused for breath. By now, Liz was determined James must not get away. She must have and secure him before any passing strumpet, like Jezebel Lucy Greshing, could lure him. She reached across and undid some more of the remaining buttons on his shirt.

Taking her cue, James quickly released the remaining

shirt buttons, letting it slip onto the floor, revealing his compact yet firm torso. He looked at Liz expectantly as if daring her to reciprocate.

Liz unzipped her dress and let it drop, leaving her standing in her underwear. James wasn't satisfied. He reached around and fumbled with her bra fastenings. Liz stood still and watched him indulgently as he struggled with the awkward catches. Eventually, the bra was undone. Liz let it drop off her shoulders, her breasts dropping free.

Liz noticed the bulge in James's pants. She couldn't contain herself from reaching out, stroking the protrusion that swelled against the fabric of his trousers.

Liz's caress only fired up James's passion. In a moment, he was reciprocating with her intimate parts. With a flurry of garments, they frenziedly discarded their remaining apparel.

The time for subtlety and seduction was long gone. They enveloped each other on the bed. Liz swept aside James's momentary hesitation, emphatically taking possession of what she had lost, swinging herself astride his body, lowering to envelop his manhood.

In Miteby, the visitors were like children, carefree under Miles, their parent figure, protective and authoritative. There comes a time when a child will question whether their parent is as all-knowing and all-powerful as they had always assumed. As one visit ended, Eddie first considered whether it was essential to comply with Miles's strict time limits. Without Eddie saying a word, Miles knew what was on his mind.

'I see you are wondering why you must return so soon.'

Eddie felt embarrassed. He hadn't meant to say anything and didn't want to appear ungrateful.

'Well, yes, but I am hugely grateful to you for guiding me to and from Miteby as you do. I appreciate it enormously.'

'The pleasure is all mine. It is part of my role as an Energy Prospector to convey people to the Other Side and back.'

'But it must get tedious for you. I don't quite know why it is something that you need to do,' queried Eddie.

'Not at all. It is what I am here for. You bring your spiritual energy with you. The Other Side is sustained by that.'

'What do you mean? How does the Other Side get sustained in this way?'

'Your thoughts, your memories, everyone that you once knew and can remember, the lost things from your childhood, those come with you to enrich us.'

Eddie paused. 'You mean, the people and things we see, hear, touch and smell on the Other Side, in Miteby, they are constructed out of our memories?'

'Exactly, that's why we must keep prospecting for more people, to provide our world on the Other Side. That's my job.'

'Oh, I see.' Eddie wanted to say more but kept quiet.

He did not have to say it aloud because Miles sensed what was on his mind. 'I see you are wondering if you could make the trip to Miteby alone.'

'Well, yes, I did wonder that.'

'People from the Material World cannot come over by themselves. A guide such as myself is necessary.'

Eddie had another concern. This time he did say it out

loud. 'Something I have noticed is that, when I get back, I feel mentally wrung out. Is that because of the mental energy the Other Side has absorbed from me while I am there?'

'Yes, being over on the Other Side draws down from your spiritual energy, so it is natural for you to feel a little flat when you return. But don't worry; your energy level will restore itself over a day or two in the Material World. A bit like making a blood donation. It doesn't do any lasting harm.'

'When you say a day or two, can you be more specific?'

'I can't. It depends on your time on the Other Side and what you do there. The more energy you expend, the longer it'll take to replenish.'

'Can you give me a rough guide?'

'You'll feel it yourself when your energy comes back. I can only say if you're still feeling drained, you should stay away. Give it more time.'

'How long is that likely to be?'

'I'd say, about three days, give or take. So, a couple of trips in any given week.'

Eddie let this sink in. Miles's explanation raised a safety concern.

'Could the Other Side absorb too much, draining me completely, perhaps?'

'Yes, that is possible. That's why I am careful to ensure you never stay too long nor come over too often.'

Eddie was grateful for Miles's explanation but not entirely reassured. He was left with the thought of the Other Side sucking him dry like some giant leech.

Larry, Karen and her Dad

It had not been Eddie's imagination that there had been two Karens in the Miteby Arms on that first visit to Miteby. Besides the Karen from the Material World, her alter ego was engaged with Larry in conversation.

Were he to be challenged, Larry would have dismissed as preposterous that he could fancy a stuck-up scrawny harpy like Karen, but the reality was, he secretly desired her to the point of obsession.

'We want the best for you,' Larry's mother had told him from an early age.

'We want you to be the best,' reiterated his father.

'One day, that'll be you, up there with a gold medal,' Larry's parents told him as they watched competitive sports on the television.

Relentlessly the message was repeated; he always had to be the best. Only winners mattered. Only the winners had his parents' approval.

'Big boys don't cry,' Larry's mother told him if he toppled and grazed his knee.

'Man up,' his father would say if he cried when one of his toys was broken.

A boy could not show weakness, a message he received loud and clear.

On arriving at primary school, Larry firmly believed he must be the best in his class to please his parents. He was brought down with a bump when, although no dunce, he was nothing special, struggling as much with the new learning as anybody else. A fellow pupil, Lucy Totkin, *did* stand out, consistently excelling in practically everything:

school work, singing, art, sports and dominating in the playground as the leader of a clique that ruled the roost.

Larry was scarred for life by his inability to accept himself as a normal average person, a solid but unremarkable performer who would get there in the end but needed time to learn. His upbringing told him that not being a winner would lose his parents' love and approval. What could have been happy formative years when he developed skills and built relationships became a nightmare of perceived failure. As he raged at his less-than-stellar ratings, he alienated those around him, not least his teachers, with compensatory aggression and bravado.

The star pupil, perceptive Lucy Totkin, observing his discomfort, took delight at taunting him for his failures and lack of effort.

Larry's parents only reinforced his desperate need to succeed. Never satisfied by his school results and sporting prowess, they were constantly pushing for more.

Despite striving in every activity, he usually did not win. Having to settle for second or third, it was this Larry put down to others, sometimes being less than friendly. It would never have occurred to him it might have been his aggressive and arrogant bombast alienating potential friends.

When Larry met Karen, later in life, he thought she was beautiful and desperately wanted to earn her admiration. He was assiduous in taking physical care of himself. He ate healthily. His gym-honed body was as near perfectly proportioned as he could manage. Short of surgery or a miracle, he could not have improved himself more. He made sure he was well-presented and dressed smartly. So when she scorned him, he assumed it must be due to his less-than-perfect competitive success.

There must be an aspect of his life where he hadn't met her high standards. He strove to make sure he had all the accoutrements a discerning woman would expect, a highly paid job in finance for a prestigious City of London firm, a Rolex watch, a Porsche, but clearly, there remained something missing. If only she had been specific about what he still lacked, he could have done something about it.

Had they simply been indifferent to each other or found each other mildly distasteful, they might have avoided contact where this could be done without offence and maintained a front of civility when communication was unavoidable. Unfortunately, Larry's ardour for Karen had made indifference impossible.

Under his competitive code, a front of hyper-confidence needed to be maintained, especially when making an amorous approach. For him, there needed to be an element of irony and raucous humour so any riposte or rejection could be laughed off as witty repartee.

Larry could not restrain himself from making the occasional unwanted saucy suggestion in Karen's direction. What he imagined was alpha male confidence and swagger, for her, came across as distasteful arrogance and entitlement. Such an attitude was intolerable, and she would brutally cut him down.

Only when alone would Larry wonder what had gone wrong and what deficiency in his achievements made her cruelly reject him. Perhaps being a wealthy investment banker was not enough, and she was holding out for a pop star or premier league footballer. She was overrating herself. Premier league footballers' girlfriends were typically way sexier. She wasn't in the same league.

On that first day in Miteby, Larry was taken aback to meet someone who looked like Karen but different to the one he had been walking with all morning, one who was clean and presentable rather than damp, sweating and mud-spattered.

'Hello Larry,' she greeted him with a smile.

He had been momentarily confused. How had she gotten herself cleaned up so fast? Why was she being friendly? Was she lulling him into a trap?

'Hello, Karen.'

'Well done for winning the Steel Man trophy. That really was an achievement. You must have worked hard for it.'

Was she going to turn it around and goad him for failures in other competitions?

'Yes, I did work hard.' He looked at her closely. She looked like Karen. It was as if she was Karen, yet not really; her identical twin sister, perhaps.

'You did alright yourself, actually,' Larry continued after a pause. 'Your record run in the Ten Peaks competition was fantastic.'

'None of that is important here.'

Was this the trap? 'What is important?'

'How we feel about each other.'

'I'm not quite sure how we feel about each other.'

'Don't you have any loving feelings about me?'

'I do think you're rather attractive. But you already know that.'

'It's nice to hear you say it because I feel the same. More than just attractive. I'm rather fond of you.'

Larry looked her in the eyes, but seeing neither irony nor mockery, only sincerity, his eyes moistened involuntarily. My God, he was blubbing. She would hate him for it.

'You wouldn't believe how fond I am of you,' he admitted.

'Why wouldn't I believe it?'

In the meantime, Karen from the Material World hadn't noticed she had a doppelgänger in the room. She had been distracted by her estranged father.

'Hello, Karen.'

As she saw him, anger, sadness, and loss welled. She wanted to yell but couldn't bring herself to. 'Dad. Why are you here?'

'I was hoping to see you. Miles said you might be popping in.'

'Did he now! What do you want, Dad?' She had not had a civil word with him since he had abandoned the family in her childhood, left her life when she was nine years old, missed her growing up, missed her teenage years, leaving her mother to struggle to raise their family alone. Did he want money or something?

'Nothing, just to see you. To make things right between us.'

'That'll take some doing, I'll tell you that.'

She had hated her father for leaving her all these years, yet yearned for him and loved him. Part of her wanted to rage against him, to flail her arms, hitting him over and over. Another part wanted to be his little girl, to have him back as her dad, to wipe away those years of separation and reset the clock to those long-lost childhood days. Yet another wanted him to explain what had happened and why to reassure her it was not her fault, not her, that had driven him away.

'It has been a long time. We've got catching up to do.'

'It ripped me apart, you leaving like that.'

'I'm Sorry Karen, I wasn't there, but I had to be somewhere else.'

He wouldn't be drawn on where that was or why he had to be there.

Karen's encounter with her father in the Miteby Arms had thrown her life off-balance more than she or anybody else would have imagined.

Karen was usually as strong and resilient as it was possible to imagine, physically and mentally. While others might be thrown into disarray by what people said to or about them, cutting remarks, and adverse comments, typically when applied to Karen, were like ping pong balls thrown at a brick wall. After her father departed from her life as a child, she had built a crust of protective armour, a hard shell that kept at bay anything threatening but left her inner being isolated from those who might have nurtured and loved her.

Karen's hurt from her father's disappearance was exacerbated by the bullying she experienced at school, instigated by one of her schoolmates, Lucy Denberry.

'What are you crying for?' demanded Lucy.

'My Dad left home,' Karen had confided.

Lucy quickly relayed and embellished the information within the school community.

'Why's your dad in prison?' fellow pupils would ask.

'He's not!'

'Where is he then?'

'I don't know.'

'How do you know he isn't in prison then?'

Lucy subsequently elaborated on the rumour by saying her father had been put away for paedophilia and incest.

'What did your dad do to you?'

'Nothing.'

'He must have done something. He's a pedo and in prison for it.'

'Bet you led him on,' said Lucy. 'It's your fault he's there.'

Karen's protective carapace, a barrier against external hurt, offered no resistance when she saw her father again. She had been in a daze completing Eddie's walk after that lunch break in Miteby. Feeling wobbly, she had not had time to understand what had thrown her off balance and how deeply it had reached inside her. After a restless night of vivid dreams the following day, she realised what her father meant to her. Scanning her map and searching online, she found no trace of the mysterious Miteby. She carefully plotted where they must have been when they first stopped for lunch in the rain, a place called Sorcerer's Copse. It wasn't Miteby, but it was somewhere to start.

Coming along the rutted tyre-churned access track into Sorcerer's Copse, she was relieved to find the familiar clearing with the felled timber and spreading oak tree.

After kicking around the damp logs scattering yellow-orange fungal encrustations, she sensed a comforting warmth from behind as if from a fire in a grate on a cold day. She turned towards the reassuring glow, and Miles stood next to the ancient oak tree at the edge of the clearing.

Karen had hoped she might encounter Miles but did not expect him to be there, leaving her startled when he appeared, frozen in awe.

Miles broke the silence. 'Hello, Karen. You are here to see your father, I presume.'

Karen hesitated before stammering, 'Ye-e-s. I was... I mean... I am...'

'He is hoping to see you, too, over in Miteby. I could take you over there if you like?'

Blinking and shaking her head jerkily as if trying to shake something out of her hair, Karen closed and opened her eyes to verify that Miles was still there. He gazed back at her expectantly.

'Could you? I mean, could you really?'

'Yes, of course.'

'You mean, now? Right away?'

'Yes, we can go now if you like.'

Karen stood still, then nodded emphatically. 'Okay, let's go then.'

Larry had been perplexed by his encounter with Karen in Miteby. While retaining some of her brittle toughness, she had been uncharacteristically engaged with things in their conversation, and her openness allowed him to relax his guard, a rarity for him. Such cut and thrust as there had been was affectionate and good-humoured.

'Sometimes I wish I had been a pottery maker,' he confessed to her. He would never usually have admitted that; it was not a profession that conformed to the stereotype of a winning alpha male.

'Oh, that's interesting. What attracts you to pottery?'

'It's the creativity of moulding the clay, having it

emerge into pleasing shapes.'

'Is that it, just the shaping things?'

'No, it would get me out of the rat race. There wouldn't be the pressure you get in something like banking. I could do my own thing and not have to always impress people.'

'I've always dreamed of living in the countryside in a farmhouse with a large family,' Karen admitted.

'Why haven't you done it?'

'Nobody to settle down with. But that wouldn't apply to you. You can be a potter on your own.'

'Doesn't pay much, being a potter.'

'Does that matter?'

'Perhaps not.'

While they were in Miteby, the version of Karen who lived there appeared to have enjoyed their conversation as much as Larry. Unprompted, she even mentioned continuing the conversation another time. With that in mind, Larry approached the real-life Karen as they returned.

'We should have another chat sometime.'

'Why? What about?'

'The things we talked about in Miteby.'

'What things? Were you listening in? You swine.'

'I don't know what you mean.'

'Yes, you do. I've nothing to say to you.'

Karen had reverted to her implacably hostile, resistant self as if it had been a different Karen in Miteby.

Larry tested the water again when they both participated in another FFWS walk.

'You know I was talking about taking up pottery. I think I might just do it.'

'Pottery? What are you talking about?'

'I told you about it.'

'Never heard you say anything like that.'

'It would be nice to continue our conversation sometime; I could tell you more.'

She glared at him. 'My diary is rather full, tidying my sock draw, and even if it weren't, I wouldn't be seeking further conversation with you if you were the last man on Earth.'

Uncharacteristically, Larry quietly withdrew, hoping something might reawaken the more congenial Karen. Could there be magic in the air of this Miteby place that had influenced her? It was odd that it wasn't on any map or online search.

Frustrated as Larry had been while Karen remained implacably hostile and unattainable, at least he had known where he stood. But Miteby unsettled him, igniting a hope that his love for her might not be in vain.

For want of other avenues, the mysterious Miteby could be the key. He had no plot for Miteby, but he had the location where they had set off: Sorcerer's Copse.

All was quiet when he arrived. He stepped over old logs crunching yellow toadstools. A glow as if from a lantern silhouetted the gnarled trunk of a great oak tree. Miles lit the gloom under the tree's canopy with a mysterious luminosity.

Larry imagined Miles could appear but did not really expect it to happen. He struggled to maintain an outward appearance of masculine bravado as his pulse raced and his palms sweated, wondering how to open the conversation.

'Hello, Larry. I believe you are here hoping to meet

Karen again on the Other Side.'

Larry nodded. 'Yes, indeed I am. Could you help me with that?'

'I'd be delighted. Karen is already over in Miteby, hoping to see you.'

Her succession of meetings with her father was akin to psychotherapy for Karen.

Reduced to tears when he told her he loved her, Karen learned the separation from her mother had been his fault when he had had an affair with a work colleague, leading to acrimony and a divorce settlement obliging him to keep away.

She shared with him her feeling of abandonment, how it had left her unable to trust any man, how she always had to keep her guard up, how much she yearned to love and trust, but had long given up hope, convinced no worthy man existed.

Coming to know her father better, getting a sense of what sort of a man he was, she appreciated that he, and men in general, were not all selfish brutes but, like all people, had emotions and finer feelings.

Larry lived for his visits to Miteby to see his beloved Karen, not the one in the everyday world who still ignored or disdained him, but her alter ego on the Other Side who enjoyed his company.

He remained perplexed about why, when she was in Miteby, Karen's attitude towards him should be so different to when he saw her in other settings.

As Miles escorted him back one day, before Larry could formulate any remark, Miles anticipated the question on his mind.

'You are wondering why Karen seems different when you see her in Miteby compared with how she is in the Material World.'

Larry was shaken by how Miles had seen straight into his head.

'Well, yes, I am wondering exactly that.'

'The Karen you know on the Other Side is the version of her in your head, the one you hope for, projected. Karen, in the Material World, is her own person. One day the two might fuse, but for now, they each have their separate existence.'

'So, what you are saying is that the Karen I have been conversing with over the past weeks is a figment of my imagination?'

'She is more than that. Karen on the Other Side is real enough, as real as I am. But that reality is spiritual rather than material. She is derived only in part from your mind. She is built from multiple sources, including Karen, as she exists in the Material World.'

If Karen was a construction fabricated from his own and others' minds, and, as Miles had said, she was as real as he was, what did that make Miles? Was Miles, too, a fabrication out of his own and others' minds? Miles demonstrated that he could see right into Larry's mind, so his spiritual energy must have flowed in. Yet, if Miles himself was a product of the spiritual energy of others, then Larry's own spiritual energy must be flowing into Miles, too, making it a two-way flow. It was bizarrely intertwined, more intimate even than sex, a fusing of souls.

To Be Together Always

Her body limp and drained like clothing passed through a wringer, Liz could have slept more, but the pale pre-dawn twilight glimmering through the bedroom window made it time to drag herself from under the covers.

Out of habit, she kept herself to the left-hand half of her king-size double bed. She reached to the right where her Trevor would have been over the past years, but it was her recently reunited first love James she hoped to find. She didn't expect him, but anything was now possible.

Her hand found only cold emptiness.

It isn't fair. They had found each other again. Why was their time restricted to the brief surreptitious trysts of adulterous lovers?

Miles had told her to leave a few days between visits, but Miles be damned, she needed to be with James today.

Rolling to the side of the bed felt as if she was heaving a heavy sack. She tipped her legs onto the floor, then, breathing heavily, hauled herself onto her feet. She felt light-headed, her feet heavy as if clad in walking boots smothered with clay soil after trekking across a ploughed field.

In a daze, she summoned dwindled reserves to dress, prepare breakfast porridge, and slump into her practical little car. She drove to a layby off the road, previously identified as the closest access point to Sorcerer's Copse. Muddy and exposed to passing traffic, it wasn't her favoured parking spot, but she lacked the energy to cope with the longer walking route from one of Gettlesdon's back streets.

Labouring uphill along the claggy mud of the access track felt like wading through treacle wearing divers' weighted boots.

Reaching Sorcerer's Copse, gasping, Liz scraped her boots against the fungus-infested logs to remove the worst of the accumulated mud.

A warm glimmer lit the few golden leaves remaining on the venerable oak tree as Miles appeared out of the mist.

'Liz, you shouldn't be here.'

'I have to see James.'

'I can't allow it. Your energy levels are too low.'

'I'll be alright once I'm over there with him. He'll revive me.'

'It wouldn't be safe.'

'Oh, please. I have to see him.'

'Not today. Come back in a few days when your energy is recovered.'

'Oh no, for goodness's sake. I need him.'

'I'm going now,' said Miles as he faded into the forest like smoke.

'Susan, I love you,' said Eddie as they lay in the summer sunshine among the swathe of meadow flowers.

'I love you too, Eddie.'

'We should be together always.'

'Yes.'

'Will you come back with me?'

'Back where?'

'To West Byfleet. There's plenty of room. You'd like it.'

'That's in the Material World?'

'Yes, I suppose. Not here on the Other Side, anyway.'

'I can't go into the Material World.'

'Why?'

'I just can't, that's all.'

As usual, Eddie did not have to voice his frustration. Miles sensed it as he guided him back to his material existence.

'You are wondering why Susan can't return with you.'

'Well, yes, I am.'

'It is because you are a being from the Material World, whereas she exists only on the Other Side. She isn't and could never be part of the Material World.'

'You mean, I can come and go, but she is stuck in the Other Side.'

'Yes. In a nutshell.'

'But you go back and forth, don't you? Why can't she?'

'Those of us from the Other Side can be summoned across in a transitory way, but we cannot exist in the Material World on our own, only within the minds of those who summoned us.'

'Susan could be brought over if summoned, couldn't she? Why can't I summon her myself? She would come willingly, I am sure.'

'Her presence would be temporary, illusory, immaterial and invisible to all but a few. Even for those conscious of her presence, she could vanish instantly.'

Eddie considered this bizarre explanation. 'You mean, she would be some sort of a ghost.'

'Yes, exactly like a ghost. It is something that does happen from time to time, but it is far from satisfactory. A thoroughly poor arrangement for all concerned. I do not recommend it.'

'Okay, so if Susan were to come back with me, she

wouldn't be real. Not tangible flesh and blood, just a will-o-the-wisp.'

'Yes, that about sums it up.'

Miles had another point to make. 'Even were it possible for Susan to be materialised in the Material World, there would be another difficulty.'

'What would that be?'

'In the Material World, you are a 62-year-old man. Many would look askance at you taking a 16-year-old as a lover, always assuming that she would have you as one. Chances are she would be off in a flash with someone of her own age.'

'Oh, I see what you mean.'

If nothing else, Eddie was reasonable. He could see what Miles had said was irrefutable.

'There is nothing to stop me coming to the Other Side myself, is there?'

'So long as I am around to guide you, I'll be glad to bring you across as much as you like, but you need to leave a little time between each visit, some days or so, to recover your spiritual energy.'

'When you say, so long as you are around to guide me, does that mean that you might not always be around?' queried Eddie with concern.

'As long as I can, I'll be here for you, but there are those who seek to stop me.'

'Who exactly might those be?'

'Agents from the Underside, Underhexes, that's who.'

'But who or what are these Underhexes?'

'You'll know them when you see them. They are not very nice. Best keep away from them, if you can.'

Jenny's now regular trips to Miteby were a guilty secret. Not that there was anything to be guilty about. Since splitting up with Paddy, she had been a free agent. Yet, disappearing into a strange place in the woods to be escorted to a fairyland for a rendezvous with a lesbian lover was all too bizarre for her to share with the world.

She would find herself a spot to park in one of the residential side streets in Gettlesdon and walk in from there, until one day, on the exact road and almost the exact spot, there was Eddie's distinctive and unmistakable classic Jaguar.

Having no wish to meet up, Jenny quickly looked at the map, finding an alternative route from nearby East Loften.

Liz was waiting expectantly in Sorcerer's Copse as Eddie arrived, returning with Miles from Miteby, the pair of them lit up by Miles's aura as if by a spotlight.

Eddie wondered if he could duck out of sight, but it was no good. She had clearly seen him.

'Hello Liz, fancy seeing you here.'

'Yes, fancy.'

Perhaps she hadn't seen Miles, and he could imply he was only out for a walk in the woods, but Miles intervened. 'Hello Liz, James can't wait to see you.'

Eddie and Liz avoided each other's gaze as Liz hurried over to follow Miles back along the path, disappearing behind the old oak tree.

Eddie knew that, because of the time compression during their visits to the Other Side, it would be only minutes before she returned, so he waited for her, taking a seat on one of the fallen logs.

Liz re-emerged presently and saw him there. 'Still here, Eddie.'

'Yes, I figured that you wouldn't be long.'

'It was quite a while. We walked along the river, had drinks, dinner and… well, spent some time together.'

'That was over on the Other Side. It's different here, in the Material World.'

'So, you go over there as well,' concluded Liz.

'Yes, whenever I can.'

She sat beside him. Eddie reflected that he had always considered her a reassuringly solid, sensible person. Until recently, he could never have imagined her having a passionate love affair with a younger man. It was a new side to her that he would have to get used to. For a short while, they sat without talking.

'How were things over there? With your young man, I mean.'

'Very nice, thank you. And your young lady, all is well there, I hope?'

'Yes, thanks. We seem to be getting on very well.'

Their cheeks reddened.

'I don't know about you,' said Eddie, 'but I am out of practice with all this young love, Romeo and Juliet stuff. It isn't something I expected to happen again at my time of life.'

'Me neither. Truthfully, I never had much in the way of the Romeo and Juliets, even when I was young,' Liz ruefully observed.

'Nor me. It rather passed me by. Or, it got killed off in me when I was young.'

'Age apparently doesn't apply anymore over there. It's like I'm young again.'

'Same here. It's odd. Like going back in time.' They sat quietly a moment until Eddie spoke again. 'Perhaps it's that feeling young again, expressing those feelings we've allowed to lie dormant, that has drawn us back there.'

'It was something that went wrong for me a long time ago, and I've been able to relive that time, but in a better way,' said Liz.

'Really? It's been like that for you too. That's exactly how it has happened for me,' said Eddie with uncharacteristic excitement.

'Goodness, you mean you're the same. Going back and putting things right?'

Eddie felt an elated new closeness developing, but cautiously told himself they should probably leave it there. The conversation was in danger of straying into very private areas. He stood and brushed himself down.

'Well, I guess we had better be going. Lovely to see you, Liz, and nice to know things are working out for you.'

Liz was reluctantly coming to terms with the limitations imposed by Miles. Although she yearned to be with James all the time, she must accept the situation if the most she could have was a delightful visit a couple of times a week.

In the meantime, between visits to Miteby, she would have to get on with everyday life, dealing with the many things she had been neglecting.

Liz was having a problem with her larder. Already crammed, there was nowhere for her latest batch of pumpkin preserve. Offloading the blackberry and apple jam, she promised Jenny to clear the required space. It was time they had a natter anyway.

'I'm planning to plant asparagus for next year,' said Liz

as they sat in Liz's kitchen eating slices of Liz's carrot and greengage cake, washed down with Liz's potent homemade elderflower wine.

'I had some lovely fresh asparagus just the other day,' said Jenny.

'It can't have been fresh. It's not in season.'

'Oh no, it was fresh. Absolutely delicious.'

'Can't have been.'

'The landlord insisted that it was.'

'Which landlord? He must have been lying through his teeth.'

Jenny blushed. She had given the game away. But it was Liz, her best friend. 'The landlord at the Miteby Arms.'

'Did I hear right? The Miteby Arms.'

Jenny blushed and nodded. 'It was the asparagus that gave you away. You can only get it fresh in May or June.'

'Ah, I see,' said Jenny, who, unlike Liz, was oblivious to such things.

'Don't worry, I've been going over there too. James and I have been seeing a lot of each other,' Liz volunteered, relieved to get it into the open.

'I see.'

'It isn't just me either. Eddie has been going over too. I bumped into him.'

'I know. I saw his car, although he doesn't know, at least I don't think so.'

'Have you noticed something? Since going over there, I've been drained. Each time I go, it takes me about three or so days before I'm myself again as if I have to recharge my batteries,' shared Liz.

'Yes, same for me.'

'I wasn't good enough for your mother,' Karen's dad told her as they sat in the summer sunshine on a bench looking out over the Miteby village green.

'In what way?'

'In just about every way. She made that very clear.'

'She must have thought you were good enough when you were married.'

'I doubt it. I can see now; she married me as second best in a moment of weakness when she didn't see other options. I neither knew nor cared at the time.'

'What happened after you were married?'

'In hindsight, I think that I only came on her radar at all because I used to talk big about myself and make myself a bit of a jack-the-lad. But that wasn't really me. She was quite angry with me when I turned out to be ordinary. After that, she'd find fault in me the whole time, putting me down.'

'I never realised.'

'When I met Phillipa from Accounts at work, she liked me as I was. I'd never met anyone before like that. With your mother always nagging and criticising, it was such a change. That's why I couldn't resist her.'

Karen considered. 'I can see how that could have happened. When you say you made yourself out to be a bit of a jack-the-lad, what did you mean by that?'

'Well, you know, making out I was a winner all the time, knowing things, things other people didn't, being able to get special deals because of people I knew, dressing in flashy clothes with bling, always having a story or jokey patter.'

'I know someone else like that,' Karen observed.

'Really? Who?'

'A man called Larry.'

Karen looked back at her dad. He was becoming increasingly like the loathsome Larry whenever she looked at him, yet she was becoming fonder of him.

Larry observed Karen make her entrance at the FFWS Christmas party, looking stunning. He beamed an open smile at her. To his surprise, no scowl appeared, only a questioning look and the faintest smile, as if she was considering whether his friendly disposition was the prelude to some sexist outrage.

Minutes later, he glanced again in her direction, expecting a glare, but while not encouraging, there was no overt hostility as she caught his eye.

'You are looking rather swish if you don't mind my saying so.' He tensed, expecting this would precipitate a ferocious response.

'Do you think so?' Karen replied, to his astonishment.

'Absolutely. That brooch and shoes go well with your dress. Very well chosen.'

Karen did not say so but appreciated his words. She had agonised over those choices, trying various combinations before the mirror; Larry had demonstrated good taste. She nodded and smiled cautiously, waiting for an aggressive or overtly sexual remark. Larry continued smiling, relaxed.

'You're not just saying that, are you?' Karen asked.

'Of course not. It just struck me that you look nice, and I wanted you to know I appreciate it.'

'Sorry, I'm not used to you *just* being nice.'

'I can be, you know. What does it make you feel, coming up to Christmas and New Year and so on?'

'I don't know. Another year has just passed; I'm not sure what there is to show for it.'

'Exactly. It feels like we're on a treadmill, pounding away but not getting anywhere.'

'Where do you want to get?'

He breathed in and exhaled. 'Something less stressful. I'd like to go out into the country somewhere. Take up pottery.'

Karen's gaze wandered to Larry's eyes. She knew he was something in the city, in finance. 'I suppose there's a company you're planning to buy in the ceramics sector?' She was poised to lay into him about capitalists stripping assets and throwing workforces onto the scrap heap.

'No. I mean making the pottery. Myself.'

'What, you mean you doing the actual work?'

'Yes, with my own fair hands.'

'Would there be money in it?'

'Not really, except I might have to sell the odd pot to earn a crust. It wouldn't be for money. I like the creativity, using my hands to mould something *I* conceived.'

'Doesn't sound like you. I had you down as a ruthless money man.'

'What about you?' Larry enquired, bearing in mind conversations he had with Karen's alter ego in Miteby. 'Ever fancied living in the countryside in a farmhouse surrounded by a large family?'

'What made you think that? You haven't been reading my mind, have you?'

'About Miteby,' said Liz to Eddie, with Jenny in the background.

'What about it?' asked Eddie, glancing towards Jenny.

'It's alright,' said Liz, beckoning Jenny. 'We're all in the same situation. We can talk frankly.'

'I see,' said Eddie.

'We've all got someone over there dear to us,' Liz explained, 'but they're stuck there, and we're still out here most of the time without them.'

'Yes. Miles says it's something to do with them not being able to exist in what he refers to as the Material World.'

'Although we can exist over there on the Other Side,' said Jenny.

'But not for long,' said Eddie. 'At least not according to Miles. He says our energy gets run down the longer we're over there.'

'Yes, that's true,' agreed Jenny. 'I feel shattered once I get back.'

'But, here's the thing. Supposing we didn't come back, we just stayed there. It wouldn't matter then, would it?'

'You know,' said Eddie eagerly. 'I'd been thinking the same. It wouldn't matter to me if I never came back; if it meant I could be with my Susan.'

'It would be a big step,' said Jenny, 'I'm worried about leaving my Sharon.'

'There's another thing to consider,' said Eddie. 'How long will Miles be around to ferry us back and forth? If we let things drift along, one day not so far ahead, we could be separated from them forever.'

'Right,' agreed Liz. 'We can't let things drift.'

'I see what you mean,' said Jenny. 'I couldn't bear to lose my Tracey now I've found her again. I'd do it. Sharon's old enough to cope without me now.'

'But might that mean we'd never get back again. Gone

for good,' said Liz.

'Would that be so bad?' Eddie asked.

'Not really,' said Jenny. 'The world can cope without us.'

'So, what should we do about it?' asked Liz.

'When Miles comes to take us back, we just stay put,' said Eddie.

'You mean,' said Jenny. 'He couldn't make us go back.'

'No, I don't think so,' said Eddie.

'So, we just stay there,' said Liz looking back and forth between the other two. Eddie and Jenny nodded.

'In that case, when?' asked Eddie.

'What have we got to wait for? Why not tomorrow?' said Liz.

They all nodded. They would meet in the morning and go to Sorcerer's Copse. It could be that they would be back, or they might not. It didn't matter.

A map's grid reference and a satellite navigation device's latitude and longitude are constants, but the place they represent is never precisely the same.

As years pass, buildings come and go, roads, paths, and vegetation change, trees rise and fall, shrubbery expands and shrinks. Seasons transform a location within weeks, winter ski resorts becoming unrecognisable as summer meadows.

On a bright frosty morning in December, Eddie, Liz, and Jenny found Sorcerer's Copse was turning into another place.

Now crunchy with frost, the mud no longer squelched and slid underfoot. Icy crystals in the air in place of damp morning mist, breathing gave out puffs of smoky condensation, winter on its way, thrusting aside the vestiges of autumn, a few shrivelled leaves clinging to semi-naked trees. Muddy sludge oozed through where their boots had broken into the surface of frozen flakes of papery leaf fall.

No mushrooms were visible where earlier copious yellow and amber toadstools grew among fallen logs, their remains reduced to mush and buried under leaf fall. Another fungus sprouted in their place, leathery, thick and resistant to the frost, a crimson blood red around its rim darkening to an earthy maroon at its centre, flecked with spots of deep purple.

They squelched the mushy remains of the decaying yellow toadstools. Liz scuffed her boot against the newly emerged reddish-purple variety.

Miles's aura, no longer warm, steady and reassuring, flickered erratically like a candle flame in a breeze. His usual unhurried demeanour gone, Miles glanced nervously at the path emerging opposite the scratchy thicket of brambles and gorse.

Following Miles's gaze, Liz sighted a dazzling woman clad in a purple cloak emerging from the path. She looked familiar, a memory from long ago, evoking a revulsion she could not explain.

She had no time to consider the mysterious woman's identity as Miles quickly rounded them up, gesturing for them to follow without delay.

'Conditions have changed,' said Miles as they skipped swiftly around the now almost bare oak tree. 'I don't know how long I'll be able to escort you to the Other Side like this.'

Nobody queried or commented on Miles's remark. A collective pang of concern spread among them, keeping them all subdued.

Worries receded under the bright summer sunshine bathing Miteby as they arrived, displaced by the joy of being there, transmuted into their younger selves and greeted by loved ones.

The following morning, the nurturing parent figure, Miles, did his rounds, suggesting it was time for them to return, but this time he found that his charges were no longer compliant children willing to come in for their tea.

Eddie, Liz and Jenny had pledged to remain in Miteby with their loved ones, and Miles could not persuade them otherwise. On earlier occasions, Miles's natural authority may have overridden the reluctance of his charges, but Miles was a shadow of his former self, his presence diminished and fading erratically.

For a second day, love-struck Eddie and Susan wandered hand-in-hand through flower-bedecked summer meadows, dangled hands in the cool water of a babbling stream, watched steam trains chuffing along the valley railway, and ended up with a passionate cuddle in the old barn where they had first made love.

Jenny and Tracey explored the tranquil path of the river Maevon, tracing it to its source in the chalk downs, diverting here and there to explore an old quarry. They explored the ruins of an old castle and standing stones placed by ancient forebears, finally ending in each other's arms in a woodland hut.

Liz and James found a hostelry on the banks of the lower River Maevon, where they had a lengthy discussion about the foresightedness of Plato in his analysis of society and politics. Their conversation was fortified and lubricated by the hostelry's excellent homemade cooking, elderflower wine, tea and scones with jam and cream. Finding themselves still in full flow into the evening, they stayed in one of the pub's quaint and cosy little bedrooms overlooking the river.

A fading weary Miles tracked the visitors down for a second morning, arguing more urgently that it was time to return to the Material World. Without his earlier spiritual strength, Miles's wayward flock felt all the bolder in their decision to remain.

More days followed, filled with carefree joy and love. Miles persisted with his appeals, but the refusals were ever more emphatic.

It was the morning after nearly a week when there was a change of atmosphere.

Eddie opened his eyes. Instead of brightness and blue sky through the window, there was a grey gloom. It was as if it was going to rain, but instead of dampness, the air had a sulphurous quality.

Eddie reached over to Susan to check if she was awake. She opened her eyes.

'It doesn't look like a very nice day.'

'Not a nice day at all,' said Susan.

'I suppose that it'll rain.'

'It'll be brimstone, not rainwater.'

'How do you mean?'

'From the Underside.'

'You mean where the Underhexes come from?'

'Yes, I'm frightened. Hold me tight.'

As they held each other in their arms, they felt a rumbling. The bed shook, and items on the dresser rattled.

'There are forces from the Underside,' said Susan, her voice shaking.

There was a banging on the front door. Miles stood there, looking unusually pale and gaunt, huddled against the wind blowing in fierce erratic gusts.

'You must go back at once,' said Miles, his voice thin and cracked. 'Don't argue. It isn't safe here now.'

Eddie looked up at the sky, filled with grey clouds. From the acrid smell, these could have been billowing smoke. Miles was right, it looked dangerous, and Miles's tone was deadly serious.

He hugged Susan, who had come with him to the door.

'What do you think?' he asked her. 'Should I go?'

'Yes, you should,' Susan confirmed. 'Underhexes could take you if you stay.'

Miles went along with Miles to round up the others. A crack in the ground had appeared across the village green, out of which hot foul mist spewed.

'The forces of the Underside are on the move; it won't be safe here anymore,' Miles explained.

Nobody disputed this. The atmosphere was ominous.

As they left Miteby, they were already feeling a deep unease in the pits of their stomachs. By the time they arrived back in Sorcerer's Copse, this had developed into more than anxiety. They were engulfed in helpless nausea, squeezing their stomachs into knots; a violent expulsion of their stomach contents twisted them like wringing out a cloth and then had them still retching over and over, long after nothing was left to come up. Their faces were a pasty grey, the cold air chilled them, and their bodies were devoid of energy.

Lesser mortals might have attempted to call for help, but members of the FFWS are made of sterner stuff.

'How are you feeling,' Eddie asked Liz.

'Terrible.'

'But not keeling over or anything.'

'No, still upright.'

Eddie looked over towards Jenny.

'I'll be alright,' she confirmed.

They set off back to where they had parked the cars a week ago in Miteby time, but only about an hour before in the Material World.

They walked at a pace most walkers would consider normal. Fit and experienced walkers get into a rhythm, a groove that keeps them going, however tired or sick they feel, the same repetitive motor that had previously driven these hardcore hikers to continue without pausing for 100 miles and more.

Reaching their cars, Liz and Jenny felt that, although they were pale and woosy, if they took it easy they should just make it home, but Eddie was dead on his feet on the point of collapse, pale and sweating like he might be having a heart attack.

Jenny called an ambulance, which, based on the description of the symptoms, arrived within minutes. On seeing them, the paramedics advised not just Eddie but all three to be admitted urgently to hospital.

Nightmares from the Past

The ambulance paramedic radioed ahead to the Accident and Emergency Department, providing their estimated arrival time and the condition of the patients.

The symptoms of all three, a man of 62, a woman of 57 and another woman of 46, were the same, tachycardia, dilated pupils, pale complexion, vomiting, confusion and hallucinations.

The A&E staff were struck by the terrified expressions of the three ramblers. Each had the appearance of experiencing something unnerving, constantly referring to someone called Lucy. When asked who Lucy was, they pointed to the middle distance and said she was over there as if there was a figure only they saw.

A&E called on the advice of a toxicology specialist. Blood samples were taken. In the meantime, a decision was made to keep the three patients in hospital for observation, at least until the toxic agent was identified. The patients were sedated to dampen their agitation and confusion before being admitted to the ward.

The subsequent memories and impressions of the patients were a vague and confused mixture of their hospital environment, the health care they received, and the flurry of hospital personnel bustling around, blending with their nightmare hallucinations.

As he was conveyed to hospital, Eddie was confronted by the dominatingly sexual figure of Lucy Lansburg. She appeared before him in a clingingly tight-fitting glowing red outfit, mesmerising him with her curvy body, seductive face and alluring eyes.

'It is me you desire,' she informed him, 'only me. Now that you have seen me, nobody else will measure up; you can desire no other.'

Eddie wanted Susan. He tried to desire only her. But he couldn't help himself. Lucy had him spellbound. He tried desperately to look away, but out of the corner of his eye, he would glimpse Lucy's flesh quivering, and involuntarily his eyes would be drawn back. It did no good if he managed to tear his eyes from her; she would instantly reappear in his line of sight.

Eddie desperately tried to conjure a mental image of his lovely Susan, but his imagination of Susan was pale and washed out compared to the distilled essence of sexuality that Lucy was feeding him.

Eddie tried to put distance between them, but there was nowhere he could go, and even if he were to retreat, Lucy would follow, mercilessly enticing him.

Lucy advanced. Eddie didn't want this. He wanted to save himself for Susan. He twisted his body and turned his head from side to side to fend her off.

She came up close, her body in front of him, threatening to envelop him. She was near enough he could smell her animal scent. The rampant male animal inside him responded.

'You want me, don't you?' cooed Lucy, 'You want to have me right now. You can't resist me, can you?'

Eddie was ashamed. What she had said was right.

'I will visit you in your dreams,' Lucy whispered in his ear. 'Whenever you have the slightest carnal thought, it will be me, and only me, you will see. Only my charms will work their magic for you. You will yearn for me always.

You will do my bidding always, out of your desire for me.'

Eddie knew she was right. He hated that she was right.

Liz's heart raced. She felt sick as the woman's figure clad in the reddish-purple cloak loomed, the one she had seen earlier in Sorcerer's Copse just before Miles had hustled them to Miteby that last time. Overwhelmed by hate and fear, Liz recognised her nemesis, Lucy Greshing, the unscrupulous floozy, seductress of her true love, James, those years ago in their youth.

The woman flung off her cloak revealing her body clad in a skin-tight slinky crimson catsuit, flaunting her figure.

Liz's heart leapt as she saw her beloved youthful unspoiled James emerge from the shadows. Surely James will rescue me from this apparition, thought Liz.

But James did not acknowledge her. He appeared not even to have seen her. His gaze was directed only towards Lucy. He walked to where Lucy stood, reaching out with his hand and fondly stroking Lucy's hair.

Lucy looked over towards Liz with mixed triumph and derision. 'You don't imagine a clodhopping frump like you could compete with me, do you?'

Lucy reached down and stroked the bulge that pushed up from within James's pants.

'This is what drives men. Reach this, and they are putty. They can't resist,' observed Lucy with a satisfied smirk. Lucy turned her head towards James, they kissed, and Liz felt tears well. Breaking off from the kiss, Lucy turned back to address Liz. 'Now he has me, your former beau can't even see you. You don't exist for him.'

Liz called out James's name, but he showed no sign of hearing.

Unscrupulous hussies endowed with sexy looks could seize anybody and anything they wanted, leaving decent, loving, but plain women with no one.

'I know what you're thinking,' said Lucy. 'If only you looked prettier, you might have a better chance. Sex appeal is not all a bed of roses, you know, as I will demonstrate to you one day.'

Jenny cringed as Lucy Fanshow, the pitiless bully of her school days, appeared.

With her confident look of innocence and superiority, Lucy spun every encounter or situation into one where she was right: all-knowing, virtuous, pure as the driven snow, fashionable and in the know. Effortlessly, she portrayed anyone who might oppose her as reprehensible, ignorant, disgusting, contemptible, unstylish or out-of-touch, using their weaknesses and peculiarities as weapons.

'Oh, it's you, the dyke.' She looked at Jenny as if she was flawed. 'What you do shouldn't be allowed. It's disgusting. Touching each other up, playing with each other's pussies. Dirty. Yuerk.'

'Don't look at me that way.'

'You needn't think you'll get any bean flicking or gash gobbling from me, you filthy pervert,' Lucy taunted. 'You need to be taught how to have decent sex like normal people. I know a guy, Duncan, a football player. He fancies me, but I could do you a favour, point him in your direction. He's quite a stud. He'd put you right. Show you what proper sex is. What about it?'

As their cases were linked, the hospital consultant, a

toxicology specialist, initially saw the three of them, Eddie, Liz and Jenny, together to inform them of the findings before visiting them individually.

The analysis of their blood samples showed the same results, the presence of toxins from two varieties of rare fungi.

The first was Psilocybe Latusaversus. He showed a picture of a brightly coloured toadstool, a glowing lemon yellow flecked with white around its rim, darkening to an amber orange at its centre. This one was principally a hallucinogen, mildly toxic but rarely fatal. The effects were pleasurable, and it was sometimes used as a recreational drug.

The second was Psilocybe Latussubterensis. He showed a picture of a giant leathery tough-looking toadstool, bright crimson blood red around its rim, darkening to an earthy maroon at its centre flecked with spots of the darkest deepest purple. It was hallucinogenic and toxic, with a high enough dose causing multiple organ failure and death. Even if the person taking it was lucky enough to survive, its hallucinations were reported as exceedingly unpleasant, like a person's worst nightmares, persisting over months, perhaps indefinitely.

He enquired whether they knew where they might have encountered these fungi.

Eddie, Liz and Jenny looked at each other. Each was calculating whether to say anything. Each wanted to keep open the possibility of getting back to the Other Side but wondered whether one of the others would speak. Eddie shook his head. Liz and Jenny made a slight nod in acknowledgement.

'No,' said Eddie. 'I can't imagine where it could have

been.'

The doctor's face suggested he did not believe it but he did not press the point. 'Well, wherever you might have encountered these fungi, I strongly advise you avoid that location in future, and most especially, if you find yourself there, don't touch anything.'

Having seen them, the consultant was happy for them to be discharged. After a few days of recovery at home, they slipped back into their everyday routine before visiting Miteby, except it was not and now never could be the same.

Eddie so loved Susan, yearning for the delightful carefree days in Miteby, but a malign force prevented his enjoying even her memory. Each time Susan came into his head, which was often, the dreaded Lucy Lansburg intervened, thrusting the vision of Susan to one side.

'It is me you desire, Eddie, just me,' Lucy would coo. 'None other but me.'

To his shame, Eddie's body responded to Lucy's charms. Nothing could prevent it. Distraction didn't work. Whatever he looked at or focussed on was shoved aside by images of Lucy's exaggerated feminine body, huge like a visitor from Brobdingnag, the land of the giants, a bouncy castle of smooth breasts, bottom and thighs, overwhelming his nostrils, eyes and even his sense of touch.

Eddie shook and panted from huge climaxes, involuntary orgasms triggered by the unwanted attentions of the phantom Lucy, her sexuality crushing resistance.

'Your sex is reserved for me only,' she would whisper in his ear. 'Always for me, no one else.'

Eddie wondered if he exhausted himself physically, would this intrusive sexuality diminish. He took brisk hikes on hilly terrain, sometimes running so hard he gasped. Breathing hard only made him more helpless to resist Lucy's blandishments. Disgusted by his infidelity, he yearned to return to his lovely Susan in Miteby but knew that he dared not while he remained possessed by Lucy.

Whenever Liz thought of James, she would see him with Lucy Greshing. Initially, they would interact in mildly flirtatious ways but quickly escalate into lewdly energetic coupling and moaning, with shuddering culminations.

As each encounter subsided, Lucy would turn and taunt. 'You must be crazy if you imagine James could fancy a graceless lump like you now that he has me.'

To emphasise her point, Lucy would return to James and entice him into another round of frenzied copulation.

'You see,' said Lucy. 'After tasting the delights I offer, James is mine. Mine forever.'

Over and over, daily, Lucy forced Liz to relive the betrayal, dejection, and hopelessness she had felt from the loss of James those years ago. Desperately she yearned to return to Miteby but knew it could not happen while Lucy had her James in thrall.

Each time Jenny tried to conjure a vision of her Tracey, she found she could hold it for no more than a second or two before Lucy Fanshow appeared to scorn her for her disgusting lesbianism.

'Oh, you want your precious Tracey? What did you imagine you might do with her then? You're dirty, aren't you? You fancy women, so perhaps you fancy this?'

Lucy would then flaunt her feminine charms. It was no good for Jenny to turn away as Lucy would follow her. To her disgust, Jenny was powerless to resist, hopelessly aroused.

Jenny desperately wanted to save herself for Tracey, but Lucy would not allow that, remaining in front of her, oozing sexuality. All the while, Lucy would taunt her for her Sapphic responses, mocking revulsion over Jenny's involuntary attraction while doing everything she could to excite it.

Bringing Jenny almost to climax, strung up tense as steel cable, Lucy would break away with sham aversion. 'I have a cure for dykes like you,' said Lucy, 'and here he is.'

A grinning image of a hairy hulk of a man, a muscly football player, filled Jenny's head, his face leering towards her, a pronounced bulge under his tight pants. Both nauseated by the threatening vision and disgusted with herself for allowing Lucy to affect her, she knew there could be no return to Tracey in Miteby while Lucy remained in her head.

'You're on good form today,' said Larry.

'What's that supposed to mean?' retorted Karen.

'Just the way you vaulted over that stile.'

'How is one supposed to go over a stile?'

'Ideally, just like you did. But not everyone can do that.'

'Why should the way I go over a stile be any concern of yours?'

'I thought it looked elegant and graceful, that's all.'

'Keep your personal remarks to yourself.'

'You make a lot of effort to keep yourself in good shape. Surely you shouldn't object when someone appreciates that.'

Karen looked at Larry through narrowed eyes. 'It rather depends on what their intentions are.'

'You know I said I'm interested in taking up pottery.'

'Yes, I remember you saying.'

'What do you think about that?'

'I think you should follow up on it. It would be good for you.'

'There is a weekend course I was thinking of going on. A potter in Devon is giving it. He's got a good reputation. Makes nice stuff.'

'Oh, that sounds nice.'

'Why don't you come too? It'd be fun.'

Karen wrinkled her nose. A weekend with Larry? She looked at him up and down. He smiled back. At that moment, he recalled her dad; he wasn't so bad.

'Alright, send me the details. I'll think about it.'

Founders Memorial Challenge

Sorcerers Copse featured on the route of the Far and Fast Walks Society (FFWS) Founders Memorial Challenge event held annually in mid-January, situated on the leg shared by the 30- and 50-mile routes a short distance after the 20-milers split off.

Surrey FFWS took delight that their event was held when weather conditions were toughest. Other FFWS branches observed it was only in a soft southern place like Surrey such an event could be in January. In the Scottish Highlands, Cumbria or the Yorkshire Pennines, conditions would not only have been harsh but logistically impossible.

Conditions for the event were typical. The temperature hovered around freezing point, with light snow and patches of freezing fog. Some snow was settling on the higher ground, hardened by frost, ice making the soil slippery. On the lower sections, the earth was slightly warmer, above freezing, resulting in a thick quagmire of sticky mud overlain with a slush of melting snow.

In the late morning before the arrival of event participants, Sorcerer's Copse was a quiet, peaceful idyll within the tranquil woodland, the ground and surrounding trees blanketed under an immaculately thin dusting of snow, looking decorative enough to feature on a Christmas card.

The perfection of the scene was sullied by the panting figure of the first runner slipping and heaving up the main track, normally used by timber handling machinery. His every step broke through the thin layer of snow and frost, embedding his foot deep into the wet sludge. With gasping effort, every stride compelled the runner to haul his foot out strenuously from the clinging clay. Each time his foot popped from the muddy cavity, clods flew off his sodden trainers, spraying brown stains across the formerly unsullied surface of the snow.

The runner continued, leaving the scene quiet again, its virgin cleanness now besmirched by a dark trail of footprints and brown spatters.

The scene did not remain quiet for long. Within a minute, two more of the fastest runners appeared, loping ponderously and competitively side by side, making further deep indentations and muddy stains on and beside the path.

Larry and Karen were among the event's runners on the 50-mile route, vying to be among the overall leaders. To their chagrin, despite both being super-fit, they would never be the first home. Invariably, the front runners were the elite athletes, whose lives centre around touring ultra-marathon races, iron man competitions, and fell-running events across the country and beyond.

Once Larry and Karen arrived on the scene ten minutes behind the lead participant, more than a dozen previous runners had trampled over the course, leaving a trail of pockmarks along the route like the ravishes of a virulent disease.

In common with most of the more seriously competitive participants, Larry and Karen were clad in tight-fitting Lycra, their footwear consisted of lightweight trainers, their tiny rucksacks crammed with skimpy, eye-wateringly expensive versions of the safety gear insisted on by the FFWS: waterproofs, compass, map, navigation device, hat and gloves.

Larry, slightly in front, lumbered on without stopping, focussing on keeping up with and hoping to overhaul the elite athletes at the front.

On her own in the clearing, Karen hesitated, wistfully recalling her previous visits to see her father on the Other Side. She stepped off the path and wandered across the snowy clearing to where the fallen logs lay. She stepped between them, kicking aside the thin covering of snow, her running trainers squelching onto the pulpy remains of a toadstool.

Hearing a muffled crunch from a familiar direction, she turned expectantly to see a diminished Miles from behind the trunk of the giant oak, its now bare branches ornamented with snow and frost.

Miles, crumpled and weather-beaten, his face haggard, still had a glow of sorts, but cold and dim like moonlight through a mist.

As she turned, her heel struck another fungus, a sturdy leathery variety, its deep reddish-purple glowing like a blood stain against the snow. There was another sound from the other side of the clearing, where a scruffy path could just be discerned emerging from a thicket of gorse and brambles. Next to the shrubbery stood a woman dressed in a brilliant reddish-purple cloak.

As soon as she saw the mysterious woman, Karen felt an icy coldness grip her heart, a surge of horror at the woman's appearance. She did not quite know why.

Before she could figure out the root of her dread, Karen heard Miles's hoarsely rasping voice. She took her eyes from the menacing woman to focus on him.

'Hello Karen, your dad has missed you and would love

you to come over,' said Miles croakily.

'I can't stop now,' Karen objected, flustered. 'I'm in the middle of running the Founder's Challenge.'

'Time runs differently on the Other Side. You could be back within minutes.'

Having already experienced this strange passage of time on visits to Miteby, Karen readily accepted Mile's reasoning. Miles hadn't mentioned what she also knew from experience, that visiting Miteby would leave her tired when she returned. Still, she didn't feel any compulsion to compete in this event, so that wouldn't matter unduly.

'Alright, I'd like to see him. I'll come over.'

As she followed Miles, conscious of an ominous presence behind them, Karen turned, glimpsing the strange woman in red. She had an eye-catching quality, the colour of her clothing shining with an eerie luminescence, spiritual tentacles Karen sensed feeling their way into her mind. In a shuddering realisation, Karen knew who the woman was, Lucy Denberry, the source of her years of malicious rumours, bullying and torment in her school days after her father had gone. The hairs on Karen's neck stood up, and her skin felt so tense it might tear. The prospect of that woman following them into Miteby was hideous.

Fortunately, as Karen and Miles continued along the path, the woman dropped back, remaining on the edge of Sorcerer's Copse. Karen's tension slowly unwound as she and Miles approached Miteby.

Having observed the exchange between Karen and Miles, the unearthly woman in red resented Miles taking possession of Karen. She had moved forward to seize prey rightfully hers, but on this occasion, she had not been fast enough, Miles having seized his quarry and ushered the victim away. She would be quicker when Miles was out of the picture next time.

As she waited a while in Sorcerer's Copse, there was the sound of another runner. She moved back into the shadows beside the oak tree and watched him run past.

Minutes later, another runner came through. He left the main path and ducked into the wood for a call of nature. On reemerging, he stomped through the fallen logs, his foot landing in the same spot Karen had stepped moments before, squashing the fungal remains. The runner heard snow being compressed on the path beside the oak tree and turned.

The noise the runner heard was Miles approaching along the path, but this time Miles never emerged. The woman in red was waiting. As an enfeebled Miles came up beside the spreading oak tree, the woman swept out before him. In her hand was a knife with a gleaming blade fabricated from the hardest, sharpest and coldest metal, purer and keener than anything mortals could produce. She plunged the dagger deep into the weakened Miles's chest. He gurgled, blood gushing into his punctured lung. He fell back, letting his body weight pull away from the knife his assailant held. She grabbed him by the hair to keep his head held up as she again plunged the blade, this time straight into his throat.

The woman smiled with vengeful satisfaction. She wiped some blood that had splashed her onto her cloak, its colour blending in perfectly.

A wave of dread washed over the man as he heard the muffled scuffle. He tried to rationalise it. There was nothing to be frightened of. It would have been one of the deer he had seen earlier in the wood. He ran on, fast, more to escape the foreboding hanging over Sorcerer's Copse than to make up time in the race.

It was early in the afternoon when Liz arrived in Sorcerer's Copse.

She was participating on the 30-mile route without aspiration or expectation of being fast, content keeping a brisk walk rather than running, except for one or two more accessible downhill sections.

In common with others participating for fun and enjoyment, Liz was attired in a utilitarian style, with sturdy hiking boots and thick warm socks, topped with gaiters stretched over tough, comfortable trekking trousers. She had a couple of cosy base layers topped with a quality rainproof jacket and a battered, practical rucksack.

An energetic walker rather than a runner, she approached briskly, though slower than the frantic front runners. Over 100 participants had already trampled past, leaving the main path a lumpy morass of mud and dirty slush.

On arrival, Liz felt a tug of emotion about her James. She had felt terrible about not seeing him during the weeks after she fell ill when hideous nightmares plagued her. She took a minute to reminisce and speculate whether she might return to Miteby and see James again. She was anxious about history repeating, with James again preferring Lucy's superficially seductive charms to her, as happened in her nightmares. Perhaps she should have one last attempt to head off that catastrophe.

She wandered around the fallen logs, crushing the already pulverised fungal remains. Would Miles appear for her now? she wondered.

She heard a sound behind the oak tree, like when Miles arrived. She looked in that direction. A figure stood there, but not Miles. It was the woman in red who she had seen in Sorcerer's Copse before, the one who had reminded her strongly of the unscrupulous Lucy Greshing. Liz almost choked from the distaste and hatred welling inside her.

Yet as revulsion swelled from one direction, the woman's strange charisma and seduction counteracted those feelings. The two women stared at each other. With Liz mute from fear and apprehension, the woman in scarlet broke the silence.

'Are you wanting to go to the Other Side?'

Liz hesitated. 'Well, perhaps. I'm not sure. Where's Miles?'

'Miles can't make it today. I'm Lucifix, but you can call me Lucy. I'm here to take you.'

Liz didn't want this woman taking her anywhere. Her head was ricocheting with confusion and mistrust. Then she thought of James. She couldn't leave James at the tender mercies of this horrible apparition. She couldn't lose him like that again.

'If I come, can I see James?'

'James is waiting for you in Miteby.'

'How is he? Does he want to see me?'

'He has missed you. He would like to see you; you may be sure of that.'

Liz neither liked nor trusted this woman. But if she didn't go, James could fall into her clutches, lost to her forever.

'Well, do you want to go or not?'

'Alright, let's go,' she said.

The Underside

Liz turned to the path beside the venerable oak tree with the spreading branches, but Lucifix shook her head. 'Not that way. We're going over here.'

Lucifix made a direct line to the narrow-overgrown path on the opposite side, which Liz had emerged from on her second visit to Miteby with Jenny and Eddie.

Liz hadn't liked the path then and didn't like its look now. Besides, as far as she knew, that was not the way to Miteby. She hesitated, uncertain and suspicious.

Lucifix stood by the beginning of the path, looking back. 'Come on! This way!'

'But that's not the way to Miteby, is it?'

'It's the way we are going today.'

'But Miles never took us that way,' Liz objected.

'It doesn't matter what Miles did. If I'm taking you, it's this way,' said Lucifix.

Liz held back; her mind full of foreboding.

'Well, do you want to come or not? I haven't got all day,' snapped Lucifix.

Lucifix radiated a commanding dictatorial power that tolerated no opposition and a seductive persona that enticed compliance. Liz did not like Lucifix, but liking her had nothing to do with it. Lucifix's powers beguiled into a person's soul.

Reluctantly, Liz followed Lucifix in through the scraggily tangled undergrowth. There was barely a way through, with branches of gorse and long strands of brambles crisscrossing, snagging and tearing Liz's clothing as they edged along.

The path began as Liz had remembered, but, as Miles had done on the other way, at some indefinable point, the path deviated. There was still snarly undergrowth, but now it was situated in an abandoned orchard. Neglected for years, scrubby bushes had been allowed to run riot under the remaining old fruit trees, untended, unkempt and diseased. The path followed the line of electrical pylons cutting across the old orchard and beside an electrical substation, humming and buzzing, its exterior graffitied.

Until this point, vegetation obscured the broader surroundings, but now a vast cityscape spread into view, revealed as they emerged from the side of the electrical installation.

As far as the eye could see was a jumble of buildings, roads, areas of asphalt covered in various vehicles, and industrial complexes stretching into the distance, perhaps endlessly beyond the pall of murky haze.

Dense clumps of high-rise buildings were set among low-rise tenements giving out to industrial areas and railway sidings. Once grand buildings from an earlier age were jostled aside by modern towers spread like orbiting planets around a glitzy financial district boasting the most prominent and striking skyscrapers. There was a clear separation between the clusters of brilliant and expensive residential blocks and the rougher brutalist residential towers. Further out in what had once been open spaces was a ramshackle shanty town of temporary shelters.

Liz had been uncertain from the start, but seeing the unsightly landscape, she felt a surge of panic. 'This isn't Miteby! What's going on?'

'We're going a different way this time, that's all,' purred Lucifix.

'I think I want to go back now.'

Lucifix looked round at her, lips curled in contempt. 'Come on, don't be so timid. We need to be getting along. Don't dawdle.'

Lucifix kept walking; Liz had no option but to follow, Lucifix's commanding presence drawing her along.

Now in an area of derelict scrubland on the outskirts of the city, spindly shrubs, their sparse shrivelled leaves encrusted with dust, struggled to gain purchase in the cracks of the fragmented remnants of a paved surface. Moss, dandelions and tussocky grass fought their way among fragments of asphalt and uneven lumps of concrete. Mounds of fly-tipped building rubble interspersed the burnt-out rusting remains of vehicles and battered shopping trolleys, once shiny and chromed but now stained with spots of rust. Used condoms and old syringes were strewn alongside a more general litter of smelly mouldering fast food remnants, empty drink cans and assorted packaging.

Huddles of people looked furtively from side to side, conducting little bits of business while others slunk around nervously alone, poor folk who looked as if they were stalking their prey from those even less advantaged.

Liz noticed a tipsy man ogling her. He was flabby and overweight, with the prickly spikes of several days' beard growth forcing out of the greasy skin of his jowly neck and chin, his lank unkempt hair receding off his leathery forehead. When she glanced nervously in his direction, he spread his mouth into a hideous leer showing the gaps between his neglected, stained, crooked teeth.

As they walked past, Liz backed away to put as much distance as she could between her and her pursuer, but the man lurched, pawing her breasts and puckering his lips.

'Come on, love, gizza kiss,' he said, breathing out fumes of beer and curry.

'Get off me,' shouted Liz, backing off.

Lucifix smiled. 'Who's your new admirer? Come on, we don't have time for flirtations now.' Lucifix pressed on, forcing Liz to scamper on hurriedly behind, hands shaking and heart pounding.

They approached the main highway, a multi-lane dual carriageway clogged with traffic, an assortment of heavy lorries belching out thick clouds of toxic diesel fumes, delivery vans, buses and cars. On the road, wealthy businessmen and their wives sat in their luxury limousines, isolated from the surrounding ugliness in the comfort of their ergonomically designed leather seats by darkened windows, soundproofing and surround sound music systems.

The path led down an underpass beneath the highway. Homeless people had set up bedrolls and cardboard shelters inside the tunnel, permeated with the smell of cannabis, urine and other odours of human bodily functions, unlit and gloomy, revealing the people and their meagre possessions only as vague shapes.

Part way in, Liz almost leapt as high as the low ceiling when she felt a large hand reach from behind, groping her bottom.

'Hello darling,' said someone with a gruff voice.

Liz swung around in horror, seeing the outline of what looked like a hairy gorilla. She did not wait to learn more about the gorilla or his intentions but scampered on as quickly as possible.

Emerging towards the daylight that shone in from the

far end, another figure rose to block her path. Silhouetted against the light, bent over with a hunched back and casting long shadows reaching out towards her like sinister ghosts, the figure looked like a goblin. A thin, gnarled hand came across and patted her on the cheek.

'You're a sight for sore eyes, dear, and no mistake,' said the figure in the cracked rasping voice of an elderly man with a chronic chest infection.

Lucifix stood impatiently at the top of the sloping access path on the far side.

'Come on now, we don't have time to waste on dalliances.'

Liz's eyes welled and her heart pounded as she walked fast to keep up with Lucifix, who led them into the city's flashy financial quarter. They passed the tallest and most ostentatious of the modernist skyscraper buildings, which prominently declared itself as the Continental and Oceanic Securities Bank. In the foyer, a flashy banner welcomed delegates to an event hosted by the bank, the Military Automation Consortium. It would feature new technologies they financed, including such wonders as robots for removing hostile forces from the battlefield, eliminating enemy units without putting one's personnel in harm's way. Area denial agents could render an area of several square miles fatal for enemy forces, but no mention was made of these also being fatal for civilians, livestock and wildlife.

Liz saw herself reflected in the building's cladding of mirrored glass, except that it seemed to be someone else, a glamourous nymphette of about twenty. Yet, the figure moved as she did, as a reflection would. This person was outstandingly graceful and beautiful, which Liz would have been the first to admit she was not, at least until now. Still, the figure retained aspects that were still recognisable as hers but beautified to an extent that it would have been almost impossible to imagine.

Lucifix observed Liz looking spellbound and incredulous at herself in the glass.

'What's the matter? Don't you like what you see? You always wanted to be beautiful, didn't you? Well, now you are. You've got what you wanted.'

It came to Liz why she had been accosted three times in the previous few minutes, something she had never experienced. Her new glamourous image was a beacon to the hordes of uncouth men frequenting this unpleasant city area. 'Can I go back, please? I don't want this.'

'No, you can't. You will follow me,' insisted Lucifix.

'But I don't want to go on. I want to go back,' Liz whined like a petulant child.

'Well, you can't, and that's it.'

'I can't go on. I won't. I want to go back,' Liz howled.

'You will do as you are told,' replied Lucifix with cold certainty.

Liz, streaming with tears, knew she was beaten. Her spirit, crumpled by the waves of domination Lucifix was radiating, acquiesced, following Lucifix down a side alley leading from the wealthy financial quarter into poorer and grittier territory. They took a path alongside a little used railway branch line, every scrap of flat space painted with lurid graffiti. Eventually, after a considerable distance, they emerged where buildings had been cleared and repurposed as allotments.

As they threaded between the plots, Liz felt a growing unease. Out of the corner of her eye, she sensed she was being observed by a figure standing beside one of the ramshackle huts. Although she wanted to know more about this threatening spectre, she didn't want to make eye contact. She glanced in its direction and instantly returned her gaze to her front, where Lucifix was striding ahead. She didn't get a good view but had a sufficient glimpse to ascertain it was an ugly man. He had a prominent beer belly, a big red nose, a purplish tinge to his cheeks, and a leering grin revealing a mouth of crooked nicotine-stained teeth, most definitely not someone with whom she wished to become better acquainted.

Lucifix led the way amongst the marked-out strips of land, eventually stopping when they had reached a small shed set in one of the plots.

'This is yours,' announced Lucifix.

'I don't understand,' said Liz, 'weren't we going to Miteby? Why are we here?'

Lucifix said nothing, looking across at Liz with contemptuous triumph. Liz gazed back. Eventually, Lucifix deigned to break the news. 'You're not going to Miteby.'

Liz looked back crestfallen. She had already guessed this might be the case but was still shattered.

'You won't be going there ever again.'

'But you promised. You said you were bringing me over to see James, who was waiting for me,' said Liz with anguish.

'I did say that James was in Miteby, waiting to see you, and that was true. But I never said I was taking you over to see him. You just assumed that for yourself.'

'You tricked me. You lied to me.'

'I didn't lie, actually. It was you tricking yourself by

assuming too much.' Lucifix had an icy tone.

Liz's heart sank deeper. 'Okay, but if I can't go to Miteby, can I just go back home?'

'Oh no, you're staying here.'

'But how long for?'

'Eternity.'

As she lay on her bed, improvised from old compost bags and sacking, it was almost too much effort for Liz to turn over due to the dead weight of dread she felt in her stomach. It was as if she was a prisoner on her first night in jail after being sent down for a long stretch, except worse. There would be no bail and no end to her sentence.

Mercifully it was getting light. She had hardly slept. It wasn't only the torment of her situation that had kept her awake, nor even the cold, uncomfortable make-shift bed. Principally, the unwelcome visitation from her new neighbour had left her rigid with terror lest the fiend returned to resume his unwelcome attentions.

It had happened after Lucifix abandoned her in what was now, apparently, her abode, a draughty rickety wooden hovel on an allotment from which she would be obliged to feed herself. Wanting to shut herself away, Liz had retreated inside the hut. It hadn't been more than minutes before there was a knock on the ill-fitting rectangle of crudely nailed planks serving as her front door. She hadn't answered because she had no desire to meet anyone, fearing it might be someone she would not wish to meet. It made no difference. There was no means to secure the door shut, and the person who had knocked swung it open from the outside.

Her fear had been justified. Framed in the doorway

was the man she had glimpsed, leering as she came across the allotments with Lucifix. Closer inspection did not improve his appearance. She could see broken veins on his face that gave him his ruddy complexion, the greasy shine on his skin and the floppy flesh of the jowls that hung on his thick neck. She heard him wheezing out the fumes of stale cigarette smoke and the mass-produced beer he had been drinking copiously from aluminium cans.

'Hello, I'm your neighbour. Just over there on the left, second plot along. Sid's the name. Welcome to our community.'

'Thanks. Nice to meet you,' Liz had lied to keep good relations.

She hadn't invited him in, but he entered anyway.

'Thought you might like company, seeing as you're on your own.'

'Thanks, but I'm a bit tired just now. Some other time, perhaps.'

'Come far then?'

'Walked over from Sorcerer's Copse.'

'Where's that?'

'In the Surrey Hills.'

'Not sure I know where that is.'

'Ask me another time. I'm a bit tired now.'

'I'll get you a beer. That'd perk you up,' Sid suggested, shuffling closer.

'No, thanks.'

'Oh look, you're shivering,' observed Sid, putting his arm around Liz's shoulders.

'I just need to get some rest, that's all,' said Liz, pushing his arm away.

Most people would have taken the hint, but not Sid.

'Gets lonely out here,' said Sid, 'when you're on your own.'

'Sometimes it's nice to be on your own.'

'You need a bit of a cuddle to cheer you up,' said Sid as he clumsily rolled over onto her and attempted to plant slobbery kisses on her.

Beyond the end of her rope, Liz screamed, kicked and punched like a demented ninja until the beast beat a retreat.

Now in the first light of dawn, Liz took stock of what she had. There were vegetable seeds and rusty gardening tools. She looked at her meagre patch of land. It was in horrible condition. The polluted ground was littered with lumps of stone, broken pieces of concrete, rusty metal, and old bones. Liz couldn't be sure of the pedigree of the bones, which could have been animal but just as easily human, perhaps from an earlier use of the land as a graveyard.

Liz shuddered to think of what nasty toxins might be in that degraded soil to be taken up by her future crops of vegetables. An ironic thought came into her mind, which fractionally raised her mood. She had once encountered a Site of Special Scientific Interest that had been so designated because it was one of only a few habitats of some obscure species of wort, something weedy with tiny white flowers. The wort liked it because the ground had been covered with debris from an almost 2000-year-old ancient Roman lead mine. It needed preservation solely because of people from long ago who had horribly tarnished the environment. Perhaps one day, this location might qualify for eternal preservation in its degraded state to preserve a living slime that had come to thrive in contaminated conditions.

Fusion

Karen sat in the sun with her father outside of the Miteby Arms.

Nothing was said. She wondered when Miles might appear.

Initially, it had been difficult to broach the painful feelings arising from his departure from her life. Then, with painful issues confronted, it had been tearful and cathartic. The drama and repertoire of emotions having been drawn out, examined, and discussed, the range of subjects to be explored was dwindling.

Karen found her attention drifting towards a couple of children cycling around the Miteby village green with a scampering little dog.

'Do you still wobble when you ride a bike?' Dad asked.

'No, I don't think that I wobble at all.'

'I remember you wobbling. You slipped over once and cut your head.'

'Did I? I got the hang of it afterwards, but you weren't there then.'

Karen would have liked to have made up for lost time by working through the father and daughter activities and conversations she had missed during childhood, adolescence and young adulthood. But that could not happen now. She wasn't nine, ten, thirteen, or sixteen.

'I could show you how to make a kite,' said Dad.

'Perhaps some time,' she acknowledged without enthusiasm.

Karen wondered about the future of their relationship at their current ages. She was finding it hard to be optimistic because her father was increasingly coming to resemble that odious oaf Larry Bettersby, which was unappealing.

Yet, she had seen another side of Larry at the FFWS Christmas party. Perhaps the loud, cocky, brash, confident and competitive aspects of Larry's character were not the real him but a façade that hid his sensitive side. If only he would shed that outer shell of unrelenting bravado, he could be nice.

She was confused. If her father and Larry were alike and she detested Larry, she should dislike her father too. But if she could see the good in her father, who was similar to Larry, there might be good in Larry.

'What do you feel about me, Dad?'

'I regret not being there for you after I had to leave.'

'Why do you regret it?'

'Because I loved you, as I still do.'

Karen looked at her dad. She felt love for him, too. She was about to say so, but the words stuck. An image of her schoolyard tormentor, Lucy Denberry, sprang into her head, taunting her with accusations of their supposedly incestuous relationship. Karen felt dirty, unable to confess her love.

But her father was like Larry. Perhaps a relationship with Larry was unappealing because of his swaggering arrogance, but if only he showed his softer side, it wouldn't be. So why did her love for her father feel so shameful?

'Fancy a cup of tea, Dad?'

'Not really, we just had tea and cakes not half an hour ago.'

It was hard for Karen to admit it, but conversation with her father had become stilted. She hoped Miles would be along shortly to convey her, ostensibly reluctantly, back to the Material World. She would have expected him to be there by now, hovering in the background.

As time drew on into the evening, Karen dug deep to keep the conversation with her dad going, finding safe topics devoid of emotional content.

'Do you like gardening, Dad?'

'Not really. Don't know much about it, to tell the truth.'

'There must be flowers that you like.'

'Roses. I like a good show of roses.'

'What, climbers or hybrid tea?'

'Couldn't really say.'

Miles still hadn't appeared, so they sampled the traditional English cuisine offered by the Miteby Arms. Karen had the vegetarian option of a potato, onion and courgette bake, and her dad had the Cumberland sausage and mash, which they washed down with refreshing Meadow Dew ale.

Since Miles still did not show, they stayed for the dessert of treacle pudding and whipped cream, helped along with a bottle of English sparkling wine.

The meal was over, and there was still no sign of Miles. It now felt probable he would not appear that evening at all. Karen arranged with the landlord about a room for the night, and they left it so that Karen's dad would look in at breakfast.

She had the attic room, known as the Room at the Top. The bed was cosy, welcoming, and comfortable, yet Karen had a far from restful night.

No sooner had she drifted off than a phantom loomed ominously out of the gloom—the woman in red she had seen at Sorcerer's Copse.

'He didn't love you, you know,' taunted the woman.

'He did. I know he did.'

'But he left you, didn't he? He wouldn't have gone had he loved you. He didn't want you.'

Karen woke, sweating and her pulse racing. There was nobody in the room, which was again cosy and comfortable. She settled, allowing her nerves to relax before her eyelids could droop once more into sleep.

No sooner had sleep come than the phantom woman was there again, glowing a blood red and taunting her mercilessly.

'What he wanted was your body, wasn't it?'

'No, it wasn't.'

'How do you know?'

'He didn't do anything.'

'What, he never picked you up and held you? Never swung you round? Never hoisted you onto his shoulders?'

'Yes, he did.'

'Excuses to get close to you for his sexual gratification.'

'No, it wasn't.'

'Why did he suddenly leave then? Inappropriate touching, wasn't it? That's all he wanted you for. His sexual gratification.'

Repeatedly Karen woke in a horror-struck state before drifting away only for the dreadful spectre to return.

'It was your fault, what he did; you encouraged him.'

'No, I didn't.'

'Go on, admit it, you enjoyed it, bouncing on his shoulders, your pussy rubbing up against his neck.'

It went on repeatedly, only finally banished by the welcome pre-dawn twilight.

Still bleary-eyed, Karen went down to breakfast in the

Miteby Arms bar. After washing down her vegetarian version of the full English breakfast with a pot of well-brewed tea, she felt revived.

There was still no sign of Miles, but her dad showed up and sat with her drinking a cup of tea as she finished her breakfast.

Karen and her dad had more or less run out of anything beyond the most superficial conversation, and Karen did not wish to mention her restless night.

'What shall we do today?' asked Karen.

'How about we go for a walk in the countryside?' Dad suggested.

'Oh, alright,' said Karen, without enthusiasm. They could look at the scenery, even if they had little to say.

'There is a pottery that I'd like to look at,' said Dad.

'Did you say a pottery?'

'Yes, that's right. Why, do you like pottery?'

'Well, yes, sort of. I know someone who does like it.'

'It isn't far, just a few miles, an easy enough walk.'

They spent a pleasant morning strolling along the quiet country lanes. On the outskirts of the nearby village of Lower Coudeby, they looked around a converted barn, made into a dwelling with an adjoining workshop equipped with a potter's wheel, kiln and other pottery accoutrements. Karen's dad tried out the wheel and inspected the kiln.

'It's up for sale,' said Dad. 'We could live here, the two of us, make up for lost time.'

'What you mean, us living together here?'

'Yes, why not?'

Karen shivered involuntarily as her head filled with the nasty insinuations that Lucy, her tormentor of old and now her successor, the woman in red, had made.

'Let's talk about it later,' said Karen, blushing.

There was still no sign of Miles when they arrived back in Miteby, so they enjoyed another evening meal in the Miteby Arms, and Karen stayed in her attic room for another night.

Karen settled for the night with trepidation. As she had feared, the red woman returned.

This time her identity was unmistakable Lucy's, the bully from her school days.

'He is setting up a love nest for you in Lower Coudeby.'

'No, it's nothing like that.'

'But, even if it were, you wouldn't mind, would you? You'd like it if he gave you a cuddle now and again, wouldn't you? You quite fancy him, don't you?'

'Don't be disgusting.'

'It is you who are disgusting. Fancy shacking up with that vile incestuous paedophile. You're as dirty as he is.'

'You're lying. It's nothing like that.'

Lucy's cronies from her school days gathered behind her, joining the taunts.

'You shouldn't be in Miteby,' said Lucy. 'You don't belong here. You should come back with me.'

The scene zoomed out from Miteby, flying back in for a bird's eye of Sorcerer's Copse. Karen could see herself lying there on the ground, unconscious. She heard her rasping breaths gradually dying away, then her body lying still, losing its colour as her life ebbed away.

Waking even more disturbed than she had been the previous night, Karen was again heartily relieved to be rescued by the dawn.

At breakfast, Miles remained absent, but another figure appeared, one even stranger than the infernal Lucy Denberry.

Karen had been feeling calmer in the reassuring light of day, just beginning to relax, recovering from the traumatic effects of her nightmares, when this new apparition shook her to the core.

As she caught her first glimpse, her first impression was that this person was close to her, someone she knew well. A moment later, she recognised the other person as a version of herself, as perfect an image as if she was looking in the mirror. But there was no mirror, and the figure stood while she was seated.

Panic swept through her as she grappled to make sense of this vision and its implications. It was like she had become detached from her body, a free spirit. Is this what it was like when you died, and your soul departed your physical remains?

Yet it couldn't be that because this other version of herself was no corpse and undoubtedly alive.

She considered for a moment the possibility of some electronic trickery, a projected hologram perhaps. If so, it was a very realistic hologram.

Stunned with her thoughts in disarray, Karen was speechless.

Her doppelgänger broke the silence. 'Don't be afraid. I am your alter ego on the Other Side.'

The material Karen found her voice. 'You mean, you are some separate version of me. Is that what you are saying?'

'Yes, that's right.'

'But how can that be?'

'You are from the Material World, but I exist only on

the Other Side.'

The material Karen, her mind still whirling, sweat beading on her forehead and pulse racing, in her panic hardly able to form a single logical thought, grappled to make sense of this explanation. Her mind gyrated ineffectually like the spinning tyres of a vehicle floundering in axle-deep mud.

'But I am on the Other Side too, now. How can we both be here?'

'We have different roles. You are here to see our father, but I am here for Larry,' replied her doppelgänger.

The Material World Karen felt fractionally calmer. There was something tangible for her mind to work on. She fought to formulate something useful to say.

'You are saying I am here because I wanted to work things out with... my... I mean our... father, but that's not why you're here. You being here has something to do with Larry. Is that it?'

'Yes,' Karen's doppelgänger confirmed.

'But why would you come here about Larry? Why should we care about him?'

'It wasn't me that wanted to see Larry; it was Larry who wanted to see me... or, rather, you, us... well, the same thing really, we're the same person.'

Material Karen forced her racing mind to slow so that she could think. It was several seconds before the significance dawned. 'You mean, you're here because Larry had you... well, us, me... on his mind, just like Dad is here because I had him on my mind. So you're sort of like Dad, in a sense.'

'Yes, we're both, Dad and I, people from the Other Side, whereas you and Larry are from the Material

World.'

Material Karen pondered this. 'It's very confusing, us both being here, the same person, yet different. It's difficult to get my head around.'

'Yes, it is confusing, but we can straighten that out.'

'How can we do that?'

'We should become one, join forces; it would be better that way,' proposed Karen's doppelgänger.

'How do you mean, join forces?'

'By uniting ourselves.'

Material Karen found herself forced back again into thinking mode. 'Uniting ourselves, how do we do that?'

'Don't worry. It'll be easy. Leave it to me.'

Material Karen was apprehensive, but she had no tangible reason to object. After a few more seconds of deliberation, she consented.

'Well, alright then. What do we do?'

'Come over to me,' said the doppelgänger.

Material Karen stood, facing her double. The doppelgänger stepped forward as if to stand on the same spot. Material Karen stepped back to make way.

'Please don't step away,' said the doppelgänger.

The doppelgänger stepped forward again, but this time Karen remained where she was. The doppelgänger stepped into the space material Karen occupied so that the bodies of the two overlapped and superimposed.

While there was no collision of flesh because Karen's doppelgänger was ethereal, there an explosive spiritual collision as the contents of their minds poured themselves together like the confluence of two rivers. The memories and thoughts swirled like watery vortices, initially distinct but fragmenting and merging as they ricocheted within the confines of their newly unified space.

The unified Karen had a combined recollection of her doppelgänger's conversations with Larry, her conversations with her father, and her torments from the bully Lucy Denberry in her recent nightmares.

Karen was struck by the pleasant, charming conversations her doppelgänger had with Larry in Miteby; simple and loving, nothing like the brittle brashness of the Larry she had thought she knew.

Simultaneously Karen's recent conversations with her father merged in her brain with her fresh impression of Larry. Her father now faded into just a distant memory in her childhood.

As the fusion progressed, the sense that they were two bodies occupying one space receded. A united Karen emerged, struggling and straining in the unification process like a butterfly emerging from a chrysalis.

As the ripples on the surface of the pool of recollections faded and the reverberations in her consciousness subsided, anxiety about returning to the Material World receded. She felt at home now as a creature of the Other Side.

Casualty Evacuation

As the rescue marshal on so-called Blood Wagon duty for the Founders Memorial Challenge event, Eddie received the call about the casualties, a woman of about 30 and another in her mid-50s, found at Sorcerer's Copse.

As one of the event organisers and a long-standing member of the Surrey FFWS committee, Eddie and the wider team had discussed and planned for these eventualities.

Making the call was one of the event participants who had found the casualties.

'They look in a bad way,' the man reported.

'Have you called the emergency services?' Eddie enquired.

'Yes, they're on the line to us now.'

'Did they say when they would be there?'

'Due to the area's inaccessibility by road, they're sending the Air Ambulance. It's on its way.'

Eddie could hear the helicopter over the phone.

'Here it is now,' the man confirmed. 'I'll need to hang up to talk to them.'

Eddie called the emergency services to make himself known to them as the contact for the event organisers. A police officer called back a short while later.

'The area will need to be cleared to facilitate the emergency services,' advised the policeman. 'Could you help us take care of that?'

Eddie consulted the map and found a diversion to avoid Sorcerer's Copse. He rapidly typed in brief alterations to the route instructions to take in the diversion. He ran off 200 copies on the printer they used for completion certificates.

While waiting for the sheets to run through the printer, he grabbed the large diversion sign he had already prepared to cover such an emergency. He gesticulated to Jenny, preparing the soup and pizzas for the finishing participants.

'Sorry, Jenny, we've got an emergency. Two casualties, and we need to set up a diversion. Could you give me a hand?'

Jenny, as always, had everything under control and could confidently leave the culinary duties with her team. The two set off from the local parish hall in Dorking in Eddie's classic Jaguar, heading towards the diversion point.

The location Eddie had designated for the diversion also happened to be the nearest point to Sorcerer's Copse reachable by road vehicles. They were greeted by multiple sets of flashing blue lights shining brightly in the now fading light of the late afternoon.

Eddie and Jenny worked hammering poles supporting the diversion sign into the ground. Eddie left Jenny, directing the arriving participants onto the alternative route and handing out the altered route instructions while he sought the officer in charge of the rescue operation.

There was an ambulance, a specialist off-road rescue vehicle and a police car present.

'At this stage, we can't rule out foul play,' the police inspector informed Eddie. 'We'll need to search the area for further casualties and secure it for forensic examination.'

'Goodness,' said Eddie. 'Is there anything we can do to

assist?'

'The rescue team could use some help,' said the inspector, gesturing towards a member of the ambulance team.

'Could you direct us to the scene, please?' said the ambulance man.

Eddie joined them in their all-terrain vehicle to point out the way.

The specialised rescue vehicle's wide, grippy tyres and flexible suspension facilitated its way into Sorcerer's Copse, twisting, dipping and bouncing to accommodate the steep rutted, muddy, churned-up track customarily used for hauling timber. They were met by the man Eddie had spoken to earlier on the phone.

'They were taken away by the Air Ambulance.'

'What was their condition?' Eddie enquired.

'They were comatose, and the paramedics had to put in breathing tubes.'

A police officer was standing nearby overseeing the scene.

'Do we know anything about them?' Eddie enquired.

'Not much,' replied the officer.

'Such as who they are, for instance.'

'We are unable to reveal their identities until their next of kin have been informed.'

Back in the Dorking parish hall, there was a buzz in the room from participants sitting around tables chatting animatedly, tucking into slices of pizza, mugs of soup, and hunks of French bread. Volunteer marshals checked people in as they arrived before guiding them over towards the trestle table in front of the hall's kitchen, from which other volunteers dispensed warm welcome sustenance. Fortunately, Jenny had been relieved from her diversion duties in the Sorcerer's Copse area and had been back in time to take control of the catering before the main rush of finishers descended.

For Eddie, there had never been a dull moment. The Ladies' toilets were blocked, obliging him to wade through the stinking pool spread across the floor with a plunger. There were also complaints about the showers running cold as early finishers had used up the hot water. In the kitchen, the volunteers were forced to use hot water from the tea urn for washing up.

The pace had slackened as the main surge of 20- and 30-mile finishers passed through and the bulk of the 50 milers had yet to arrive.

Jenny brought Eddie over a mug of tea. 'You look frazzled.'

'Yes, it's been quite a day.'

'There's a lull. You should be able to relax for a bit.'

'Not for long.' Eddie sighed. 'I'm sure to be called out on Blood Wagon duties before long.'

'Do we know who the casualties are?'

'Yes, I figured it out from the tracking information. They must be Karen and Liz. They're both long overdue at Checkpoint 3.'

Jenny's face went blank and white. 'I had better get back,' she said after a few moments, turning to the kitchen area.

Eddie's mobile rang. 'Here we go.' He had barely had a chance to sip his tea.

It was Guildford Hospital.

'Just to inform you about the two participants rescued

from your event.'

'Right. Thanks. What can you tell me?'

'They are Karen Doddleston and Liz Lenbury.'

'Thank you. What condition are they in?'

'They are both in a coma but stable. We have transferred them from Accident and Emergency into Intensive Care.'

Eddie took his tea mug over to the kitchen area.

'They're over at Guildford Hospital, in Intensive Care,' he informed Jenny.

She paused and nodded. She took Eddie's hand for a moment and squeezed, then turned to take care of a pan of soup about to boil over.

Somehow Larry's tired legs propelled him, still running for the final few hundred yards of the 50-mile course of the Founders Memorial Challenge.

The route extended over the wide variety of terrain offered in Surrey. The boot-clogging clay soil stretches across ploughed fields; the thoughtful inclusion of semi-submerged water meadows for cleaning off the mud-encrusted boots before resurfacing them through cattle trampled quagmires; a succession of steep ascents and descents on and off the North Downs; dense deciduous woodland littered with tree-roots and brambles that stretched across paths like steel hawsers, nearly invisible in the hours of darkness, and pine forests on sandy ground strewn with needles that sapped energy like running along a dry sandy beach. Then to sandy bracken and heather-covered heathland that could double for Scotland; indeed, it was so convincingly Scottish that budget-conscious film directors used the terrain for highland dramas, keeping costs down by filming near studios in Pinewood or Shepperton.

Larry's entire body was tired. Mud weighed down his trainers, clogging the treads and making the soles flat and slippery, sliding erratically and unpredictably on the pavement's icy slush. His knees, ankles and hips ached, the sinews of his legs taut as violin strings, strained by his body twitching one way or another to regain balance over the challenging course. Yet, near exhaustion, his feet were pounding in a relentless rhythm.

He squeezed out the energy to propel himself at a run up the final steps to the front door of the Dorking parish hall, straining to maintain the countenance and grace of an elite athlete. Although Larry sought to convey boundless athleticism and energy, as he checked in for the finish, his haggard grey features gave away the punishment he had imposed on himself to complete the course.

He stood waiting at the desk; his participant number was logged into the system. His body was already sagging, yet his leg muscles twitched rhythmically as if still trying to run. Formalities complete, he felt almost faint from exhaustion, but somehow his legs did not get that message, still straining forward, propelling him quickly over to the trestle table from where the food and drink were handed out.

Loaded with a generous helping of soup and pizza, chocolate biscuits and sweetened tea for quick energy and rehydration, Larry eventually took the weight off his feet, placing the sustenance onto one of the tables as he slumped onto one of the stackable chairs. At last, the muscles in his legs accepted it was time to stop. The weariness that had already enveloped the rest of his body flowed into his lower limbs. The aching fatigue spreading down his thighs, through his knees, sending twinges of cramp into his calves, locking his ankles into immobility and sending a cold stiffness through his feet into his toes.

Larry's mind switched off for a few minutes, focussing only on rest and taking in the warmth and calories to restore his depleted energy reserves. When his mental batteries were charged, he wondered where Karen might have gotten to. He hadn't noticed her come in. He looked around the room. She had been up with him until Sorcerer's Copse, but he hadn't seen her since and hadn't noticed her overtaking him, so he figured he must have come ahead of her. From experience, she usually came in hot on his heels. He would have expected her to have arrived by now or, if not, soon. He decided to wait.

As one of the 50 milers, Larry was unaware of the incident. His brain was sufficiently rested to take in the background conversation by now.

'That diversion around Sorcerer's Copse must have added half a mile.'

'Yes, and that back path beside the woods was a quagmire. Took me right up to my knees.'

'What was it all about?'

'Someone said there were a couple of casualties. Had to be rescued by Air Ambulance.'

Larry slid his chair over. 'Excuse me, but does anybody know who the casualties were?'

'No, afraid not. Two women. That's all I heard.'

It had been nearly half an hour since he arrived in the hall, and Larry was apprehensive about Karen. He wandered to the check-in desk, where Eddie kept a general eye on things.

'Hello Eddie, you couldn't tell me if Karen Doddleston's been through yet, could you?'

Eddie looked uneasy. Despite his tiredness, Larry was fast to read the body language. Eddie knew something but didn't want to say it.

'Look, don't get all cagey with me. I can tell something has happened.'

'Sorry, but it's confidential information.'

'It wouldn't be confidential unless it was something serious. Come on, spit it out. I'm concerned about her.'

Eddie frowned. 'Alright, she has been admitted to Guildford Hospital.'

'What's wrong with her?'

'They said she was in a coma. That's all I know.'

The police had postponed carrying out a thorough forensic search of the area around Sorcerer's Copse until first light.

Pale hints of dawn were apparent in the sky as the assigned specialist officers fortified themselves with a warming cup of tea out of a flask, dunking chocolate digestive biscuits into their plastic mugs.

The sergeant in charge decided there was sufficient light, so they slurped the last dregs of tea and stood ready for action. The officers spread out into their assigned search sectors.

One made his way to where a footpath curved around a large spreading oak tree. The officer peered around the corner. He stepped back, startled. In front of him, only dimly lit in the shadows, was what appeared to be another casualty lying on the ground, a man dressed in bright, high-visibility yellow amber.

'Hey, sarge, I think we've got another one.'

He switched on his torch to cast a better light onto the scene. Taking a step towards what he had taken to be another body, he realised his mistake. A mass of fungal growth of tightly packed stalks and yellowy amber toadstools had erupted, forming itself into the appearance of a human form.

'Sorry, sarge, false alarm. Light playing tricks on me.'

Larry's alarm woke him the morning after the Founders Memorial Challenge event.

While he had been in the Dorking parish hall the night before, he had been shocked more than he might have expected on hearing Karen had been one of the casualties. He had felt the urge to dash straight over to the hospital.

Realism prevailed. He would probably have been too tired even to make it. When he got to the hospital, there would have been no chance of him being allowed to see her. He needed to get some rest. So he went home and set his alarm.

Arriving at the hospital at the earliest reasonable hour, he enquired about her at reception.

'Are you related?'

'We are close friends.'

'When you say close, how close?'

Larry thought quickly. They weren't going to let just any old friend in. 'Well, I'm her partner,' he lied.

'I'll phone through to the ward. It's up the stairs and on the right.'

Karen's mother was already at her bedside, and Karen

was lying still, comatose and on life support.

'Hello, I'm Larry,' he announced, breaking an awkward silence.

'So, what brings you here?'

'Karen and I are very close.'

'Oh, I see. How long have you been close?'

'Just the last few months.'

'Funny she never brought you over to see me,' remarked Karen's mother, looking him up and down. 'Were you taking part in this thing she was doing?'

'Yes, we often do these events together.'

'Do you care about her?'

'Yes, of course I do.'

'So how did you let this happen?' she demanded, looking at him accusingly.

'I don't know what happened to her, but it wasn't anything I did.'

'Must be dangerous out there for this to have happened.'

'I suppose it must.'

'So why did you let her go out there if it was dangerous?'

'I didn't. She enrolled for the event herself.'

'But you must have encouraged her to do it.'

'Both of us were already doing these events. That's how we met.'

She looked at him doubtfully. 'You're not going to run away from her, are you? Not now, in her hour of need.'

'No, of course not.'

She was unconvinced. The challenging atmosphere was relieved when a doctor came in.

'The toxicology report identifies that she has been

exposed to two rare and highly toxic species of fungi,' the doctor explained.

'So, what does that mean?' asked Karen's mother.

'Her condition is stable, so the signs are hopeful that she will pull through, but if she does recover, it could take time. It is going to be a waiting game.'

Larry was finding the atmosphere with Karen's mother tense, and he clearly couldn't talk with Karen herself, so he beat a retreat.

He suspected that there was more to Karen's sickness than the fungi. He felt in his gut it must have something to do with Miteby and the Other Side. He resolved to find out.

Eternal Competition

It was around midday when Larry brought his Porsche towards the nearest point on the road to reach Sorcerer's Copse.

Larry's car was an integral part of the persona he aspired to present, a display of ostentatious wealth, impeccable taste in the latest fashion, and a supreme physique combined with a ready wit and humour, all achieved without apparent effort.

The grass verge and turning into the rough trackway typically used by forestry staff was taken up with police vehicles, within one of which several police officers, some in white coveralls, were chatting and eating sandwiches.

Assuming they would not allow him access, Larry drove on another mile, figuring another route would bring him into Sorcerer's Copse.

Leaving his mud-spattered prestige motor parked precariously on a grass bank at the roadside, he set off on foot, trespassing across fields well-trodden by grazing cows. He reached the path up the gully between overgrown banks, where the gnarled oak tree spread out over Sorcerer's Copse.

As he approached the oak tree, Larry was blocked by a length of blue tape marked with the words 'Police—Keep Out'. He looked around and saw that the entire clearing was taped off. There were signs that people, presumably police forensic specialists, had been at work on the site. Still, at that precise moment, there was nobody there. Probably taking their lunch break where he had seen them earlier.

Nobody being there to challenge him, Larry stepped over the tape and into the clearing among fallen logs, scuffing his feet against a tough fibrous fungus, scarlet red around its rim, darkening to a purplish maroon at its centre. Hearing a rustling from the far end of the clearing, he saw the figure of an imperious woman dressed in a glowing reddish-purple cloak, standing where an overgrown path emerged from a dense scrub of gorse and brambles.

The woman's piercing gaze impaled him. She beckoned. Impelled, he walked over zombie fashion until he was about five yards distant, whereupon she stretched out her hand, flat and palm facing down, halting him with a quick flick towards the ground. Instinctively he obeyed, standing straight and still like a soldier on parade.

'Looking for somebody?'

Larry would typically have demanded to know who she was, introducing himself, or overtly making a move to seize control of the conversation. But this was not a normal encounter. The mysterious woman was unquestionably in command, and Larry was under her spell.

'Well, yes. I was hoping to find someone called Miles. I have found him here in the past.'

The woman nodded slowly. 'Yes, I know, Miles. He can't come today. I'm here instead.'

'Ah, right. Well, glad you could come,' said Larry compliantly.

The woman said nothing, penetrating his soul with her gaze.

'I'm Larry, by the way,' Larry stuttered.

'Yes, I know. I'm Lucifix, but you may call me Lucy,' the

woman informed him.

Larry was confused. She already knew him, and she did look somehow familiar. He didn't want to offend her by confessing he had forgotten.

'Hello, Lucy,' he said. 'It's been a while,' he added, hoping it might prompt her to save his embarrassment.

'It was a long time ago,' she said, not overly helpfully, although it ruled out recent contact, making his forgetfulness a little more forgivable were he forced to confess it.

'I'd been hoping to find Miles because he might have been able to get me in touch with Karen Doddleston,' said Larry, wanting to move things along.

'Were you now,' said Lucifix, looking at him quizzically.

'It probably sounds strange because she is actually in hospital, in a coma. I know that. I've seen her there. I hope this doesn't appear ridiculous, but I thought that there might be a part of her in Miteby; oh, I expect that feels ridiculous as well because it's not on the map,' Larry said, babbling.

Lucifix put out her hand to stop Larry. 'I know where she is, yes.'

'You couldn't take me over to see her, could you?' asked Larry, hopefully.

'You should come with me,' announced Lucifix.

'Thank you,' said Larry meekly.

He half turned back to the giant oak tree, anticipating following Lucifix down the familiar path Miles used.

'No, this way,' said Lucifix, gesturing to the barely discernible track threading into the dense thicket behind her. Larry followed her among the tangle of snagging, scratchy gorse and brambles. She led the way at speed, gliding through effortlessly like a phantom. Larry found himself running to keep pace.

The path led through a neglected, overgrown orchard when it emerged from the scrub. Lucifix kept up her blistering pace leaving Larry panting and gasping, and his legs, still fatigued from the relentless 50-mile run the previous day, ached with stiffness and cramp.

Larry's feet slipped on loose gravel that had accumulated around the workings of a graffiti-plastered electrical sub-station. He was too tired to take in more than a vague, blurred impression of the cityscape that came into view.

Doubts formed in Larry's mind. It didn't look anything like Miteby. But he was now so close to exhaustion that he could not even consciously consider such a concern. Every scrap of energy he could muster was expended on staying on his feet, keeping pace with Lucifix. She sped forward across derelict scrubland without pausing. To add to Larry's difficulties, there were heaps of dumped building rubble, rusty carcases of abandoned vehicles, old shopping trolleys and miscellaneous rubbish for him to manoeuvre around. The effort from running diverted his attention from unsavoury detritus: used condoms, old syringes and the like. He was vaguely aware of other people but had no energy to take in who they might be and what they might be doing.

She led him through an underpass that took them under a major highway. Breathing heavily, Larry could not avoid sucking in lungfuls of noxious exhaust fumes from the traffic.

They were now in the city's financial quarter, with

Larry gasping from the exertion and coughing from the urban jungle's polluted air.

Lucifix halted as they came up to the most grandiose of the plush skyscrapers dominating the banking district, announcing itself prominently as being the offices of the Continental and Oceanic Securities Bank.

Larry was like a faithful hound, held at heel in unquestioning obedience to his owner, standing still and compliant awaiting Lucifix's command.

'We need to get you signed up,' Lucifix announced.

Larry, still gasping, was unable to speak. When his brain could function again, all that came into his mind was confusion. 'Sign up for what?'

'You like challenge events, don't you?'

'Yes, I do, actually.'

'Well, you are indeed privileged. I have you lined up for something special, the ultimate in challenge events,' purred Lucifix.

'Oh, the ultimate? I'm not sure which that is.' He could think of several well-known ultra-marathons, Iron Man competitions, etc.

'It is very special, sponsored by the bank, the Perpetual Mountain Ultra-marathon.'

It was not one Larry had heard of, but he was intrigued. It wasn't what he thought he was coming for, but he was up for it. Karen's fate was still nagging him, though. 'But what about Karen? When do I get to see her?'

'All in good time. Perhaps we can get her along to see you compete. You'd like that, wouldn't you?'

'Yes, it would be nice to have her there.'

'I'll see what I can do about that. Leave it with me. In

189

the meantime, we need to get you signed up,' Lucifix insisted.

She gestured for him to follow her through the bank's grand entrance into an immense atrium embellished with acres of the finest marble, ornate urns containing exotic indoor plants and other opulent decorative features. The low seating and raised timber-panelled reception desks emphasised the visiting supplicants' relatively lower importance than the all-powerful bank.

A banner across the foyer welcomed attendees to a forum hosted by the bank, 'The Role of Competition in Sustaining Economic Growth'. According to the headlines proclaimed on the welcoming poster, continually rising productivity, frictionless global distribution of goods, expansion of commodity supplies for industry, elimination of trade barriers and streamlining regulation were to be discussed.

After signing Larry in at a modest desk towards the back of the foyer, Lucifix led them out onto the street, around a corner and down an escalator into an underground train station. The platform was heaving. A short while later, a train pulled in. The already dense mass of humanity was obliged to compress even tighter to permit a surge to come off the train. After half a minute jostling, it was time for those on the platform to board. Lucifix was assertive in forcing a way onto the train so that she and Larry were crammed hard against their carriage's sliding doors when it eventually moved off.

They trundled underground an hour, constantly buffeted and squeezed as passengers forced themselves on and off the train at each dozen or more stations.

On reaching their destination, emerging into daylight,

Larry found himself in a ski resort town absorbed as a suburb of the megacity from which they had come.

Encroached on either side by towering mountains, it was situated within a valley that rose towards a distant glacier. It was summer, and the only visible snow consisted of small remnants tucked away in north-facing rocky crevices. In their natural state, the mountains would have been heavily wooded on their lower slopes, but there was now almost no trace of forest cover. The slopes were covered in the paraphernalia of mass tourism, bare ski pistes, ski jump installations, bob sleigh runs, ski lifts, snow cannons, a gondola system, apres ski bars and restaurants.

Not far from the station, a large banner marked the event for which Larry had been signed up, 'The Perpetual Mountain Ultra-marathon'.

Lucifix led Larry to a table set up for checking in. As other competitors laboriously jogged past, Larry was allocated a number and a timestamp was recorded.

Lucifix's seductive influence and commanding charisma had taken over Larry's body and soul, leaving no room for personal autonomy. In the absence of a specific command, he stood around looking uncertain.

Lucifix was irritated. 'Go on. Get going. You've been booked in as having started already. You're wasting time.'

Lucifix shoved him towards the track where other participants assembled.

For want other guidance, Larry joined the melee of runners staggering strenuously up the steep incline of the mountainside. He ran a few steps with difficulty but dropped back to a walk.

'Get moving,' shouted Lucifix. 'Go on. Run.'

Larry's legs felt as heavy as concrete, yet with Lucifix's chiding voice ringing in his ears, he found reserves he did not know he had to resume a heavily plodding run up the forbidding slope. Feeling Lucifix's withering gaze boring into him, Larry kept moving, forcing himself to at least keep pace with his fellow participants as he struggled past the infrastructure for winter sports, pylons supporting ski lifts, barriers separating off-piste areas, huts housing maintenance equipment. Already shattered from this participation in the Founders Memorial Challenge and the frenetic pace Lucifix had set earlier, Larry felt that every step would exhaust him. Yet, Lucifix's commanding influence compelled him to keep going relentlessly, struggling uphill for hundreds of meters into the thinning air of the higher mountain slopes.

Hours of remorseless toil brought him towards the mountain summit, where a café bar sat atop the station for the gondolas carrying tourists who did not have the energy, physical capability or inclination to make it under their own steam. It was a checkpoint for the Perpetual Mountain Ultra-marathon event. Larry could see that this was only the end of a stage rather than the finish because he saw participants ahead of him moving on further. He anticipated that he might be allowed the luxury of a short break before being compelled to press on, but as he paused for a second or two, Lucifix was waiting for him.

'Get moving, you lazy swine,' she taunted.

It was at that moment Larry realised where he had encountered her before. She was Lucy Totkin, the fellow pupil who had made his life a misery in his primary school days, showing him up when he could not match her precocious skills and taunting him for his inadequacies.

Despite recollecting the hell Lucy had put him through, he did not resent her. She had been right to deride him for his failures. He should have strived harder and not been so lazy. As Lucifix, she was rightly chiding his laziness, driving him to achieve more, compete, and win.

The following section, downhill along the line of electrical supply pylons, was less arduous but ferociously fast and slippery, requiring constant alertness and nimble footwork to avoid slipping over precipitous rocky cliffs.

The path flattened off for only a short stretch before setting off up again, scaling another peak, steeper and more challenging than the previous one, alongside more ski pistes and a zip-wire attraction before zigzagging up around and among outcrops of jagged granite rocks. Towards the summit, they were obliged to clamber over and around an elaborate mesh of heavy welded steel girders concreted into the bedrock, installed for avalanche protection. After more than three hours of what felt like an endless ascent, he reached a second higher summit topped with a panoramic restaurant served by a cable car.

Lucifix again was present at the summit checkpoint driving him on, now unmistakably in the guise of his tormenter of old, Lucy Totkin.

'Go on, move, you worthless turd. Stop slacking.'

She is right to goad me, Larry told himself. He must work harder to prove himself worthy.

Another treacherous descent felt to Larry as if it would destroy his knees as they absorbed the impact of his weight coming down relentlessly hard and awkwardly with every lurching stride.

The path consisted of lumpy uneven cobbles made slippery by dangerous patches of ice and snow, turning and twisting his ankles as he ran. To the side of the path was an assortment of litter and yellow stains in the snow, accompanied by soiled tissues where people had relieved themselves.

The route turned upwards again, harsher, steeper and higher than ever, over a glacier before reaching another mountain eyrie, served by what was described as the world's highest mountain railway. Besides the steepness and ruggedness of the terrain at this altitude, the thin air left Larry breathless and light-headed.

Utterly spent at the summit checkpoint, Larry could not move again until he had taken a breather.

'No time for idleness; get moving,' shouted Lucifix as she leapt from nowhere.

'Where… is… the… finish?' Larry enquired, gasping each word. Surely it must be soon, he thought. Nobody could maintain this pace for much further.

'There is no finish,' Lucifix informed him derisively. 'It is a perpetual marathon, for all eternity. This is your life now. You enjoy competitive endurance running, don't you? You should feel grateful, being allowed to do what you enjoy forever.'

Back at the Continental and Oceanic Securities Bank offices, the forum on the role of competition in sustaining economic growth was underway.

The need for continually rising productivity was emphasised. At the very least annual improvements of 2-3%, but enterprises should ideally be aspiring for a stretch target of 5%. Technology, keeping staff continually available online by electronic means, with smartphones, wi-fi, 5G and so on, was a key enabler. Culling the the passengers from the workforce by laying off the least productive 10% of staff annually was recommended to raise average productivity and motivate personnel to excel.

Automation was also a helpful enabler. Supervisory systems could use machine learning to acquire knowledge of worker expertise, encoding operational best practices into persistent organisational memory enabling the human element to be phased out.

For optimum profitability, organisations must avoid sentimentality about the fates of those automated out of a job or burned out by stress. Weeding out the weak was an essential part of the eugenic improvement of the human race and a necessary process for sustaining economic growth.

Jeremiahs constantly warn about the depletion of the world's resources, but their concerns have always been unfounded. Year after year, peak oil was supposed to be just about to happen, yet never materialised. Historically new supplies have always been found, and human ingenuity always succeeds.

Someone objected that even at an annual growth rate of 2%, that represented a 7-fold increase in the rate of consumption over a century, rising to a 100-fold at a growth rate of 5%. Simple mathematics showed that must be unsustainable. This was dismissed as simplistic. New materials and techniques would be devised, as demonstrated throughout history.

A further objection was raised that even if the resources were available, consuming them resulted in degradation of the environment, pollution, global warming, destruction of natural habitats and loss of biodiversity.

There was general annoyance at the presence of these people attempting to hold back economic progress. Global warming has been demonstrated to be fake news; even if it were true, it would be good. Swathes of new farmland would become available in sub-arctic tundra, and crop yields would improve because CO_2 was a fertiliser. Urban pollution was generating lucrative opportunities for businesses providing face masks and filtration systems for building air conditioning and ventilation.

Attempts at further objections temporarily halted the proceedings. Chief bank security officer Duncan McTaggetty and his burly assistants Sean and Kevin moved in to eject the troublemakers from the premises.

Into the Infernal Depths

Eddie stared at his plate of meat pie, potatoes, peas and gravy, slowly getting cold. Twenty minutes earlier, it had looked and smelled appetising, but now it had a glazed, congealed look. He found the lingering stale wafts nauseating. He had taken a corner out of the pie, half eaten a couple potatoes and spread the peas around.

Eddie told himself it was daft to stare at the food. He must eat. He levered a piece of the pie with his fork and brought it to his mouth. He chewed on it without enthusiasm. It gave him no enjoyment. He wasn't in any hurry to swallow, but for want of anywhere else to go, he gulped it down. He heaved involuntarily, somehow containing it in his stomach where it sat uncomfortably. He was forced to admit he couldn't face eating just now.

About an hour before, fixing himself a meal had felt like a good idea. He had enjoyed the first few mouthfuls until he received the call.

The police had called to inform him of another poisoning victim found at Sorcerer's Copse by the search team when they returned from their lunch break.

The man should not have been there but had crossed the police exclusion tapes. He had been rushed to hospital. Fungal poisoning was suspected, similar to the other two casualties. The police could not provide his identity, but they let it be known a Porsche was found nearby and that he had been to the hospital earlier to visit one of the two women victims. Having spoken to Karen's mother earlier, Eddie had deduced that the new victim must be Larry.

Disturbing as it was having Liz and Karen so dangerously ill, with them as the only victims, the situation had felt grave but manageable, but now it was spiralling into chaos. Eddie reflected that the authorities could not deal with the problem effectively because they lacked a full understanding, seeing only the medical consequences of toxic fungi. It would take someone like himself, with the wider perspective of Miteby and the Other Side, to tackle the situation adequately.

Eddie felt convinced Liz, Karen, and now also Larry were somehow entrapped on the Other Side. Getting them released would be essential for their physical recovery. He must enlist Miles to bring this about.

Surmising that Larry would have reached this conclusion too, bringing him to Sorcerer's Copse, Eddie realised Larry's mistake was going alone. While duty-bound to seek Miles's assistance, Eddie should enlist support. He tipped the contents of his plate into the food recycling bin before picking up the phone.

'Larry's been found unconscious at Sorcerer's Copse,' Eddie informed Jenny.

'Oh, my goodness, how is he?'

'He's at Guildford, in Intensive Care. They're saying due to toxic mushrooms.'

'Why has he only just been found?'

'He only went over there today. He went through the police cordon.'

'Why would he have done that?'

'I don't know, but I can guess.'

'Oh, so what do you think?'

'I'm guessing he was there trying to rescue the other two. I can't think of any other reason.'

'Rescuing them? How?'

'He must have believed, as I do, that they are stuck in Miteby.'

'But they are in Guildford hospital, aren't they?'

'Their bodies, yes. But not them, as such, not their spirits, souls, whatever you want to call it.'

'Does that mean our bodies have stayed behind in Sorcerer's Copse whenever we have been over there?'

'I think so. It's the only way I can figure it out.'

'Golly.'

'I have a horrible feeling about this,' said Eddie. 'If we don't figure out how to get them back from Miteby, they might die.'

'Isn't there anything the doctors could do? Or the police?'

'If we went to them with what we know about Miteby, what would they do?'

'It would be difficult to explain, that's for sure.'

'They would most likely certify and lock us up in the funny farm. We couldn't involve them.'

'So where does that leave us?'

'We're the only ones who might be able to get them rescued, with the help of Miles.'

'So does that mean going to Sorcerer's Copse?'

'Well, yes, but it will be taking a huge risk. We could get stuck over there too, like Larry seems to have been.'

'So, if we went, we could end up like the others?'

'Yes, that might happen.'

'What should we do then?'

'Well, I'm going over there. Someone's got to do something.'

'In that case, so am I,' said Jenny.

'Are you sure? It'll be very dangerous.'
'I'm sure.'

Eddie pulled his classic Jaguar to the side of the road where the forest track led off towards Sorcerer's Copse. The grass verge was churned with tyre tracks from the recent presence of departed police and rescue vehicles.

Although the steep track was theoretically accessible for vehicles, generally it was only for off-road timber handling machines, enforced by a heavy metal barrier preventing unauthorised access. They would have to take it on foot.

A little way up the track, a new barrier blocked the way with a sign telling them 'Danger—Keep Out' together with a biohazard symbol. They looked at each other and nodded, stepped around the obstacle and continued up the slope towards the danger area.

Sorcerer's Copse, having been heavily disturbed and trampled by the recent activity, was now calm and silent. The clearing appeared unthreatening, yet Eddie and Jenny approached cautiously, keenly apprehensive of the unseen supernatural hazard. They looked around the places where Miles might appear, but nothing occurred in the ten minutes it took to check the area thoroughly.

Completing their circuit, they looked at each other and shrugged, mystified yet relieved nothing demonic had emerged.

'Perhaps we should go around again,' said Eddie.

'May as well.'

Fifteen minutes elapsed. They had completed their second circuit, and still, nothing emerged.

'One more time?' suggested Eddie.

Jenny shrugged and nodded.

Their third inspection finished without incident.

'Looks like nothing is going to happen,' Eddie observed. 'Perhaps we should call it a day.'

'I guess so.'

As he followed Jenny towards the vehicle track Eddie's boot tripped up against the chunky fibrous mass of a dark purplish-red fungus throwing out a smoky cloud of spores. Looking up from where his foot had been, he caught a glimpse of a figure, a woman wrapped in a red cloak standing next to the barely discernible beginning of a path among an untidy thicket of gorse and brambles.

The woman was staring intently in Eddie's direction. She caught his eye, and he was trapped by her gaze, unable to move his eyes away. Eddie stopped and faced her. Oblivious, Jenny continued walking along the track away from Sorcerer's Copse.

The woman in red gestured with her hand for Eddie to approach. Ensnared, Eddie obeyed.

The woman gave out an attractive force Eddie found impossible to resist, an allure that held him in an overpowering enchantment. Unthinking, Eddie walked up close to where she stood.

'You are looking for your friends, Liz, Karen and Larry, I suppose,' the woman said softly.

'Yes,' said Eddie.

'I am here to take you,' she said soothingly.

'Yes,' repeated Eddie.

'You should come with me.'

'Jenny should come too, shouldn't she?'

The woman looked along the track to where Jenny was still walking away, unaware Eddie had been diverted.

Annoyance flicked onto her face as if she was irritated that Jenny was getting away.

'We'll come back for her later.'

'Yes,' agreed Eddie meekly.

'I am Lucifix. You may call me Lucy,' the woman announced.

Already vaguely feeling the woman was familiar, it came to Eddie who she was, the seductive Lucy Lansburg from his school days. She had lured him behind the bicycle sheds to be beaten up by Duncan McTaggetty, the school bully.

He might have felt hurt and anger for what she had put him through those years ago, but the attraction swept aside such feelings. Lucifix now was just as she had been in those hormone-flooded teenage years, her seductive power so strong he could only feel subservience and devotion.

Lucifix led the way onto what could faintly be made out as a footpath leading through a dense thicket of snagging strands of gorse and brambles. Eddie followed in zombie-like compliance, unmoved by the straggly lengths of bramble stems that slashed and whipped as he threaded along the overgrown path.

Lucifix was a guiding beacon for Eddie, glowing and radiating her attractive power, outshining other features within the landscape. Eddie barely noticed where she was leading him as he marched with a steady purpose behind her.

He had only vague impressions. He walked through an abandoned orchard, by a humming electrical installation, through an immense cityscape laid out before them, and then to more derelict scrubland. That led down into the city, sullied by detritus and dirty, desperate people who somehow managed to exist there. An underpass took them beneath a colossal highway that cut through the landscape.

Usually, Eddie would have taken an interest in these surroundings, assessing them and figuring out where he was, but now Lucifix possessed his mind. Instead of leading or controlling Eddie's thought processes, her influence shut them down, leaving him with only an overpowering wonderment at her radiance, beauty, feminine perfection and majesty.

Eddie was vaguely aware of the seediness dropping away and the ambience of the city streets becoming more prosperous as Lucifix led him into the central hub of the financial district. In front of them was the monumental modernist edifice of the Continental and Oceanic Securities Bank.

Within the foyer, the bank proudly announced an expert discussion entitled 'Population-wide Micro-targeting and Influencing'. Top psychologists would demonstrate proven methods for achieving business and political goals using algorithms to tailor messages to individuals and artificial intelligence to automatically take them through the stages of Attraction, Questioning, Conversion, Convincing, Recruitment and Message Propagation.

Eddie hesitated on the steps leading up to the grand entrance.

Lucifix shook her head. 'Not that way. You are joining the staff.'

She led him around the side of the building where another more modest entrance was labelled as 'Staff

Only'. She beckoned for him to follow, leading inside a modest entrance hall. They took the lift to the depths of Basement Level 3, an expansive utilitarian area. The walls were painted a plain white, scuffed and chipped by objects. The floor consisted of a rigid non-slip heavy duty plastic covering laid directly onto the rough concrete. There were corridors radiating out in various directions, lined with plain painted doors.

'I am the Building Services Manager,' Lucifix announced. 'You will be joining my team as a Building Services Operative.'

Eddie had no problem with working for the majestic Lucifix, but for a moment, he remembered what he thought they had come for. 'Are we going to see Liz, Karen and Larry?'

'Liz and Larry are already here in the Underside. You can see them when you get a day off duty. I am making arrangements for Karen to join us shortly.'

Eddie remembered what Miles had said about the Underside, that he had mentioned Underhexes lived there and how the folk from Other Side were terrified of Underhexes.

'So this is the Underside?' Eddie queried.

'Yes.'

It occurred to Eddie who Lucifix might be. His heart raced. 'You're not an Underhex, are you?'

'Folk over there on the Other Side use names like that, but you needn't get too concerned. It's only superstition,' said Lucifix dismissively.

'But I thought we were going to the Other Side.'

'Really? I never said that.'

'But you let me think it.'

'You said you wanted to see Liz and Larry. They're over here now, and Karen is on her way.'

'But I wouldn't have come if I'd known.'

Lucifix gripped Eddie by the chin and held it so his eyes met hers. 'I think you would,' she said with a quiet purr.

She held his mind in a vice, gripped between overwhelming arousal and spiritual reverence for her divine majesty. He knew there could be no escape, that he had no wish to escape even if he could. He wanted nothing more than to be hers forever.

'The Other Side is no good,' she assured him. 'All they have there is unreal nostalgia, a syrupy imagination of how things might have been if only inconvenient reality had not intervened. Here in the Underside, you will experience life as it is.'

Eddie stood dazed, letting the reality of his situation sink in.

'Enough of this chitchat,' said Lucifix abruptly. 'Time to get you kitted out.'

She led him into one of the rooms. There was a man behind a desk dressed in uniform overalls with the bank's name and logo displayed on the front. The man handed a set of uniform clothes similar to what he was wearing.

'Put those on,' commanded Lucifix.

Eddie hesitated.

'Come on now. We haven't got all day,' she barked.

Eddie complied, and she led him out further along the corridor and through another door, which led into a large open area around which were stalls, giving it the appearance of a set of stables for horses. In the central area between the stalls were a few tables and chairs on which men in uniform overalls were seated.

Lucifix led Eddie to one of the stalls. It was small, with just enough space for a bedroll and a small cupboard.

'These are your quarters,' she informed him. She turned to walk away.

Eddie felt an intense pang of loneliness as if he had been stabbed. As if he was an infant whose mother was about to abandon him, the thought of her leaving him now was unbearable. He lunged and seized hold of her shoulder.

'Please don't go. I love you,' he pleaded.

She glared at him, but he persisted. He clung to her, burying his head into her breasts. She pulled out a whistle and blew it hard.

Almost at once, a bulky figure emerged, a man wearing the same uniform as the others except, in his case, he had sergeant's stripes sewn onto his arms. The man grabbed hold of Eddie and hauled him away from her.

'Teach him manners,' commanded Lucifix.

The man smirked. 'Yes, madam, I will.'

He punched Eddie hard in the guts, then hit him repeatedly in a relentless torrent of blows, every one of which knocked the stuffing out of him. Eddie toppled, but the colossal man picked him up and held him against the wall. After a minute of non-stop beating, the man released his grip and allowed Eddie to slump onto the floor.

The man turned to Lucifix. 'He has been taught, madam.'

Lucifix nodded appreciatively. She crouched and leant over Eddie's battered body. She took hold of his chin and lined up his head to face her. 'You may look, but you may not touch. Do I make myself clear?' she said quietly.

Eddie nodded.

'Let's hear you say it,' she demanded sharply.

'Yes.'

'You will address me as madam.'

'Yes, madam.'

'That's better. The penalty for infringement of that rule will be severe. Understand?'

'Yes, madam.'

The man with the sergeant's stripes stood nearby, his chest thrust out.

'By the way, this gentleman is Duncan McTaggetty. You may recall that he already had cause to deal with you some years ago. He helps me keep order around here. If you're wise, you won't give him cause to deal with you again. Clear?'

'Yes, madam.'

'This group of men here, of which you are now a member, are what I like to call my stable. I own you, every one of you. You need to understand that. You will scrve and obey me in all matters. Is that clear?'

'Yes, madam.'

'Owning a man is like owning a pit bull terrier or a fine stallion. He is a powerful beast, especially those like Duncan here. He needs to be broken in, trained and brought under control. Then he will serve you faithfully. You will serve me faithfully, Eddie dear, won't you?'

'Yes, madam.'

'You desire me, don't you? You yearn for me. But you won't have me. You are my plaything, but I will never be yours. Your unattainable desires will torture you. Your desires are now your curse. They will be there constantly, but they will never be satisfied. Understand?'

'Yes, madam.'

'But don't worry. When my slaves serve me particularly well, it amuses me for them to slake their lust on another one of my minions. If they are gay, that could be another man. I enjoy seeing them getting their sexual relief that way. I may reward you like that if you behave yourself for me.'

'Yes, madam.'

Eddie might have expected to be appalled by his predicament, but such was her enchantment, he was more in awe of his supreme mistress Lucifix than ever.

'Get into your stall and rest,' commanded Lucifix. 'Duncan will show you to your duties later.'

As Eddie went into the open-ended cell to be his home, he saw someone familiar peering out at him from the neighbouring stall. He rested on the bedroll for a few minutes, partly to recover and wait until he could be sure Lucifix and Duncan McTaggetty had gone.

When it felt safe, he stood and peered around the corner of the partition. His neighbour, a powerfully built man in his early thirties dressed in the same uniform as himself, looked up at him but didn't say anything. Eddie recognised him as the taciturn visitor from the Thames Valley branch of the Far and Fast Walks Society who had attended the fateful walk when Miles had first led the group into Miteby.

'Hello, it's Tim, isn't it?' said Eddie.

'Er, yes, I'm Tim.'

'Thought so. You were on the walk I led back in October, weren't you? The one where we went to that strange pub at lunchtime.'

'Yes, that's right.'

'What brings you here?'

'Wanted to meet someone again, but met up with Lucy. She brought me here.'

'You mean, meet someone you'd seen in Miteby, I'm guessing,' said Eddie, trying to fill in the gaps.

'Yes, that's right.'

'Someone you had met on that day we ended up at the Miteby Arms?'

Extracting information from Tim was like drawing teeth. Eddie recalled that Tim had been hard to talk to when he met him, and he hadn't got any easier.

'Yes.'

Eddie decided against enquiring about who that someone might be and why Tim wanted to see them again. For one thing, it would be too much like hard work, for another, it was private. Tim could tell him another time if he felt like it.

Eddie noticed Tim had visible bruises on his face and, Eddie thought, if his ordeal was anything to go by, probably more hidden by his clothing.

'Did Duncan have a go at you too?' Eddie enquired.

'Yes, he did.'

Eddie paused, expecting Tim to elaborate on what had happened to him, but Tim remained silent. Eddie decided against attempting to extend the stilted conversation further. He could have asked what Tim's transgression had been to cause Lucifix to set Duncan onto him, but again, if Tim didn't want to volunteer this information, he shouldn't press. Perhaps she didn't need a reason and had all her new staff beaten up by Duncan as a form of initiation.

'Well, nice to see you again, Tim. Be seeing you around, I expect,' said Eddie in conclusion.

Tim did not even nod or smile in acknowledgement. Eddie withdrew into his stall.

Deep underground in Basement Level 3, far from daylight, it was impossible to discern the time; however, it must have been early in the morning that Duncan McTaggetty reappeared. He stood outside Eddie's and Tim's stalls.

'Time to get up. You can't stay there wanking in your pits all day. There's work to be done,' he bawled, in sergeant major style.

Tim and Eddie staggered up, bleary-eyed, still wearing their uniforms, which were now creased and dishevelled.

'Stand straight,' Duncan yelled. He looked at their appearance. His lips curled. 'You look like shit. You can't go out like that. Get yourselves tidied.'

Duncan glared at them impatiently while Eddie and Tim smoothed themselves down and tidied their hair. When they got into a state that just about passed muster, Duncan thrust a bundle of new clothing into Tim's arms.

'Put that on,' he commanded.

The outfit consisted of striped trousers, a starched white shirt, a tie with the bank's logo, a tail coat, shiny shoes and a top hat.

When Tim had attired himself appropriately, Duncan escorted him and Eddie up in the lift to the bank's foyer. He led them to the main entrance. Looking at Eddie, he told him to keep himself in the background as this did not involve him.

On this day, the bank was hosting a symposium

entitled 'Use of Pharmaceuticals for Human Compliance Management'. According to the introductory material, the pharmaceutical industry had a significant role in maintaining the Established Order's stability by optimising human contentment and conformity. Products that countered discontentment, depression and anxiety would reduce the likelihood of anti-social challenges. Addictive characteristics would build dependency on the products, enhancing profitability and maintaining the beneficial effects of lowering hostility and resistance to authority. Humane euthanasia products would improve global economic efficiency by reducing the unnecessary prolongation of life beyond productive years.

'Right, you know what you have to do?' Duncan asked Tim.

'I think so,' Tim replied.

'Well, what is it then?'

'To greet visitors, engage with them in pleasantries and assist them with finding what they need within the Bank,' Tim intoned.

'Well, get on with it then.'

Tim advanced tentatively into the centre of the foyer while Duncan withdrew into the background with Eddie observing from a distance.

A man strode through the front door, walked swiftly past the reception desk, quickly used a pass to operate the electronic barrier and headed purposefully towards one of the lifts.

Tim stood in his way.

'Welcome to the Continental and Oceanic Securities Bank,' said Tim, without eye contact.

'Yes,' said the man with irritation in his voice. 'What is

it?'

'How was your journey into the city today, sir?'

'Absolutely fine. Now, what can I do for you?'

'What service are you in need of today, sir?'

'Excuse me, but why do you need to know that?'

'In order that I may direct you to the appropriate department, sir.'

'I don't need any assistance, thanks.'

'I need to know what service you require so that I can direct you.'

'I know where I am going, thank you. Will you please get out of my way,' said the man emphatically, sidestepping Tim.

'I can show you where to go if you tell me what service you require,' said Tim as he followed behind.

Duncan stepped forward, positioning himself between Tim and the man.

'Sorry, sir,' said Duncan. 'Our Bank host is a little too eager to help. Sorry to have troubled you.'

Duncan took Tim by the arm and hustled him away into a little side room. Eddie hovered outside, overhearing the exchange.

'What do you think you were doing?' bawled Duncan.

'I was greeting the gentleman and trying to assist,' answered Tim plaintively.

'Why did you stand in his way like that?'

'So I could help him before he passed me.'

'But he didn't need help.'

'How was I to know if he needed help?'

'It's flipping obvious whether someone knows where they are going. Use your common sense. And I don't want to see you standing in people's way again. Got it?'

'No, sir.'

'Now get out there and do your job properly.'

Back on duty, Tim noticed a woman entering the entrance foyer, looking around. After a few seconds, her eyes alighted on the reception desk, and she wandered over. Following a brief conversation, the receptionist handed her a pass and pointed to the electronic barriers. The woman walked over and held her pass over the side of the barrier. Nothing happened. Tim remained where he was, looking in her direction.

There were awkward seconds while the woman continued to wave her pass around, but the electronic access gate remained firmly shut. Tim remained where he was, his eyes on her, but taking no action. The woman noticed his gaze, then looked away unnerved before resuming her futile gestures with her pass. After a little while, another visitor showed her the pad that would read the pass, the barrier opened, and the woman stepped through hesitantly. She took several steps into the large atrium and looked around uncertainly.

Tim took a few steps towards her, placing himself a few feet to one side, observing her sidelong. The woman backed away to keep some distance between them. Tim edged back towards her.

'Welcome to the Continental and Oceanic Securities Bank,' said Tim in a monotone.

'What do you want?' asked the woman, nervously looking for an escape route.

'How was your journey into the city today, madam?'

'Look, I don't know what you want, but I'm not interested.'

'What service are you in need of today, madam?'

'Nothing from you, thanks. Please leave me alone.'

Duncan intervened again. 'Can I be of assistance, madam?'

'Yes, get that creep away from me.'

Duncan waved Tim away in the direction of Eddie standing in the background on one side of a pillar.

'Thank you,' said the woman.

'Can I direct you anywhere, madam?' Duncan enquired.

'Yes, I'm here for the Pharmaceuticals Symposium.'

'It's in the Conference Suite, madam. Just over there through those doors.'

Back in the side room, Tim was again reprimanded. 'What do you think you were doing, creeping her out like that?'

'I don't know what you mean?'

'Staring at her in that creepy fashion.'

'But you said I was supposed to make eye contact.'

'Not like that. You're supposed to smile and engage, not stare.'

'Oh right, smile. I'll do that.'

'Why didn't you help her when her pass didn't work at the barrier?'

'I'm supposed to help people find where they need to be.'

'Well, they're not going to get there if they can't get past the barrier, are they?'

Eddie cringed. It was evident that for Tim, striking up a conversation with a stranger was the most stressful thing he could imagine. He didn't know how to initiate the interaction or what to say. Presumably, he had been given social rules and guidelines over the years, but clearly, the more guidance he had been given, the more confusing the whole small talk business had become.

As Tim and Duncan emerged from the bawling out, Lucifix appeared.

'You wanted to be more sociable, didn't you?' she whispered in Tim's ear. 'Well, now is your chance. Make the most of it.'

She is enjoying this, thought Eddie, revelling in Tim's discomfort. Lucifix drifted off again, and Duncan turned his attention towards Eddie.

'Now it's your turn. Come with me.'

After seeing what Tim had endured, Eddie wondered what horrors were in store for him.

Duncan led the way via the lift, taking them deep into Basement Level 5, where they came out into a gloomy underground cavern full of ducting, pipework and machinery. On one wall was an array of computer screens that displayed the status of the many systems within the building.

Duncan informed Eddie that his new role was to be Building Systems Support Technician. His duties were to monitor, maintain and repair the technical systems within the building. Eddie's years working in information technology meant he was used to complexity, but the extent of what he could see on the screens looked daunting.

In a flood of jargon and acronyms, Duncan took Eddie through the various systems within the building. The filtration and air conditioning system circulated air through a maze of ducts, computer networks, video conferencing, a phone service, robotic window cleaning system, automated window shades, water supply, building security, fire suppression system, sewerage system and the electrical supply cabling. Some displays provided information on the status of each system, including alarms highlighting malfunctioning components.

Having taken Eddie through the overview, Duncan acquainted him with primary mechanical components. Heavy-duty pipework led into the central sewerage collection vessel. Eddie needed to monitor this for build-ups of methane.

The heaviest piece of equipment was the standby generator to provide continuity of power to the building in the event of an interruption to the electrical supply. Duncan took Eddie through the intricacies of the machinery and his maintenance duties. There was a large bank of batteries that carried the load in the event of a power outage until the standby generator fired up, the automatic starter motor, various control circuits and a large storage tank for the gloopy sulphurous bunker oil that powered the generator, an adapted marine diesel engine normally used in ocean-going cargo vessels.

Finally, Duncan handed over a smartphone to him. If any detected or reported malfunction occurred, an alarm would be raised. Any of the monitoring systems Eddie needed could be called up on the device to facilitate dealing promptly with support issues wherever he happened to be within the building.

Lucifix appeared just as Duncan had finished giving Eddie his instructions.

'You are used to working in data centres full of humming machinery, aren't you?' she purred. 'You should be at home here, which is just as well because this will be your domain for all eternity.'

Lured to Oblivion

Lucifix liked to get to know her slaves. She occasionally subjected them to rigorous interrogation. While gratifying Lucifix, this was not as enjoyable for the enslaved. She would subject victims to stress, humiliation, pain and degradation, as much to impose her authority as to extract information.

Not that she would dirty her hands with the rough stuff. She had staff to oblige her with that sort of thing, such as Duncan McTaggetty, who had a talent for violent enforcement.

Eddie had been with her for days. Time enough to have found his bearings and get to grips with his duties in Basement Level 5. It was time for her to have a little chat with him.

Eddie was applying lubrication to the drive shaft bearings of the monstrous stand-by generator engine when Duncan McTaggetty arrived to escort him into her presence in the Basement Level 4 interview room.

Several bright lights were directed onto a single flimsy folding chair in the centre of the room.

Lucifix was seated on a high back office swivel chair upholstered in black leather set behind a substantial mahogany desk, as issued to the bank's senior managers. She was in the shadows, yet dominating the room, her controlling influence permeating every crevice.

Lucifix observed Eddie as Duncan brought him in. He was straightforward, this one. But then, most men were. All too readily driven by their lust.

Eddie felt Lucifix's seductive and commanding essence

soaking into his soul. He was compliant, unable to resist her power. He welcomed her possession of him. He yearned for her to always be there. He knew she was cruel. He didn't mind. He would do anything for her. He would gladly accept any indignity.

'Sit down,' Duncan commanded.

'Yes.'

'Yes, what?' barked Duncan.

'Yes, sir.'

'That's better. Show respect.'

Eddie obeyed. For a while, nobody spoke. Duncan stood upright and to attention a couple steps behind where Eddie sat on the brightly lit folding chair. Lucifix observed silently from behind the desk. About a minute elapsed.

'I am going to ask you a few questions,' she eventually announced.

'Yes, madam.'

'If you fail to answer fully and truthfully, there will be consequences.'

'Yes, madam.'

'Duncan, show him what that means.'

Duncan sprang forward from behind and struck Eddie hard on his face. The force of the blow tipped Eddie off the chair, leaving him sprawled on the floor.

'Get up and sit yourself back down,' Duncan commanded.

Dazed, Eddie complied. Lucifix waited for half a minute while Eddie regained his composure. His head was ringing, and his cheek smarting from the impact.

'So, you understand now what I expect, don't you?'

'Yes, madam.'

'I would like to know about your friends and associates in the Material World, in case any of them might be useful to me.'

Eddie didn't say anything. Lucifix waited, tapping her foot.

'Well, what have you got to say?'

'What would you like to know, madam?'

'That's better. Let's start with the woman you had with you in Sorcerer's Copse before you came here. Who is she?'

'Jenny Binglett.'

Over the next twenty minutes, Lucifix questioned Eddie on all he knew about Jenny. She was particularly interested when Eddie mentioned her undisclosed lesbian tendencies with Tracey Trubb on the Other Side.

'I have been finding it increasingly tedious dealing with males. I need some female meat to amuse myself.'

Eddie's heart pounded. She must have extracted all that detail about Jenny because she had designs for her. He blushed a deep crimson but said nothing.

Lucifix was annoyed he had not spoken. 'Well, what have you got to say for yourself?'

'Yes, madam.'

'I have better things to do than talk to a brick wall. When I say something, I expect you to be listening and acknowledge me. Clear?'

'Yes, madam.'

'Duncan, he has been going to sleep on me while I was talking. Wake him up.'

'Yes, madam.' Duncan stepped forward and struck Eddie across the other side of his face. Eddie tipped and sprawled across the floor in the opposite direction.

'Get up, sit down and listen properly to what I am going to say,' Lucifix ordered.

Once Eddie was seated again, she continued. 'You are to go out from here and collect this Jenny woman and bring her back to me.'

She was demanding he entice Jenny back to this world of eternal torment. She was asking him to betray his friend. He sat in stunned silence.

'Well, speak to me,' demanded Lucifix.

Eddie wilted under Lucifix's enthralling and imperious power. 'Yes, madam.'

Eddie was back in Sorcerer's Copse.

In the Material World, only moments had passed since he had made his way to the Underside with Lucifix. She was with him now, waiting in front of the gorse-encroached entrance to the entangled path to the Underside.

Eddie's instructions were to follow Jenny and persuade her back into Sorcerer's Copse. He saw her walking away down the forestry track a couple hundred yards along. Leaving Lucifix, Eddie walked fast to catch up to Jenny.

In theory, safely back in the Material World, it would have been possible for him to have disregarded Lucifix's instructions and abandoned his new existence in the Underside. In his material form, he had been with Jenny moments before. She had no inkling anything might have happened to him, so there would have been no need to explain a thing unless he had chosen to confide his experiences.

But that was in theory. In practice, Lucifix's controlling tentacles extended into every crevice of Eddie's being, her steel grip on his mind compelling him to obey without question. He was aware he was about to betray his friend, luring Jenny to the same torment to which he was condemned, riddling him with guilt and shame, yet overriding this was the imperative of obedience to Lucifix. Under her spell, he had no desire to escape, yearning only to serve her for eternity.

Eddie called out, 'Hang on a moment.'

'Why?' Jenny stopped.

'I saw something in Sorcerer's Copse we should look at.'

'What?'

'Well, more a somebody, a person. We should check it out.'

'Well, alright, we probably should,' Jenny agreed, turning.

As they emerged back into Sorcerer's Copse, Jenny caught sight of the person Eddie had mentioned. She was a striking woman in a glowing reddish-purple cloak.

The woman's eyes fixed on Jenny, her gaze drawing her in. Jenny was simultaneously shaken and captivated. The most potent sensation was attraction. For no apparent reason, Jenny felt an overwhelming desire for her. Exceeding the capacity in Jenny for mere physical arousal, the woman's unstoppable allure overflowed into surrender and adoration. Yet underneath these feelings, Jenny felt an unease that there might be a malevolence veiled in the woman's undoubted beauty and charisma. She felt she knew the woman from somewhere, from long ago.

'You are Jenny, aren't you?'

'Yes.'

'I am Lucifix. You may call me Lucy. I understand you

want to know about the fate and whereabouts of your friends.'

'Yes, I do.'

'Your friends are Liz, Larry and Karen, aren't they?'

'Yes, that's right.'

'I know where they are.'

'Really, where?'

'I can take you.'

Jenny looked to Eddie for guidance. He grinned sheepishly, embarrassed.

'Should we go?' Jenny hissed to Eddie urgently.

Eddie nodded.

'Alright, we'll come with you,' Jenny confirmed.

As they paused on arrival at the towering edifice of the Continental and Oceanic Securities Bank, Jenny was forced to take a second look at Eddie. She noticed that, though they hadn't paused during their walk from Sorcerer's Copse, somehow he had shed his outdoor winter hiking gear and was wearing uniform overalls sporting the logo on display at the front of the building, evidently the bank's emblem.

Jenny had barely noticed Eddie during their journey because he had lagged behind. She had the impression he was avoiding conversation and eye contact.

One thing for sure was that they were not in Miteby, where she had initially assumed they must be headed. She sensed Eddie might have known this but omitted to mention it.

Jenny lingered near the foyer where the bank advertised the 'Resource Industries Best Practice Convention' event. Discussions were to be held on maintaining profitability by global rationalisation of industry capacity. This would inevitably require the closure of some plant for the greater economic good, releasing assets for more profitable deployment elsewhere. There was to be a session on land clearance technology to provide for resource extraction, providing for the elimination of unproductive flora and fauna from sites required for industrial and mining activities and the growing of cash crops. Redeployment of displaced persons into new industrial activities would also be discussed.

Lucifix called her away.

'We're not going in there. Round this way.'

She led them to a side entrance marked 'Staff Only', where they took the lift to Basement Level 2.

As they arrived, Lucifix turned to Eddie. 'Thank you, Eddie. You may return to your duties.' He stepped back into the lift and took it down to his workplace on Basement Level 5.

As he went down, Eddie checked his on-call device. There was already a backlog of faults. A phone on the 10th floor, blocked Ladies toilet on the 24th floor, overheating from the air conditioning supply in the 30th-floor conference room. The most urgent was the malfunctioning automated methane release valve on the central sewerage collection vessel. Eddie would have to operate the release valve manually with a spanner.

'Right, we had better get you kitted out,' Lucifix announced, leading Jenny into a room off one of the corridors radiating from the vestibule in front of the Basement Level 2 lift. There was a woman behind a counter dressed in similar uniform overalls Jenny had observed Eddie wearing, except tailored for her female figure. She placed a similar uniform on the counter for Jenny.

'What is going on?'

'I am the Building Service Manager, and you have the privilege of joining my staff as one of my Building Service Operatives,' Lucifix announced calmly.

As Lucifix spoke, Jenny felt the same awe and unexplainable attraction, deference and reverence she had felt initially in Sorcerer's Copse, entrapped, apprehensive, yet compelled to acquiesce.

'But we came to see Liz, Karen and Larry, didn't we?' Jenny protested feebly.

'And so you shall, in good time.'

'But where are we?' pleaded Jenny.

'The Underside.'

Jenny's heart pounded heavily, and her face went pale. In Miteby, she had heard the Underside spoken of in fearsome terms. 'But, the Underside. I don't want to be here. Can we go back?'

'There is no return from here.'

The significance slammed into Jenny like a death sentence. Her head felt heavy, and the room spun. Her legs went rubbery and gave under her. She slumped onto the floor.

Lucifix walked over to Jenny and prodded her with her foot. 'You can get up now and put on your uniform.'

Within seconds Jenny's senses returned. Still in shock, she meekly complied. Dressed for her new role on the bank's staff, Lucifix led Jenny to her new home, a stall in the female staff sleeping quarters.

'You can rest now,' Lucifix purred.

Jenny stretched on the bedroll while Lucifix watched.

Jenny could see Lucifix silhouetted against the light. By the laws of physics Lucifix's shape should have been no more than a dark shadow against the lit background, but such laws did not apply here. For Jenny, Lucifix's body was lit and glowing with a mysterious energy, like the glow from a radioactive substance. It was more than light, but a seductive warmth as if from a fire burning within, aglow with incense carrying an aroma of sexuality spreading around Jenny's stall, a delightful scent as pleasing as freshly baked bread but stimulating different appetites.

Besides altruistically seeking her friends, Jenny's other motive for making the trip was to reach her beloved Tracey. Now, whatever amorous feelings Jenny may have felt for Tracey were swept aside by Lucifix's intense eroticism.

Lucifix did nothing but sway sensuously in the stall's entrance, but such was her mesmeric power there was no need for her to touch Jenny to bring her to a peak of arousal. Wet and glowing, Jenny's libido was wound up like a spring. But Lucifix would not release her, only wind-up Jenny's tension ever more.

Eventually, Jenny could hold out no longer. Spreading her legs, she reached down with her fingers.

In a flash, Lucifix's demeanour flipped from seductress to contemptuous tyrant. 'You disgusting dyke. I might have known.'

In that instant, all eroticism evaporated, and it came to Jenny why Lucifix had appeared familiar. She was Lucy Fanshow, the bully from her schooldays who taunted her about being a lesbian, vehemently denied at the time but now acknowledged.

'You'd like to make out with me, wouldn't you?' said

Lucifix, again teasingly.

Jenny's amorousness switched back on. She knew Lucifix was playing with her, yet her allure overrode doubts. She lay prone and ready for whatever it would take.

Lucifix stepped into Jenny's stall and knelt. Her hand hovered over Jenny's thigh as if poised to unleash Jenny's passion.

'Come on now, you want me to touch you down there, don't you?' whispered Lucifix, her voice a low purr.

'Yes, please, oh, yes, do it,' Jenny squeaked.

'Don't be so disgusting,' snapped Lucifix. The tyrant was back. Lucifix jumped up. 'I'm not going to do that for you, but I have someone who will. Someone who will cure you of those filthy Sapphic tendencies.'

The profile of a heavily built man loomed to join Lucifix against the light of the entrance to Jenny's stall.

'I want you to meet Duncan McTaggetty. You'll get to know him because he will supervise your duties here in the bank. But just now, Duncan has pleased me. As a reward, I have promised him the pleasure of feminine company for intimate relations, and here you are, ready and waiting.'

Jenny wanted to be sick. 'No, no, please, no, not that. I don't want it,' she screamed.

'Really? What a pity. And Duncan has been so looking forward to it,' said Lucifix mockingly.

'No, no, please no.'

'Oh well. We'll have to make alternative arrangements for Duncan, won't we?' said Lucifix. She turned to Duncan.

'Duncan, there is that woman on the allotment. You

may bring her in.'

'Yes, madam,' Duncan acknowledged before departing. Lucifix turned back to Jenny.

'You may rest. Duncan will be back for you later.'

Jenny felt panic.

'No, not later either. Not as all.'

'Don't worry, he won't be back for that. You are spared from sexual relations,' said Lucifix. She paused. '…For the time being. Duncan will be back to show you your duties, that's all.'

Lucifix left, leaving Jenny alone and relieved. She wasn't looking forward to being acquainted with Duncan but had been spared the worst.

Liz's hours of valiant struggle on her allotment, arduously digging and forking over the derelict ground, had made visible improvements. At one end, she had accumulated a tidy heap of miscellaneous debris embedded into the hard ground: masonry, stones, hunks of rusty metal, broken glass, plastic, bones. The cleared land was dusty and unpromising but at least friable and suitable for planting. As time passed, she would work in organic matter to nourish it.

Liz felt a familiar dread as she heard footsteps behind her, saw a shadow move in her direction. Once again, she would have to fend off the attention of the odious Sid.

The work had been hard and tedious, but what Liz found most trying was being constantly pestered by her unsavoury neighbour, forever attempting to strike up a conversation, making sordid suggestions and innuendo. Most disgustingly, he insisted on coming close to her, invading her personal space, his oversized belly brushing against her, breathing fumes of stale tobacco smoke and cheap beer.

When she faced the invasion, she was relieved to see a stranger. He was a bulky man in a uniform with a familiar company logo, although she could not place it.

'I take it that you are Liz.'

'Yes, that's me.'

'Good. Lucifix wants to see you. You are to come with me.'

Liz did not have much to do except work on the allotment, so she was happy to comply. It would be nice to get away from her disgusting neighbour.

'Right you are.'

The Building Services staff had been called together in the communal area on Basement Level 3.

As she came in, Jenny, vulnerable and alone, was relieved to see Eddie. She sought him out and stood close, holding his arm.

Eddie was nervous, yet happy for her to be close. Neither spoke, feeling but not mentioning Eddie's betrayal.

It was not only Eddie who felt guilt and embarrassment. Jenny felt it too, after her ordeal and fright from her encounter with Lucifix and the terrifying Duncan McTaggetty. Any reasonable and objective observer would have exonerated Jenny, but she could not escape a lifetime of disgust about her sexuality that Lucifix exploited to humiliate and terrify her, guilt that weighed on her about her powerful if involuntary arousal. Her shame prevented her from sharing her feelings with Eddie, other than conveying her vulnerability by clinging

228

to his arm.

They remained quiet and still, close, yet not connecting mentally, each gazing ahead, lost in their thoughts and avoiding eye contact.

Around them was a buzz of conversation and expectation from the staff, uncertain and speculating about what might require their presence.

Eddie's neighbour, the strong and silent Tim, looked at Eddie and Jenny from a few feet away. Among the crowd, it was only Eddie that Tim had any connection with unless he counted the overbearing oppression from Duncan McTaggetty and Lucifix as a kind of connection.

Seeing Eddie preoccupied with Jenny, Tim was impeded from connecting with him. Even if he hadn't been, Tim would have struggled. Since they had been there, invariably, Eddie had struck up a conversation between them, which, while friendly, quickly fizzled out. Tim would have liked to sustain a dialogue but didn't know how. As usual, his conversations were within his own head.

The buzz came to a rapid halt as Lucifix entered and made a proclamation. 'I look after the needs of my staff. Those that serve me well are rewarded. Duncan McTaggetty is a man who has served me particularly well, and for that reason, I have decided he should be recompensed with some intimate pleasure.'

Those around the room had come to know that intimate pleasure arranged by Lucifix for one of her favourites would involve humiliation and abasement for someone else.

Lucifix looked accusingly at Jenny. 'I had arranged for him to have his reward earlier, but a new staff member would not cooperate.'

Those who had been in Lucifix's service for some time knew that had Lucifix been determined that Duncan have had his way with this newest staff member, he would have. She had some purpose for sparing Jenny, probably other humiliations. Sometimes straightforward suffering is easier than the guilt of being spared.

Lucifix faced the room's entrance. '…So we have made alternative arrangements.'

At this point, Duncan McTaggetty advanced into the room with Liz walking behind him, oblivious to Lucifix's and Duncan's plans.

Eddie and Jenny could identify Liz, yet simultaneously, she appeared different to the Liz they were familiar with. The plain, solidly built, unglamorous, late middle-aged woman had transformed into a shapely young woman.

Lucifix turned to look in Eddie's and Jenny's direction. 'You wanted to see your friend, Liz, didn't you? Here she is. I expect you have already noticed she's prettier over here than she was in the Material World.'

Lucifix turned to Liz. 'You wanted to be attractive to men, didn't you? You lamented that men wouldn't look at you, abandoning you for prettier women. Well, that has been fixed.' Lucifix turned back again to Eddie and Jenny. 'Your friends Eddie and Jenny are pleased for you about that, aren't you?' She addressed Duncan. 'She is attractive, isn't she?'

'Yes, madam, very much,' Duncan confirmed.

Lucifix looked at Liz with a wry smile. 'I hope you are suitably grateful for your good fortune. This impressive hunk of a man wants you, and he won't be looking elsewhere.' Lucifix addressed Duncan again. 'This woman is your reward. Take her and show her what a virile man can do.'

'Yes, madam.'

Duncan took hold of Liz's wrist and hauled her towards his sleeping quarters in a booth at the end of the room, a slightly more spacious and better-appointed version of the stalls provided for the more junior staff. Liz attempted to resist and hold herself back, but that was futile.

Eddie and Jenny watched in horror. Eddie felt the urge to protect Liz but couldn't see how. As Lucifix had intended, Jenny felt a renewed guilt.

Duncan and Liz disappeared, and the sounds of Liz's violation could be heard.

Eddie felt Liz's pain as if it was inflicted on him. Futile or not, he felt compelled to act. Abruptly he ran forward to where the foul deed was taking place.

Lucifix glanced to two members of her staff, men who were Duncan's assistants as supervisor and enforcer, their rank denoted by the corporal's stripes on their uniforms. They sprang forward and seized Eddie, dragging him over to face Lucifix. While they held him on the floor before her, he could hear Duncan's animal grunts and Liz's screams.

Lucifix was unmoved. She was in command of the others present, and her presence and approval sufficient for her followers to tolerate the unacceptable. Even Eddie, held in the iron grip of Lucifix's goons, despite attempting to intervene, felt himself coming around to the idea that her wishes were paramount.

Lucifix considered for a minute. 'It is not only Duncan who deserves to be rewarded. Sean and Kevin deserve their reward too.'

Those around the room waited expectantly. Sean and Kevin were heavily built ruffians.

'Your tastes are different to Duncan's, aren't they, boys?'

Sean and Kevin nodded.

'You like your meat to be male, don't you?'

The boys nodded again. Lucifix looked at Eddie's prone figure. 'This fellow is well proportioned, isn't he? You could make use of him, don't you think?'

'Yes, madam,' answered Sean and Kevin.

To Rescue Our Friends

Many people have found that a holiday destination can be a wonderful oasis of delight as a temporary visitor but less idyllic as a permanent inhabitant.

Karen's change from a transient guest in Miteby to a long-standing resident came about unintentionally when Miles did not appear to escort her back to her material existence. Even as she hoped Miles might reappear, she continued to feel like a guest, as might tourists stranded in a holiday resort after a hurricane or tsunami.

She was like someone retired in their favourite foreign holiday destination, devoid of purpose, cut off from their roots, discovering that only so many rounds of golf and refreshing sangrias in the clubhouse can be enjoyed before the pleasure wanes.

The strange fusion of Karen with her alter ego from the Other Side had left her a constipated chaos of conflicting thoughts and memories, like someone obliged by politeness to consume two Christmas dinners in succession. As these settled and reconciled, she developed a growing fondness for Larry.

Despite its beauty, tranquillity and nostalgic charm, Karen did not feel at peace in Miteby. Her mission had been to reacquaint and reconcile herself with her lost father, but that business was done. The fusion with her alter ego had brought a synthesis in her mind between her father and Larry. Now it was Larry she yearned to see, but he wasn't there.

Making matters worse was the lack of restful sleep, plagued in her dreams by the infernal woman in red, Lucy

Denberry.

'He doesn't care about you, your dad, does he?'

'Yes, he does.'

'Why did he go away then?'

'It was because of someone at his work.'

'So, he cared more about her than you?'

'It was my mum; she didn't want him around.'

'Why would your mum keep him away?'

'I don't know.'

'It was because of what he was doing with you, wasn't it?'

'No.'

'And you liked it, didn't you?'

'He didn't do anything.'

'Liking it makes you as dirty as him.'

Lucy repeated these insinuations so often that she felt they might be true. Later, when Karen was in her dad's presence, Lucy's accusations in her nightmares resurfaced, making his presence distasteful.

Confusion reigned in Karen's head. While Larry was synonymous with her father, her fondness for him felt unnatural and loathsome. Her dad arrived one day after she had endured a particularly vicious nocturnal taunting from the merciless Lucy. As he appeared, she could barely hold herself back from throwing up.

'Dad, I can't cope with seeing you just now. Being with you has become too confusing and difficult,' she blurted.

'I see,' he said sadly.

'I'm sorry.'

'Is it just for now that you can't cope with seeing me, or will that always be the case?'

Karen squirmed. She hated rejecting him. Blushing,

she answered, 'I think it will always be like this. I'm sorry.'

He nodded sadly. 'Okay, I understand. I'll just go then.'

But he didn't move. He remained still with a sad smile. As Karen watched, he became less bright, greyer and translucent. Initially, she didn't understand. Perhaps the lighting was changing. After half a minute, it became apparent he was fading.

'Dad?'

'I'm on my way now. I'll be gone soon.' His voice was so faint she could barely hear him.

As she continued to watch, he slowly dissolved, becoming less distinct, his colour fading, becoming transparent.

'Oh, Dad, I'm sorry.'

There was no answer—his lingering presence a vague smokiness, then nothing.

Karen felt desolated by what she had done. In shock, she reflected. It was true he had walked out on her, and as far as she was concerned, he had just disappeared. She wasn't to blame. It was also true she could not face him anymore, so it was a blessing for him to be gone. Realising that people could abruptly disappear here on the Other Side was sobering.

Karen urgently wanted to reach the resolution of her feelings for Larry, which were oscillating between hate and love. She despised his shallow materialism and boastfulness, yet, as with her father, sensed underneath that brittle front there was a fundamentally decent man. But in Miteby, Larry, like Miles, was nowhere to be seen.

In the Miteby Arms, Karen found solace by filling her days in companionship with fellow exiles: Susan, Eddie's lost lover; James, Liz's former beau, and Tracey, Jenny's close friend from her school days. Karen found that, while pleasant and friendly, these folk lacked depth, existing only in their relationships with their respective lovers. When she attempted to draw them on other aspects of their lives, she got only vacant stares or a change of subject back to their respective loved ones.

Another person hung around the Miteby Arms, an uncommunicative woman with round glasses on a round, unadorned face. This woman had her hair in two plaits, aged around thirty, but with the manner of someone older, like a solitary elderly woman who lived alone with her cats. Karen discovered her name was Tina, but not much else. Tina's conversation exclusively involved the characters and happenings in the *Citadels of Vallborg* series, a subject Karen had neither knowledge nor interest in. Not wishing to appear unfriendly, Karen would nod and smile as she went past but avoided getting further involved.

On a day while Karen sat on benches outside the Miteby Arms alongside James, Susan and Tracey, trying fruitlessly to find something of substance to discuss, Miles reappeared. Karen's pulse quickened as she felt a new hope that, with Miles's help, she might now escape the rut she had found herself in.

Miles was wasted, gaunt and old, the skin on his face like dry flaking tissue paper. He lurched, wincing, lacking his customary glow except the faintest speck of starlight in one eye. He sat heavily on a bench and clasped his hand to his chest. His shirt was saturated with blood, which oozed between his fingers.

'What happened?'

'An unfortunate encounter with an Underhex on my last visit to the Material World,' Miles croaked. 'But I'll be alright soon, now I'm back in Miteby.'

'What can we do to help?'

'Pop over to the Miteby Arms and fetch Bob, the landlord. He'll take care of me.'

The landlord brought a pint of Meadow Dew ale and a jar of ointment. As the landlord spread the ointment on the wound by some magic, the blood flow went into reverse, shrinking the stain on Mile's shirt as if in a movie run in reverse. Meanwhile, Miles quaffed the ale. At last, with a flourish of his finger, the landlord vanished away the last fleck of blood. The tear in the cloth of Miles's shirt knitted itself together seamlessly.

Miles had visibly filled out; his skin was smooth and supple, and his aura had returned to its fullest warmth and strength.

Karen, now accustomed to supernatural happenings, was less surprised by the spectacle than she might once have been.

'Does that mean that you are mended now, cured of whatever that Underhex did?'

'Yes, I'm intact again now.'

'I've been thinking. It must be well over the time I should have been here in Miteby. Shouldn't I be getting back?' said Karen, getting straight to what was on her mind, now the immediate priority of Miles's survival had been addressed.

'That's as may be, but I can't take you back to Sorcerer's Copse any more. By what she did to me there, the Underhex has closed that route for me. I'm dead there now.'

'What am I to do then? Does that mean I am stuck here?'

'Not necessarily. But first, between us, we have a more urgent undertaking.'

'Oh, right. What?'

'Several of our friends are marooned in the Underside, entrapped by the Underhex who did this to me at Sorcerer's Copse. We must get them out of there.'

'Our friends? Who?'

'Larry, Liz, Eddie, Jenny and Tim.'

'Who is Tim?' Karen enquired.

'He was here with us when the FFWS group first came from Thames Valley.'

'Oh, I vaguely remember,' Karen mused. 'He didn't leave much of an impression. Didn't have much to say, as I recall.'

'He struggles with conversation,' Miles agreed.

'How did they get to be in the Underside?'

'The Underhex I told you about, her name is Lucifix. She will have used her enticing powers.'

'You mean like you did to get us over here.'

'You could say that, but my intentions were good. Hers are evil.'

'What is their fate if they remain?'

'They will be under her spell and in torment for eternity unless we rescue them,' replied Miles, shaking his head.

'What sort of torment?'

'Suffering devised for each of them. Lucifix is inventive in that regard.'

'How are we to rescue them?'

'There is a way from here to the Underside. It will be difficult and dangerous, but we should try.'

'Yes, of course,' said Karen.

'The risks are considerable. It will involve conflict with Lucifix. She has awesome and dangerous powers.'

'So, we have to fight her to get them out?'

'Yes.'

'What if Lucifix wins?'

'We could be trapped eternally in the Underside where we would suffer too.'

Miles embodied the kind of inspirational leadership that sweeps aside fear. Like Scott or Shackleton recruiting a team for Antarctic exploration, dangers served only to inspire. With Miles leading, all felt willing and obligated.

'We'll come,' chimed James, Susan and Tracey.

'And me,' said Tina.

I'm trapped here as it is, which is losing its charm if I'm honest, Karen reflected. May as well take my chances. 'Alright, I'm coming too.'

Back into the Light

Despite Miles's warnings, like the perils of war for army recruits, the hazards of their undertaking felt remote to the rescue party. The magnitude of the dangers only became real when confronted by the smoking pit behind the mountain village of Hollingsby, a short train journey from Miteby.

This tunnel, which Miles informed them was their passage to the Underside, belched foul sulphurous fumes, dropping into a dark, apparently bottomless abyss. The rocky sides vibrated with ominous rumbling reverberations. Their descent required scrambling over a jagged rock face, taking care with every move to keep a grip lest they slip into the inky chasm.

Were they alone, it is doubtful any could have summoned the courage to descend, yet each took the plunge collectively, inspired by Miles's determination, conviction, and confidence.

The fear subsided slightly once they were over the rim, tentatively picking up pace as they gained confidence.

Descending deeper was more challenging as the light faded. Without obvious reason, Miles appeared brighter than the others. Perhaps he was wearing more reflective clothing, Karen speculated. Deeper still, Miles was clearly acting as a source of light, not mere reflection, illuminating objects. It was a curious luminosity, not light from a distinct source, but a glow emanating from his person. From above, a mere distant glow left only Miles's ghostly radiance.

The rumbling vibrations swelled as they descended.

Karen sensed the weight of the bedrock, looming above, closing from the sides and extending to unimaginable depths. They plodded deeper and deeper, one careful step at a time, with only Miles's strange glow to light the scene. Arms and legs were tawt and fatigued from relentless effort.

A new fainter glow appeared, a cold synthetic light like that from factory strip lights, accompanied by a mechanical thumping, clanking and clatter.

The noise and light intensified as the rocky passage flattened into a lit cathedral-like cavern. Their passage was one of several emerging here, a central hub within an extensive mining operation. People dashed about like ants, dressed in grubby orange overalls with white hard hats mounted with miners' lamps, working heavy earth-moving equipment and towing waggons piled with mineral ore.

A miner with a striped hat, presumably in authority, strode forward to meet the rescue party. 'This area is for authorised personnel only. What is your business?'

'We have come to free our friends,' said Miles.

'Who are these friends of yours, and what do they need to be freed from?'

'I include you among our friends if you want to be freed from this place.'

The supervisor formulated a rebuttal, but the words stopped in his throat, halted by a beam of understanding light from Miles that illuminated the physical surroundings and shone its radiance into people's souls and long-hidden corners of their beings. At that moment, the supervisor remembered that his life had a deeper purpose than facilitating the extraction of mineral wealth

241

from the Continental and Oceanic mine. Lit within him was the mouldering remains of an almost forgotten desire, his yearning for freedom.

No sooner had this long-decayed thought appeared in the supervisor's mind than another idea loomed: a dread of the repercussions this seditious liberation might unleash. He peered around nervously in expectation of the brutal enforcers of the Established Order that must appear to snuff out this budding insurrection.

'When you include me among your friends, do you mean just me, or my colleagues too, those you see around here?' whispered the supervisor.

'Any among you who desire freedom.'

The supervisor was looking acutely anxious. Furtively, he told Miles and the party to remain momentarily while he hailed five or six other nearby miners. Out of earshot, he explained to them quickly what had transpired, casting his eyes sideways in Miles's direction.

The reaction of his colleagues was dismissive, but like their supervisor, their rejection was curtailed by Miles's spiritual light. After a short exchange, the group nodded and walked apprehensively yet purposefully towards Miles.

'How do you propose that we be freed?' asked the supervisor.

'You can just climb along the tunnel from which we have just emerged.'

'What, you mean right now?'

'No, not right now. First, we must rescue our other friends.'

'Who are these other friends?'

'They are the nearest and dearest of my companions

242

here, trapped deeper within the Underside, beyond this place.'

As Miles spoke, a bright red glow became visible from one tunnel leading out from the cavern. Fear and awe appeared on the faces of the miners. The ominous light swelled, spreading knotted feelings of foreboding within the guts of those present. Moments later, Lucifix appeared, radiating both terror and devotion.

'What kind of conspiracy is this?'

Waves of mingled commanding dominance and seductive sexuality flooded the space as she sought to reestablish her domination and adoration. Her spiritual energy would have typically crushed resistance, but she faced a counterforce.

Miles's spiritual light also shone out, illuminating not only the space of the cavern but Lucifix herself. Her observers now saw her differently. Where they usually saw only majestic power and irresistible beauty, under Miles's light, they saw tyrannical cruelty, malevolence and the ugliness of evil.

'These are my friends, and I am setting them free,' announced Miles.

Lucifix strained her spiritual muscles and sinews to overcome everyone's resistance, from Miles, the members of Miles's party and the miners' hearts.

After a minute, realising she could not prevail, Lucifix made a final ominous pronouncement. 'Be assured, those who have defied the Established Order will be crushed and punished.'

Those gathered watched motionless while Lucifix made her retreat along the tunnel. Miles's spiritual light spread across the cavern, sweeping up and ejecting every trace of Lucifix's lingering malevolence.

'Do you want to be free from her?'

There were nods and murmurs of support.

'Very well, but I will need your help. Are you with me?'
Everyone nodded.

'She will be mustering her forces against us; we must move swiftly.'

Mining work ceased, and the remaining miners joined the group.

'You need only believe, and you can be free,' Miles assured them.

'Lucifix is too strong,' said one miner, shaking his head. 'She can read our minds and knows when anyone imagines freedom or escape.'

'I, too, am strong,' Miles assured him. 'Have trust in me, and you will be free.'

'Once, many years ago, I imagined I might be free, but it was not to be.'

'What happened?' Karen enquired.

'I was on the Continental and Oceanic Securities Bank staff,' the man recounted. 'I led a rebellion of the Building Services Operatives, strike action for better conditions.'

'Did you succeed?'

'She knew immediately. We were rounded up, beaten to a pulp and sent here to the mines.'

'How long ago?'

'I lose track. Must be about forty or fifty years, I'd say.'

'I led a rising on one of the plantations,' said another miner.

'When?'

'Over two centuries ago.'

'In my case, I led a mutiny on one of the galleys. That

was close to two thousand years ago.'

'So how long is she going to keep you here?'

'For all eternity,' said the supervisor.

'What do you have to fear from her?' asked Karen. 'She has already denied you the light of day in this hell hole. What else can she do?'

'There are worse places,' said the supervisor. 'The sewers, for instance.'

'What do you have to do down there?'

'You get to dig out the fatbergs.'

'What's a fatberg?'

'A giant encrustation of solidified cooking fat, excreta, compacted wet wipes and used sanitary tampons. They can fill the pipe and extend for hundreds of metres; no sooner have you cleared one, there is another.'

'We need a plan of action,' said Miles. 'To release Eddie, Tim and Jenny, we must enter the Continental and Oceanic Securities Bank. It won't be easy; it is well defended.'

'There is a hydro-electric plant that works off the flow from the underground river Styx,' said the supervisor. 'If we took that out, it would cut off the city's power.'

'How would you do that?' Miles asked.

'We'll take out the machinery with the dynamite we use for blasting.'

'Okay, good. We have a couple of other rescues to do first, so could we time it for ten hours from now?'

The rescue party tracked through a tunnel that housed the electrical cables running from the underground power station, emerging on the surface at the electrical sub-station overlooking the great city of the Underside.

Before moving on to the city, there was a detour, a cable car up to one of the mountain summits on the route of the Perpetual Mountain Ultra-marathon.

Larry had long since lost count of the summits he had clambered up since entering the competition, hundreds probably, but what did it matter against the infinity he must scale over eternity?

In the Underside, the usual constraints of the Material World do not apply, so Larry could run indefinitely without food or rest, should Lucifix decide. Without respite, Larry was not spared the exhaustion, aching muscles, shredded joints, blisters, breathlessness, emptiness, hunger and dehydration from his exertions.

Supremely fit and physically tough as he was, the relentless strain showed in his haggard appearance, hollow cheeks, grey complexion, eyes sunk deep into their sockets, dried out leathery skin and lank matted hair.

The constant slog up and down steep mountain tracks was now Larry's existence. So besotted was he with Lucifix, if she expected it of him, he would comply without question. He lived for those brief moments she would be there at a summit, waiting. She never had an encouraging word, only scorn and derision, taunting him for his lack of commitment, demanding he put in more effort.

Yet, despite her manner, it was her presence that encouraged Larry. He revelled in her being there, concentrating on him, oozing the overwhelming sexuality that made his mind and body want to worship her forever from one mountain to the next.

Larry gasped and struggled up yet another summit, concentrating every scrap of his remaining energy into a show of speed to please Lucifix, should she be there. Experience told him she would never give him a hint of praise, however hard he strived. Yet he could imagine she might be at least somewhat pleased by his effort.

At the top, Larry saw Karen, Miles and the others, but, to his disappointment, no sign of Lucifix. Such was her domination of his mind; Lucifix was all he could think about. By now so strongly programmed to keep going, he didn't stop when they called to him, nor barely acknowledged their presence.

Miles intervened, stepping across Larry's path. Larry was so focussed that if it had been almost anyone else, apart from the divine Lucifix, he would have just stepped around and pressed on. But Miles shone out at him with a revealing light that reached into his psyche. He was reminded of Karen and his feelings for her. She was there. He was compelled to stop.

Karen's eyes lit as Larry cast his own on hers. For a moment, they just gazed fondly into each other's eyes.

Before they could exchange a single word, another voice rang out. 'You don't have time to engage with your admirers. You have a race to run. Get yourself moving.'

It was Lucifix. Larry panicked. He had let his beloved Lucifix down. Yet he did not want to move on; Karen was there for him. He stood in confused indecision for seconds, switching his gaze between them.

It was the presence of Miles that broke the deadlock. His spiritual light illuminated the scene, casting Lucifix in a different perspective. Larry no longer saw her dominating power and overwhelming sexuality but her cruelty, vindictiveness, and expression distorted by scorn and hatred.

Lucifix tried again to regain control over him and spur him on. 'Come on. Get moving. Get on with the race. Run,' she commanded, but her spiritual leash had snapped. Angrily she turned to Miles. 'This is not finished, meddler. I will be back, and you will be punished.'

Larry was free, reunited with Karen.

Miles's rescue posse, including Larry, arrived searching for Liz at the allotments. They found only her plot. An unkempt, unhealthy, overweight man wandered from the neighbouring plot.

'Looking for someone?'

'Yes, Liz, a friend of ours.'

'I'm a good friend of hers too,' he said, with an oily obsequious look of faux helpfulness. 'Name of Sid. I look out for her.'

'Do you know where we could find her?'

'I wouldn't know. I keep an eye out for her. Make sure she is alright.'

'That's nice, but do you know where she is?'

'I couldn't say.'

'So, how well do you know Liz?'

'We're close if you know what I mean.'

'We'd really like to find her.'

'I wouldn't like her to get into trouble.'

'It's trouble we are trying to rescue her from.'

'If she's gone somewhere, that's her business, isn't it? She might not want anyone to know about it.'

'Yes, but do you know anything about where she might have gone.'

'You wouldn't have anything that might jog my memory,' said Sid, holding up his hand and rubbing his thumb against his fingers.

Miles pulled out a banknote but kept it firmly in his grasp. 'Come on, out with it. Tell us what you know.'

Sid mused. Perhaps the authorities at the bank would reward him if he kept quiet. He felt a surge of concentrated spiritual energy emanating from Miles. 'Alright, there was this man in a uniform who came looking for her,' said Sid, taking hold of the banknote.

'Go on,' said Miles, still holding the money.

'He had sergeant's stripes on his shoulder and a logo. Continental and Oceanic Securities Bank, I think, on his uniform. She went away with him.'

It was quiet on Basement Level 3.

Duncan McTaggetty had finished demonstrating his virility with Liz and, having no further use for it, dumped her violated body onto the floor outside his quarters.

Likewise, fellow enforcers, Sean and Kevin, had taken their pleasure with Eddie and slung him out like garbage into the main thoroughfare of Basement Level 3.

It had been an awful and humiliating experience, but Eddie was resilient.

His call device bleeped in his pocket. Out of habit, he pulled it out to take a look. Two new alarms had appeared. One of the robotic window cleaning units had become stuck on an obstruction on the 17th floor. A drink dispensing machine on the 26th floor was leaking sticky brown coffee over carpet tiles. He shoved it back into his pocket.

Eddie picked himself off the floor. He could hear Liz whimpering. He looked around and saw her laid out at the other end of the room. With Lucifix's entertainment session finished, just the two of them remained, the other members of the bank's Building Services staff having dispersed back to their duties.

Liz was curled in a foetal position, shivering, as Eddie approached her. In her magically beautified form, she lacked the sturdiness and vigour she had as her unglamourised self. She now looked fragile and broken, pitiful, like the shattered remains of an exquisite Dresden porcelain shepherdess fallen off its plinth onto flagstones.

Eddie sat on the floor beside her.

'Liz, love, I'm so sorry about what happened,' he said gently, his voice shaking.

There was no time for Liz to reply as Lucifix swept in, filling the room with an atmosphere as cold, brutal, and cruel as a Samurai sword.

'This room is for staff only. You can't entertain your friends here,' she said harshly, directing herself towards Eddie. 'She is not allowed here. Take her out. Now.'

Traumatised, Eddie could not feel anything anymore except icy cold despair. 'Yes, madam.'

She stood overlooking him as he helped Liz to her feet. 'Come on, Liz. It's time to go. I'll see you out,' Eddie said gently.

Eddie put his arm around Liz's shoulders, guiding her along the corridor and into the lift to the bank's staff entrance. He went out with her into the street, and they sat on the pavement side by side, backs to the wall.

'I'm so sorry I couldn't protect you from that,' lamented Eddie.

Liz had recovered her composure and wasn't shaking anymore. She put her hand on Eddie's knee. 'You tried, Eddie love, that's what matters. You couldn't have done more.'

Eddie's on-call device bleeped again. This time he ignored it.

Eddie knew he would soon be missed. Yet he did not want to leave Liz alone. He didn't really want to leave her at all. He would have preferred to have stayed with her all the time to love and protect her.

When he didn't get back to his station in Basement Level 5, someone would be hunting for him, Duncan, Kevin or Sean. Or perhaps Lucifix herself. Or the bank's security staff, seeing them together, they might come out to investigate. He was content to wait until one of those things happened. Right now, Liz needed him, and he would remain to provide what comfort and protection he could.

Liz saw Eddie in a new light. Until now, he had been her efficient and organised colleague on the FFWS committee, capable and knowledgeable, but not someone she had considered romantically. Now she could see that he was a fine man with a good heart, a man she should treasure.

They remained, not saying much, because what was necessary at the moment was not what was said but being together and supporting each other.

As they sat, two more alarms bleeped on Eddie's on-call device. Again Eddie ignored them. He could deal with those later.

They were still sitting when Miles's rescue squad arrived, including their respective lovers, Susan and James, Karen, Larry, Jenny's lover Tracey and Tim's Tina.

A moment before, Eddie and Liz had felt as cold as if they had been marooned on the most frozen windswept iceberg in the Antarctic Ocean. Now Miles's presence and the collective strength of his entourage shone over them like warm sunshine.

'I'm glad you're both here,' said Miles, 'because that only leaves Jenny and Tim to complete our rescue.'

'What do you mean, rescue?' asked Eddie.

'We're here to take you out of here, to get you away from the Underside.'

Eddie's heart was torn, feeling deeply protective towards Liz. Susan was his long-lost true love, but swamping those feelings was his awe and devotion to his supreme Lucifix. It didn't matter how harsh and cruel Lucifix was. She owned him.

'I don't know,' said Eddie helplessly.

'The power is due to be cut soon,' said Miles. 'That should remove the bank's security systems, allowing us to move into the bank and rescue Jenny and Tim.'

Eddie knew this plan would not work because the bank's standby generator would keep the building operational for days, ample time for the mains electricity to be restored. But he said nothing. He could not undermine Lucifix.

As Eddie anticipated, Lucifix chose that moment to sweep out of the staff entrance, projecting her majestic presence.

'What is going on?' she demanded. Looking straight at Eddie, she commanded: 'You haven't got time to idle in chat with ne'er-do-wells. Get back to your duties. At once.'

Eddie made to obey, but saw Lucifix in a different light under the strange spectral illumination from Miles. In a flash, he could perceive the malevolent core of her spirit, her cruel enjoyment of suffering, and her ruthless determination to achieve her ends regardless of how many others might be crushed.

Eddie thought fast. As Miles had planned, the rescue team's only chance was for the electrical power to fail. But that could only happen if the standby generator was out of action. Eddie could do that, but first, he would need to get back into the building. Lucifix would not allow him back if she suspected her spell over him had been broken.

'Yes, madam.'

Lucifix was gratified that whatever power Miles had to usurp her influence over her minions had not worked on this occasion. Perhaps his powers were waning; now he had come to the Underside. She smiled as she imagined the torments and humiliations she would impose on Miles when she had him overpowered, as she surely would in due course.

Jenny was at her duties in the foyer of the Continental and Oceanic Securities Bank. She was there to arrange the displays, replenish stocks of leaflets, and provide light refreshments for important visitors while looking decorative and efficient, but she was forbidden to talk to visitors. That was Tim's job.

Jenny found this excruciating. Taciturn and uncommunicative, Tim struggled, and his attempts at conversation were painfully embarrassing. Jenny, naturally chatty, would have found it a breeze, but frustratingly she was not allowed to assist him.

On this day, the bank was running a Democratic Leadership Symposium, for which the bank's Building Services Manager, Lucifix, was a keynote speaker.

A woman came in and looked Tim up and down.

'Excuse me, can you help me?'

'Yes, madam,' said Tim, a fixed false smile on his face. 'Welcome to the Continental and Oceanic Securities Bank.'

'I'm staying over for a few days. Is there anything you might suggest for me as sporting entertainment after the Symposium?'

'What service are you in need of today, madam?'

'Is there any particular service you have in mind?' asked the woman, unsure what to make of Tim's unusual offer.

'We have the Democratic Leadership Symposium today.'

'Yes, I know. I'm attending it.'

'You require something afterwards?'

'Yes, that's right.'

Tim thought. This eventuality hadn't been in his script. Then he remembered seeing material about the bank's sponsorship of sporting events and recalled words from the brochures.

'The bank sponsors many athletic and sporting activities, madam. We consider our community's holistic wellbeing paramount and encourage everybody to achieve peak sporting performance. Was there a particular sporting activity that interested you, madam?'

'Is there a sporting activity you can recommend?'

Tim looked awkward. 'Our wellness facility offers aromatherapy massage and high-intensity training.'

The woman carefully inspected his physique. 'How intense did you have in mind?'

'The training is for peak performance, madam.'

'Is that a promise?'

'We endeavour to satisfy our clients.'

'Do you, now? Satisfaction guaranteed?'

'Yes, madam.'

'You look as if you look after yourself,' she remarked, assessing him admiringly. 'What sports activities do you undertake to keep in such good shape?'

This left Tim tongue-tied, his mouth opening and closing soundlessly like a fish in a tank. Seeing Tim's embarrassment, Jenny ignored her instructions and stepped in.

'We have extensive winter sports facilities in the region. You may be interested in the Perpetual Mountain Ultra-marathon race, which can be viewed from some excellent mountain restaurants with panoramic views, accessible by convenient cable car and gondola services.'

'I was talking to him,' said the woman.

At that moment, Lucifix appeared. An icy fury in her demeanour filled Jenny and Tim with dread.

'You were instructed not to talk to visitors,' said Lucifix. 'You disobeyed me.'

'But Tim needed help,' pleaded Jenny.

'Conversing with the visitors is a job Tim must learn for himself.'

'Sorry, madam.'

'I don't have time to discipline you now, but you may rest assured, there will be consequences. I will deal with the matter later.'

Leaving it there, she advanced imperiously into the auditorium for the Symposium, where she was due to make her keynote speech.

At this point, the lights in surrounding buildings abruptly went out. There was a flicker in the bank's building, and everything carried on with lights, computers and sound systems remaining functional.

In Basement Level 5, the giant marine diesel engine that drove the standby generator shuddered and belched black smoke as it kicked into life, working perfectly due to Eddie's diligent maintenance.

The whole area throbbed with a deafening cacophony of the heavy thump and clatter from the twelve immense pistons oscillating within their cavernous cylinders, swinging their connecting rods in rhythmic motion around the engine's driveshaft. Although Miles did not know this, the success of his plan depended on Eddie stopping the generator for sufficient time for the rescue team to get Jenny and Tim out of the premises. Eddie was ready.

It would be no good just stopping the engine because it could be quickly restarted. He would stop the engine by starving it of fuel.

Eddie opened a valve at the bottom of the large fuel tank. A torrent of thick gloop spread across the basement floor. He was reminded of the overflowed ladies' toilet he had had to clear at the Dorking parish hall during the Founders Memorial Challenge event.

Eddie's on-call device bleeped insistently. He took it out. According to the device, there was a fluid leakage on Basement Level 5. Somebody else's problem. He scoffed as he slung the device into the swelling pond of oily sludge. As it sank, it bleeped again. According to its display, there was now an air quality alert on Basement Level 5.

By now, the air was thick with choking oily fumes.

Eddie did not wait to be suffocated. He made his way up to the foyer and remained out of sight in a discreet corner, ready for the power cut he estimated would occur within half an hour.

The audience clapped as Lucifix took the stage for her keynote speech at the bank's prestige event, the Democratic Leadership Symposium. Among those present were influential figures in major political parties across the reaches of the Underside.

She opened by declaring the first duty of empowered leadership is the preservation of the Established Order. Without order, chaos would reign. Democratic processes are potentially dangerous because they threaten the Established Order unless managed effectively.

Fortunately, the population and media can focus on only a few issues. Leaders must exercise control of the problems that appear to the public. They must therefore be supported by social influencers and those adept at using political platforms.

The leadership selection process must weed out candidates who might raise undesirable questions and expectations among the populace. Ideal are those who divert attention from matters that could affect the Established Order by agitating and focusing the energies of the population on emotive but harmless issues. So-called populists are suitable because they are adept at raising public fervour and controversy about trivialities and diverting scrutiny and debate from more dangerous matters.

In cases where a potentially dangerous issue inadvertently reaches the public domain, detailed public scrutiny can be averted by simplifying debate. Reduce issues to binary choices. Simplified in this way, exploration of the fine detail and nuances can be avoided. Ideally, the issue should be neutralised by formulating both binary choices so neither option threatens the Established Order. If that isn't possible, present the choices as Good versus Evil, to build up hatred and distrust against the choice threatening the Established Order.

Galvanise unquestioning loyalty to the leadership and group the leader represents by portraying other groups, foreigners and so on, as threats to the nation.

Use public voting to pose loaded questions to the population, including an emotional pull in the desired direction. When the desired result is obtained, close off any further examination or debate by presenting the result as the established will of the people so any opposition may be presented as, at the very least, undemocratic, if not treasonous.

Lucifix was closing off her presentation when the generator sputtered deep underground as the fuel flow petered out. Batteries took over, but these could carry the load for, at most, minutes. Alarms sounded, and a recorded message played over the public address system calling on people to evacuate the building.

The doors swung open to provide unrestricted access and exit from the premises.

Miles and the team jostled their way in and found Jenny, Tim and Eddie in the foyer. From there, the group poured into the street with the flow of other occupants. Their escape had not gone unnoticed by Lucifix because she appeared in their path like an avenging angel intent on striking them down, radiating her imperial majesty and ravishing beauty. In the ordinary course, they would have been powerless to resist, but now there was another force at play, a gentle radiance of light Miles emitted, illuminating Lucifix differently, revealing majesty in the form of brutal tyranny and beauty as gruesome cruelty.

Led by Miles, the group, immune from her influence, brushed past Lucifix as if she wasn't there, heading out of the city towards the now cold and silent electrical substation from where they could access the deep mines through which they had entered Lucifix's infernal realm. They would soon depart, returning along with the miners now released from Lucifix's enchantment and slavery.

Reality Restored

The whole of Miteby was partying in celebration of Miles's triumphant rescue of their friends and in welcome to their new villagers, the miners who had migrated with them from the Underside.

Colourful bunting bedecked the streets above grotesque effigies of Underhexes spread throughout the village; fairy lights strung out like streams of stars above rows of stalls offering tasty goodies; everywhere, there appeared amusements and protective talismans against evil. Raucous fun was had by all on the pretty painted wooden horses galloping around steam-powered merry-go-rounds. Flags and ribbons bedecked the maypole. Folk quaffed tankards of Meadow Dew ale and goblets of mead as they listened to and joined in rumbustious rustic songs to the tunes played by the village band.

Amidst the celebration, gaiety, and joyous delight, bittersweet adjustments were made to personal relationships.

Eddie, Liz, Susan and James made an awkward foursome.

Eddie and Liz had reverted to their older selves. They had a new connection, no romanticised Romeo and Juliet, but a mellow attachment. Still, in their youthful form, Susan and James could almost have been Eddie's and Liz's grandchildren, mere distant memories of youthful passions from long ago.

Susan and James looked mournfully from the sidelines as Eddie and Liz, bonded by their shared trauma in the Underside, held hands and looked fondly into each other's eyes. Sensing Susan's and James's discomfort, Eddie and Liz looked at them sheepishly but were unable or unwilling to reach back out to them.

James broke the deadlock. 'You two look happy together.'

After appreciating how it must have made James and Susan feel, Eddie and Liz looked embarrassedly at each other, looked back, and nodded.

'I suppose this means Susan and I are in the past now, as far as you are concerned,' stated James. There was no rancour in his voice, just an objective clarification.

Eddie's and Liz's toes curled at the thought of the pain they were causing their erstwhile lovers, but they could not deny it.

'You don't need to say anything. I can see it in your eyes. James is right,' said Susan with a hint of sadness.

Eddie felt that he had to say something. 'I am so sorry, Susan, you have been very dear to me. I do still love you.' He reached out towards Susan, but she pulled away from him.

'No, your place is with Liz now. I can see that.'

'Oh, James, I can't tell you how dear you have been to me,' said Liz.

'I know,' James acknowledged, 'but we have served our purpose.'

'What do you mean, your purpose?' Eddie enquired.

'To straighten things out for you, in your souls,' Susan explained.

James looked at Susan. 'I think that we should go now, don't you?'

Susan nodded. As Eddie and Liz looked on, Susan and James became less tangible, translucent as if made from coloured glass, then fainter, fully transparent. Their presence lingered as a smoky mist, gradually diffusing, losing shape as the wisps of their existence dispersed by gentle currents in the air. Eddie and Liz felt panic and wistfulness as their former loved ones vanished, presumably forever.

In his heart, Eddie knew what was happening. Susan and James were spiritual apparitions, conjured to fulfil a need. He felt a sense of mourning for a loved one who was now gone but, in reality, already departed long ago, persisting in haunting him in a ghostly form over the intervening decades but now exorcised.

The last vestiges of Susan and James having evaporated, Liz broke the silence. 'It's just us now, Eddie.'

'Yes, just us.'

'You will always be there for me, won't you, Eddie?'

'Yes, always. I'll be stuck to you like glue. Don't you worry.'

While Tracey was embarrassed by ecstatic displays of emotion, she might have expected some demonstration of affection from Jenny when they were reunited.

As they departed from the Continental and Oceanic Securities Bank building on the Underside, the priority had been to get as far as possible from the clutches of the malignant Lucifix, leaving no time for more than momentary shows of affection. Despite this, Tracey might have expected a fond look or a smile of happiness. Jenny caught her eye and smiled fleetingly, but the smile lacked warmth and quickly faded. Tracey might have rationalised Jenny's lukewarm reaction as reflecting the horrific traumas and terror she suffered.

A little later, when they stopped for a breather at a safe distance, Tracey could have hoped for a more fulsome show of affection from her lover. Jenny came close for a hug, but her clasp was less than wholehearted, as one might greet a distant relation at a family reunion. Tracey tried to press herself closer, but Jenny broke away. Tracey attempted to initiate a conversation, but after the briefest of exchanges, Jenny was diverted by something Miles said.

On stopping in the deep mining cavern to rendezvous with their new allies, the band of rebellious miners, Jenny had, perhaps intentionally, diverted from being with Tracey to make introductions with the miners. Likewise, during the lengthy clamber out of the mine and back to where the long tunnel emerged into the Other Side in the quarry behind Hollingsby, Jenny had preoccupied herself with chatting with her new friends, the miners.

Once they arrived at Miteby, despite the absence of any explicit rejection from Jenny, it would have been clear to Tracey all was not well. Jenny was usually outgoing in expressing her feelings, and even Tracey, who did not set much store in demonstrative displays, sensed the unease.

As the celebrations got underway, Tracey hovered near Jenny, but whenever she tried to talk to her, Jenny would be diverted into conversation with someone else. Tracey bided her time, awaiting a quieter moment, but Jenny contrived to keep within the jubilant throng.

Tracey could no longer bear the tension. She took Jenny firmly by the arm. 'Jenny, we need to talk, just the two of us,' she insisted. 'Over there, away from the others.'

'What's the matter?'

'You know perfectly well, now come on.'

'No, I don't know.'

'Yes, you do. You have avoided and ignored me since we got you out of the Underside.'

Jenny felt rising annoyance at the way Tracey was yet again pressurising her. Then, all at once, she felt relief. Until that moment, she had not been sure what she wanted, but in that instant, she knew. It was Tracey's insistent grip on her arm that convinced her. She could not allow Tracey to control her life as she had. She and Tracey were history.

Out of range of the madding crowd, Tracey came to the point. 'What is the matter? Do you still care for me?'

'I'm sorry, Tracey, but it's over. You and I aren't right for each other,' said Jenny.

'What happened? What went wrong? I don't understand.'

'It went wrong in the Underside. It wasn't you because you weren't even there.'

'You met someone else, is that it?'

'No, nothing like that. There isn't anybody else. Not yet, anyway. It's just that things happened there that brought home to me how I felt.'

'The swines. Did they abuse you? You know, rape you, that sort of thing.'

'Not exactly, but it wasn't nice, what happened.'

'What can I do to put things right? I'll do anything. Anything at all. I love you,' pleaded Tracey.

Jenny did not have to deliberate about Tracey's pleas. Her suppressed misgivings could no longer be denied. Tracey had unleashed Jenny's true sexuality, and their relationship was infinitely better than she had ever had with men, yet their relationship still wasn't what it should be. It was when Tracey grabbed her arm so forcefully

Jenny saw clearly what was wrong.

Her relationship with Tracey had been coercive from the beginning when Tracey had forced her attentions on her. Even now, Tracey had always initiated and set the pace of their intimacy. Her recent exposure to the unstoppable hypnotic force of Lucifix's hyper-sexuality and her threat to unleash Duncan McTaggetty on her had crystalised her horror of dominance and coercion.

'Sorry, Tracey love, but there isn't anything. We just aren't right for each other. That's all,' said Jenny emphatically.

'So, there is literally no way back for us. Is that it?' said Tracey, crestfallen.

'Sorry, but no, there isn't.'

'I see. I guess that I'd better just go then. It was good while it lasted, wasn't it?'

'Yes, Tracey love, it was good while it lasted.'

Jenny's view of Tracey faded. At first, it was just that her outline was slightly indistinct, as if she was going out of focus and her colour was washed out. After a minute or so, she was becoming transparent. There was only the faintest smoky indication of her presence in another minute, and then she wasn't there. She was gone from Jenny's life—forever.

Larry was finished with the rat race, his competitive impulses wrung out of him, slogging up a hundred and more mountain peaks during the Perpetual Mountain Ultra-marathon.

For someone like Larry, for whom competition and status were everything, opting out could have left an empty shell devoid of self-worth and reason for living, but

Larry had discovered previously hidden qualities in himself, a desire for peace, tranquillity, and artistic expression.

Even the one prize Larry still yearned for, Karen's love, was not something he was prepared to bust a gut for. If it happened, so be it; if not, he would accept the situation with equanimity.

She sat beside him on a bench outside the Miteby Arms as they observed the festivities. That was nice, he reflected. She wasn't so repulsed by him that she preferred to be somewhere else. For some reason, she had been more affectionate since they had been reunited. He hadn't told her about his decision to opt-out and chill out. She surely wouldn't want him then. He resolved to be straight with her. Just in case she had been developing feelings for him, he had better let her know and leave her free to seek someone with better prospects.

'I'm going to give up my job at the bank.'

'Oh, I see. Have you got a better offer somewhere else?'

'No, I don't want another job. I'm giving up that life.'

'What do you want to do then?'

'I'd like to do artistic pottery. Sort of sculpture with clay. Some things I'd make might be useful, others just decorative. I don't mind.'

'That would be a big change.'

'Yes, it would. I don't suppose I'd earn anything much from it. To start with probably nothing, and even later, if I succeed in making a name for myself, probably not much more than a pittance.'

'What will you live on?'

'I've saved a bit. I've earned quite well at the bank, so I won't starve.'

'That's good.'

'But I'd have to get rid of my fancy stuff. Car, Rolex, and so on, that would have to go.'

'But you don't need those things. That wouldn't matter.'

'I don't suppose you'd be interested in me now I've told you this.'

'Why do you say that?'

'I've decided to give it all up, opt-out. I guess it makes me a bit of a loser.'

Karen leapt up with excitement. 'No, it doesn't make you a loser,' she shouted, 'It's the best thing you could ever have done. You should have done it ages ago.'

'You mean that? Are you sure?'

'Yes, of course, I'm sure.'

'Well, okay, I'll go ahead with the pottery thing. Glad I've got your blessing.'

'Totally. Go for it.'

Larry hesitated. So far, this had gone better than expected. There was one final question, which he dreaded to ask because he feared he would not like the answer.

'I assume it's not a lifestyle you might consider sharing with me. I'm not expecting anything. I don't suppose you'd be one for the simple life.'

'Yes, you chump. I wouldn't want you any other way. In fact, if you ever did go back to the bank and got into all that one-upmanship nonsense, I would leave you there and then.'

'You would move in with me, into some shack deep in the countryside with a pottery workshop and kiln attached?'

'Yes, in a flash.'

Larry reflected. Life was strange. All that effort to

impress and win her to no avail, then, when he has given up trying, she clings to him like a limpet.

Tim felt relieved when the rescue party hustled him out of the impressive yet dreadful Continental and Oceanic Securities Bank. Those from medieval times who had been lucky to escape imposing castles such as the Tower of London must have felt the same.

Expressing how he felt was not something that came easily. Whether through facial expression, body language or speech, Tim was taciturn. To an observer, it could appear he was unmoved. He had been delighted to see Tina, his friend from Miteby, as a member of the rescue party.

'You look like Odelsdottir when she rescued Sir Gladdifon from the Whirlpool of Doom,' he told her.

'Like Sir Gladdifon, you will live to fight another day and achieve your destiny,' she replied.

'Do you think so?'

'There will be demons to fight, and you will prevail.'

As they sat opposite at a small table outside the Miteby Arms, the celebrations of their rescue in full swing, Tim felt a growing love for Tina. She alone could read his feelings, and he hers. They had both read every one of the books in the *Citadels of Vallborg* series several times and watched every one of the dramatisations incessantly throughout many an evening at home, providing them with a shared language of allusion. Tim decided the time had come for boldness.

'You remind me of Princess Beatefice.'

'Nonsense, Princess Beatefice was much prettier and courtlier than I could hope to be.'

'For me, you are every bit as pretty and elegant as Princess Beatefice.'

'No, I'm not.'

'Yes, you are. Whenever I read the Vallborg stories with Princess Beatefice in them, I imagine that she is you.'

'I don't believe it. Nobody else has thought of me like that.'

'I don't care about other people. That's how I feel.'

Tim was emboldened by the goblets of mead he had consumed. 'When you said I was like Sir Gladdifon living to fight another day and achieving my destiny, did you mean that you thought I really was like Sir Gladdifon?'

'Yes,' confirmed Tina, 'I really did think that.'

'When Sir Gladdifon slays the monster Mengelfang,' said Tim, seizing the moment, 'do you think he could win the heart of Princess Beatefice?'

'Yes,' said Tina, 'he could.'

'That's wonderful.'

'They have only ever met and talked in Miteby,' Tina observed.

'Yes, that's true.'

'They would need to meet in the Material World. Chatting online via the VallborgWorld.com website wouldn't be enough.'

'What, you mean face to face, like us now?'

'Yes. You would first have to seek her out and meet her back there in the Material World before winning her heart.'

Tim felt crestfallen. Moving on from their extensive online dialogue to a face-to-face meeting was daunting. He had tried this before with other people. It had taken all his boldness and determination to summon the courage to make such a move, but each time had ended dismally when he had failed to make a connection. He dreaded that happening again. Also, it would be a huge risk because another failure would mean losing his online soulmate. 'How should I go about it?'

'Do what Sir Gladdifon does in the stories. Keep to that, and you won't go far wrong.'

Eddie and Liz had been alone in each other's company for some time, all make-believe gone, each as they were in the Material World.

Gone was the glamour bestowed on Liz by Lucifix. Eddie preferred her that way, her sturdy no-nonsense self. Glamour was skin-deep. Character matters.

It felt good for both of them to be together, yet they were subdued. They were in mourning for their respective might-have-been lovers brought to life for them in Miteby, now faded from them in front of their eyes, probably forever.

It was good to have reality restored, but that reality cruelly squashed a fantasy world they had harboured in their dreams for decades. The excision of these fantasies had been a necessary surgery to enable them to give each other the love they deserved, but it was a surgery that carried some post-operative pain.

Eddie was the first to notice. Their surroundings were getting less distinct, colours less vivid, fading to pastel shades. He wondered if it had been the mead they had been drinking copiously. He took a swig of what he still had in his goblet. It didn't have any taste.

'Liz, do you notice anything, things fading, or is it just me?'

'Yes, they're fading for me too.'

Miles appeared, little more than a an almost unidentifiable glowing blob.

'I'm saying goodbye now,' he said faintly. 'You are on your way back to the Material World.'

It was not only their vision fading. The voices of the people around them were slowing, and the sounds were losing meaning. They felt strangely relaxed, content to rest and let things bubble away around them, slipping increasingly into the distance, vanishing out of sight.

When consciousness returned, Eddie was in the hospital. The medical staff were animated and pleased to observe him responding, coming out of his coma.

'It's good news,' the consultant told him. 'All those who had been brought in comatose from the effects of the toxic mushrooms, Psilocybe Latusaversus, and its more toxic cousin, Psilocybe Latussubterensis, have regained consciousness and are on the road to recovery.'

Walkers Reunion

Are there places, objects, and beings with a separate existence beyond the material world? A question as old as there have been people. If there are such phantoms, what is the nature of their existence? If such entities are apparent to one person, will they also be to others? Does being aware of a phantom depend on believing that phantoms can exist? Does a belief in these phantoms suggest phantoms are artefacts generated in the minds of those who believe? What is it within believers' minds that bring phantoms into existence? Angst, regrets, trauma, dreams?

Mythical beings, spirits, trolls, and goblins, reputed to lurk in the dark depths of the forest, appearing to the susceptible, take their form from the monsters that hide within the deepest crevices of their tortured souls. What of those governed by reason and logic, rejecting such superstition? Would such rationality make them immune to supernatural happenings?

For those securely framed within the architecture of convention, the cracks of their psyche rendered smooth with the cement of civility, the monsters within may lay dormant, leaving the woodland goblins unseen. Such order prevails until the brittle façade is shattered, exposing the fissures of the psyche, releasing the sprites and demons that dwell there, regardless of belief, to swarm among forest glades.

When the monsters previously hiding within were banished from their hiding places, logic suggests the susceptibility to sensing these spirits, trolls, and goblins should also be gone. Does it follow, being no longer seen, that these mythical beings no longer exist, if they ever existed? Or is it that the supernatural spectres are always there, regardless of a person's ability to sense them?

Is merely releasing and confronting monsters within the soul sufficient to exorcise them? Perhaps they burrow even deeper into the psyche, temporarily dormant, awaiting the clarion call that will unleash them once more.

It is a glorious day in July, months after the rescue of those who weathered the Other Side's joys and the Underside's terrors. Eddie is leading another walk for the Surrey branch of the FFWS, to reunite those who embarked on those adventures in October of the previous year.

Since their fortunate homecoming in the Material World, they have put their joyful passions and anguished suffering behind them and have no desire to return. Does this mean those unmaterialised places no longer exist? Do their phantom messengers, Miles and Lucifix, endure? Will they return today to haunt those who have reconvened?

Eddie's planned route is again in the Surrey Hills, but they will avoid Sorcerer's Copse. The rendezvous is a car park in the village of Sheerbeck, one of those impossibly pretty and quaint places. When people come there for the first time, it looks vaguely familiar because it has appeared in many television series and films, mostly murder mysteries and period costume dramas. As one walks past rows of higgledy-piggledy cottages, one half expects to see the legs of a corpse protruding from under the shrubbery being examined by a famous detective of modern fiction.

The village centre contains a collection of traditional shops, an inn and tea room that serves cream teas. It is only when looking beneath the surface that this apparently idyllic, unspoiled scene is revealed as a theme park version of Merrie, England. The baker provides fancy loaves and cakes made on the premises at five times the price of a factory-baked loaf in the supermarket in Dorking. The butcher provides venison, braces of pheasant and homemade spiced pork and herb sausages that the well-to-do can charge to their accounts. The inn is a gastro-pub with a Michelin star. The tea room caters for coachloads of tourists traipsing through each day to admire the scenery. Cottages in the village are advertised by prestigious international estate agents at prices starting from a million pounds.

When Eddie arrives at the car park a little after 8:30, he drives a new Tesla, Liz by his side. Eddie has traded his classic Jaguar for the Tesla he and Liz now share. The old car had been one he had shared for many years with his late wife, Margot.

Eddie and Liz are as they have always been to their friends, except they have become noticeably more relaxed. They have relinquished what they were compelled to do out of duty and virtue.

Eddie has reduced the organising he does. Amazingly, the world doesn't come to a grinding halt. Someone else picks up the slack. Liz has not brought culinary treats to share around today. She has cut back on her relentless horticulture, baking and food preservation. Nobody has yet starved as a result.

The most significant change is that Eddie and Liz are now a couple. They had always been good friends and collaborators on FFWS matters, but there had never been any noticeable intimacy or chatty conversation between them. Eddie didn't chat, and Liz tended to do hers with her female friends, like Jenny.

The last few months have started a new chapter in their lives, previously running in parallel on separate tracks, now merged into a shared path. They are in a rented cottage nearby, in a more down-to-earth village, with each of their previous homes on the market.

Jenny draws up in her modest hatchback, accompanied by another woman Eddie has not seen. Jenny introduces her as Sheila, a friend who isn't yet a member of the FFWS but would like to try it. From the intimate and affectionate manner between them, Eddie surmises they mean more to each other than just friends. Jenny can be relied on to have a cheerful demeanour whatever the circumstances, but Eddie is pleased that today she appears particularly happy and relaxed.

Eddie glimpses an unknown figure standing by the village hall near one side of the car park. He wouldn't have noticed the man but for his azure blue outfit.

Tim, a strongly built man in his early thirties with a reserved demeanour, a visitor from the Thames Valley branch of the FFWS, is accompanied in his battered four-by-four off-road vehicle by a potential new member, who Tim introduces as Tina. Eddie remembers seeing Tina with Tim in Miteby but chooses not to mention this.

Tina, a woman of about 30, seems to have transitioned directly from childhood into late middle age in a bound, bypassing adolescence and early adulthood. Her hair is arranged into two plaits, thick round-framed spectacles on her round unmade-up face, clothing selected entirely for practicality without a thought for fashion, elegance or colour coordination.

Introductions having been made, Tim and Tina retreat to one side to have a private and incomprehensible conversation between themselves consisting of the finer points of the numerous wizards, demons, heroic knights, and damsels featured in the sagas of the fantasy series, *Citadels of Vallborg*.

The two couples, Stan and Mary Potterswell and Reg and Ivy Nettleberry, are soon chatting between themselves. Eddie is irritated by how they invariably form themselves into a private enclave; they should make more effort to socialise.

Larry and Karen arrive together in an old pick-up truck. Those who had witnessed their past animosity would have been amazed by the change in their relationship. Now they hold hands and gaze fondly at one another.

Larry and Karen had always been the finest of physical specimens, supremely fit and healthy, marred only by some haggardness and brittle irritability visited on them by the stress they imposed on themselves. Today they remain in the best condition but have acquired a peace and harmony they never had before.

The man in the azure blue outfit walks towards the group, catching Eddie's eye.

'Am I in the right place for today's FFWS walk?'

'Yes, that's us,' says Eddie, gesturing to the other members.

'I'm Melvin Mycroft. I haven't walked with the FFWS before, but would it be okay if I joined you?'

'Yes, of course. New people are always welcome. I'm

Eddie. I'm leading the walk today.'

Eddie edged to the huddle formed by the chattering Potterswells and Nettleberrys. 'Stan, Mary, Reg and Ivy, can I introduce Melvin, a new walker joining us.'

At 9:00 am precisely, formalities and introductions having been completed, the group sets off out of the village in bright sunshine under a blue sky.

The path takes them alongside a stream running languidly over rocks and among reeds, within which, if you look carefully, you might see trout flicking their tails to remain stationary against the gentle flow of water.

The jumble of cottages gives to a small patch of woodland. When Eddie had walked the route what felt like only a few weeks earlier, bluebells were out in an azure blaze under the dappled sunshine that could then still break through the pale green shoots of the early leaf growth on tree branches. Eddie reflects on how fast things move with the seasons. This time the leafy canopy has filled out, obscuring the sunlight and the bluebells are gone. A few vestiges of wild garlic remain with its starry white flowers, still filling the air with its oniony scent.

They reach a small wooden bridge across the stream. Eddie halts the group and invites them to make a line across the bridge for the traditional group photo to load later onto the FFWS website.

As they set off again, Eddie takes the opportunity to discover about the newcomer, Melvin.

'Have you come far to be with us today, Melvin?'

'No, not today. I'm staying in a local guest house while on assignment.'

'So, where is home when you're not in our neck of the woods?'

Melvin looked pensive. 'I don't really have a home at the moment. I live a nomadic existence, moving where my work takes me.'

'So, what is your work exactly?'

'I'm an alternative energy prospector.'

I've heard something like that before, thinks Eddie. Not wishing to be drawn further into the web of this mysterious newcomer, Eddie discreetly lets the matter drop and positions himself to talk to others.

The walkers have now broken out from the woods, branching from the stream alongside a wheat field. Among the grain patches of wildflowers breakthrough with primary colours that sparkle under the bright sunshine: red poppies, yellow dandelions, corn marigolds and dazzling blue cornflowers.

Eddie finds himself with Jenny and her new partner, Sheila.

'Nice to meet you. Sheila,' says Eddie. 'Glad you could come.'

'Jenny has told me a lot about the FFWS, so I thought I'd give it a try.'

'We've been going around together for a little while,' Jenny explains. 'But it's taken until now before I could get her on a walk with us.'

'So, you see quite a bit of each other?'

'Yes, we've just moved in together,' says Jenny.

Eddie has already surmised from the body language they are probably in a relationship. He feels pleased for them.

The field has sloped up, bringing the group onto higher ground overlooking a vista of the Surrey countryside. Behind, in the distance, their starting point, the village of

Sheerbeck, can still be made out as a collection of cottages around a church whose steeple protrudes like a spear pointing at the heavens. At similar distances on either side are two more villages, one clustered around the remains of a ruined castle, the other the grand country home of a minor aristocrat. Between the small clusters of habitation are small rounded hills and dips in the landscape, arranged in a haphazard pattern of fields and irregular clumps of woodland.

Eddie draws up alongside Tim and Tina. Past experience suggests making conversation might be a struggle, but he has a go.

'Hello Tim, and I guess you must be Tina.'

'Yes, I'm Tina.'

'Glad to see you both.'

Silence ensues.

'You two have lots to talk about,' Eddie observes.

'Yes, we both like the Vallborg stories,' Tim explains.

'I don't know much about Vallborg,' Eddie admits. 'Are there any things about it you especially like?'

'It's romantic,' says Tina.

'The stories are nice,' says Tim. 'Like life should be.'

'Was it Vallborg that brought you together?'

'Yes,' Tim confirms without elaborating.

'How long have you shared your interest?'

Tim muses while he does a little mental arithmetic. 'Seventeen years and two months,' he announces.

'Gosh, that's a long time,' says Eddie. 'You must have seen a lot of each other over the years.'

'No,' says Tim.

'So, you only get together now and again, then?'

'We used just to post things on Vallborg World.'

'You mean the website?'

'Yes, but we met in real life recently,' says Tina.

'Oh, where was that?'

'Couple of months ago,' says Tim. 'At the Vallborg World convention in Birmingham.'

'Funny thing is,' says Tina. 'We had both been going to the conventions yearly, but we had never met in real life until then.'

'So how did that happen?'

'Tim sent me a message saying he would like to meet.'

'Well, you seem to be getting on well together now.'

'Yes,' says Tina. 'He sent me the three Symbols of Steadfastness.'

'Not sure what they are.'

'They are what Sir Gladdifon uses to woo Princess Beatifice,' explains Tina.

'Not the real ones, of course,' says Tim. 'They are reproductions. You can buy them from Vallborg marketing.'

'I don't mind,' says Tina. 'They're real for me.'

'That's great,' says Eddie.

'Just thinking, Eddie,' says Tim. 'We're going to get married.'

'Congratulations to you both.'

'Would you like to come to the wedding?' says Tim.

'Well, yes, I suppose I could. Why not?'

'You'll have to decide what character you want to be.'

'What character should I be?'

'Everyone needs to be a Vallborg character because we are reenacting the marriage of Sir Gladdifon and Princess Beatifice.'

Having almost no knowledge or interest in Vallborg,

Eddie feels unable to take the conversation further and drops back to leave them to their private Vallborg-themed chat. Eddie is fascinated to observe that almost any aspect of life has some Vallborg parallel for Tim and Tina to use as a communication vehicle, which is also because they seem unable to engage in conversation except in terms of Vallborg-related characters and happenings. Continuing to listen, Eddie discovers there is perhaps just one aspect of life Vallborg does not cover in detail, but even there, now oblivious of Eddie's presence, Tim and Tina appear only able to communicate via references to fictional characters. Apparently, according to Tina, there are things that Pinky likes Perky to do before Perky can come in. Eddie senses the conversation getting overly intimate and drops out of earshot.

Eddie finds himself again in the company of Melvin, the mysterious newcomer. He feels nervous about where this might lead.

'This alternative energy thing you mentioned earlier. What does that involve?'

'It comes in several forms,' says Melvin. 'There are heat pumps, in various flavours, air source and ground source, for example, geothermal is available in some sites, run-of-river hydro as well as the more mainstream solar and wind.'

Eddie feels relief. While he soon feels overwhelmed when Melvin expands into the technical intricacies, at least Melvin hasn't alluded to anything paranormal.

They are now leading away from the open countryside, back into woodland. The trees are packed close. The gloom under the dense leaf canopy is especially apparent in contrast with the bright sunlight they have experienced. If supernatural forces exist, they will be found in a place like this. Apart from what strange being Melvin may be, the ones who had drawn several of those present to the strange worlds of the Other Side and the Underside could be with us again today, Eddie speculates.

One might question whether the spirits Miles and Lucifix even exist, a point that cannot be proved. Supposing they do, let us imagine Miles hovering nearby among the trees, waiting to join the group, anxious to bring new spiritual energy into the village of Miteby on the Other Side.

We might perceive Lucifix there, skulking in the woodland fringes among heather and gorse, waiting to deploy her seductive charisma to entice unsuspecting victims to eternal torment in the Underside. Eddie scans the group to ensure all are present. As he does, he speculates who among them might be susceptible to the wiles and machinations of spooky emissaries from other worlds.

But who is to say Miles and Lucifix are the only spiritual agents? At any moment, we may encounter a new unknown apparition. These spectres could come from anywhere at any time. So far, Eddie has not been able to identify anything suspicious about today's newcomer, Melvin, but he can't be sure. There remains one thing yet unexplained about Melvin, his distinctively bright outfit.

'I like the bright blue you're wearing. Sort of azure, isn't it? Quite striking.'

'It's the colour of the Slovenian cross-country alpine running club I coached for one season. I had an injury to my knee ligament, so I had to give it up, unfortunately. Thought I'd come along today because I'm hoping some long-distance trekking might be a good way to improve my fitness.'

Eddie catches up with Larry and Karen as they emerge from the wood. 'Melvin, can I introduce you to Larry and Karen?'

'Pleased to meet you.'

'So, how are you getting on these days, Larry?' says Eddie. 'Anything exciting happening at the bank?'

'I'm not with them anymore.'

'What are you doing these days?'

'I'm just setting myself up doing some artistic pottery.'

'How's that going?'

'I haven't sold much, and I don't suppose I'll ever make much of a living at it, but that doesn't matter. I've got enough put by, provided we live frugally.'

'Did I hear "we"?'

'Yes, Karen and I, we're together.'

'Should have done it years ago,' says Karen.

Eddie recalls how for months, Larry had incessantly tried to impress Karen with expensive status symbols, boastful bravado, and feats of athleticism but had earned only disdain. Ironically, he has now ceased to compete, instead doing simple unimpressive things pleasing to himself, and Karen is devoted to him.

There are days people might wonder why they bothered to leave the warmth of their homes to face the cold, wet inclement weather, but on this occasion, it is a wonderful day to be out. The concerns are not wind and rain but sunscreen and where one might replenish water bottles. Eddie has thought of that and, in the afternoon, plans to take the group past a churchyard where he knows there is a tap.

They are up on the edge of the North Downs, which on this beautiful day affords a grand vista southward over the rolling countryside stretching below them from their chalky vantage. Were it not for the undulating hills of the South Downs that marks the limit of what they can see, they may have been able to see the coastline of the English Channel.

The route takes the group along the edge of fields and through a succession of woods and commons, a mix of terrain; woodland, heath and grassy chalk hillsides. At last, Eddie leads them onto a viewpoint on the crest of a hill designated for their picnic lunch break.

'There's a pub I know near,' the stranger Melvin pipes up. 'I know the landlord, and he'd be happy for the group to stop by. It's only ten minutes. There will be refreshing cold drinks. Why don't we go instead of stopping in the blazing sun?'

Eddie considers. Once, he would have been indignant about this attempt to usurp authority. But over the past months, he has regained a devil-may-care spontaneity. The beauty of walking is that sometimes you are unsure where you might end up. Why not if the group would enjoy a cold drink in the pub?

'Oh, no, I don't think so,' says Jenny. 'Better stay, I think.'

'I'm for staying put too,' reiterates Liz.

'I don't mind the sun,' says Karen.

Presumably, they can remember the joys, pain and upheaval of their adventures on the Other Side and the Underside and are in no hurry to repeat such escapades.

Sensing the mood, Eddie sums it up. 'Better not. You never know where something like that might lead.'

Milton Keynes UK
Ingram Content Group UK Ltd.
UKHW012201190124
436313UK00004B/66

9 781788 649896